The Long Pa

A Tale of the Mounted Police

H. A. Cody

Alpha Editions

This edition published in 2023

ISBN : 9789357385091

Design and Setting By
Alpha Editions
www.alphaedis.com
Email - info@alphaedis.com

Contents

CHAPTER I UNLEASHED

"Is Grey—Norman Grey—here?"

The Orderly paused on the threshold and looked around the room.

"Over there," replied a constable, jerking his thumb to the left, "in the corner."

At once the Orderly strode forward to the side of a young man leaning against the Canteen bar.

"Say, Grey, the O. C. wants you."

At these words the man addressed straightened himself up to his full height of six feet with a sudden jerk, while his dark piercing eyes flashed questioningly from beneath the broad brim of his Stetson hat. A deep silence now pervaded the room; the poker chips ceased their rattle; the rustling of the newspapers stopped; the man behind the bar stayed his hand in the act of pouring a glass of ginger beer, and even pipes were allowed to go out.

It was the quiet after supper hour in the Big Glen Barracks of the "X" Division of the North West Mounted Police, in the far-flung Northern Yukon Territory, and the work of the day was done. The few prisoners had been marched silently back to their lonely cells in the stout log guard room; the flag had fluttered slowly down from its tall staff in the centre of the big Square; the bugle had rent the air with its quivering notes, and the guards had been changed. Everything had been done speedily and systematically. It was the daily routine. Each man knew his duty, and did it.

The Canteen was the regular place of meeting, and here a score of constables and corporals, tested guardians of a lone land, were gathered, to drink the customary glass of ale or beer, read the newspapers, discuss the affairs of the day, and play a few friendly games of cards. The click of billiard balls in the adjoining room could be distinctly heard, whilst from the open door of the Sergeants' Mess came the sweet strains of a violin.

"Where's the O. C. now? In the office?" It was Grey's voice which broke the silence as he looked hard at the Orderly.

"No, he's in his house. You had better hustle."

Grey glanced down at his clothes. He was dressed as he had come off guard of the prisoners. A belt filled with cartridges encircled his waist, and his revolver sheathed in its leathern holster hung at his hip. His appearance at that moment was sufficient to win both respect and admiration from the most indifferent. Of this his companions were not thinking, but of that summons to meet the Commanding Officer. Well did they know the startling news which was agitating this northern town, causing strong men's eyes to moisten, and mothers to clasp their children closer in their arms. Had not prominent citizens hurried in and out of the O. C.'s office all the afternoon, and did not the air hang heavy with expectancy as to what move would be made and who would be chosen for the difficult undertaking? Now it was no longer uncertain. Grey was the first to be called, and all realised that the choice had been a good one.

"Grey's got a difficult job ahead of him," remarked a tall, slim constable after the former had left the room.

"He's the man for it, though," replied another, deliberately sipping his beer.

"He'll do the job if anyone can, for he fears neither man nor devil. Don't you remember how he stood up before 'Twisty' Parker and his gang in Big Gulch Road House, cowed the whole bunch, and got his man?"

"Indeed I do, but that was nothing to the way he ran down "One-eyed" Henry, the Swede, who murdered his partner at Five Fingers. He walked right up to the revolver's point when it was spitting fire like hell, knocked the Swede down and took him alive. The murderer afterwards acknowledged that it was Grey's coolness, and the terrible gleam of determination in his eyes which unnerved him and made his hand shake as if he had the palsy."

Grey in the meantime had crossed the Barracks Square, and was admitted by a quiet, passionless-eyed Jap into the presence of his Commanding Officer. Giving the customary salute he stood at attention, and awaited orders.

Major Sterling was sitting at his desk when Grey entered, with his eyes fixed upon a map lying before him. Pacing up and down the room was a small, middle-aged man whose agony of face and excited manner plainly bespoke the agitated state of his mind.

"Major, find my boy," he was saying. "Spare no pains or money in your efforts to run those villains down. They hate me, and have sworn to have revenge. They demand twenty thousand dollars. Think of it, twenty thousand dollars! They threaten the life of my child if it's not paid! Oh, God, help me! I can't pay it, and I won't. But I want my boy, my only child, Donnie. Major, for the sake of a heart-broken father and mother; for the honour of this town, and for the welfare of humanity, capture those scoundrels and save my boy."

In reply to this passionate appeal the Major swung around in his chair and faced the troubled man.

"Mr. Farwell," he began, "the best answer I can give you stands there in the person of Constable Grey. Leave the matter to us. We will do the best we can."

"Thank you, sir; oh, thank you," cried Mr. Farwell, seizing the Major's hand and wringing it vehemently. "I know you will do what you can. I shall go now, but you will keep me informed, will you not?"

"Yes," replied the Major, rising and opening the door. "You shall be kept acquainted with every move. Remember, Mr. Farwell, I am a father as well as an officer, and what more can I say?"

When the door had closed behind his visitor the Major returned to his desk, and remained for a while lost in thought. He was a stern man outwardly, and ruled with a firm hand. Unbending in the line of duty he combined rigid discipline with discriminating justice. Neither position, money, nor threats availed in the slightest degree to swerve him one hair's breadth from a purpose he knew to be right. Major Sterling was an autocrat on this ragged edge of civilisation, and yet an autocrat whose every heart beat was for the honour of his country and for the welfare of the people committed to his charge. Relentless as a sleuth hound in crushing down crime and tyranny he was feared and respected by both whites and Indians alike.

"Grey," he at length remarked, turning toward the constable and motioning him to a chair, "sit down; we've important business on to-night."

The Major's voice had lost much of its old-time sternness, and Grey was more than astonished at this unexpected order. Never before had he taken a seat in the presence of his Superior Officer. To do so was a severe breach of discipline. He advanced a step, and hesitated.

"This chair, Grey," and a slight smile illumined the Major's face as he noted his subordinate's embarrassment. "There, that's better," he continued, turning his attention once again to the map lying on his desk. With a pencil in his hand he traced a course from Big Glen out over the land away eastward toward the Rocky Mountains. At times he paused, and his brow knitted in perplexity. At length, however, the pencil rested upon a spot where a crooked stream was marked upon the map. Everything else was a complete blank, no name of town or village appearing. Here the Major made a small circle, and wrote over it the one word "Hishu."

"See, Grey," and he held up the map, "I want you to go there."

The constable started at these words, and glanced keenly at the pencil mark. His interest now was thoroughly aroused. For years that region had a strange fascination for his daring spirit. Indians had related marvellous tales of what the place contained: rivers foaming, rushing, and plunging into dark mysterious depths; monsters living in the mountains, their roars shaking the earth, and belching fire and rocks from their terrible mouths. There were tribes, too, so they said, horrible and bloodthirsty, with hair, filled with knives, hanging to their waists. At times the Indians about Big Glen had come trembling to the Police for protection. Those tribes from their mountain fastnesses, so they believed, were about to sweep down and wipe them out of existence. The Police had always succeeded, however, in allaying their fears, and upon investigation found the trouble generally started in the fervid brain of the useless Medicine Man.

So the Major was to send him there. Grey could hardly believe his ears. Into that region shrouded in mystery, like the shadow of death! What was the use of it?

"How soon can you get ready, Grey?" The Major was speaking as if certain of his line of action. There was no sign of doubt in his words.

"I can start at once, sir," the constable replied. "That is, as soon as I make ready. But do you think, sir, they would flee to a place like that?"

"Not if they knew how much I know," and the Major gave a peculiar little laugh.

"But why should they go there, sir? They must have heard about that place, and what a—"

"Look here, Grey," interrupted the Major, "I've had my eyes and ears open to that region for some time now. I've heard all those Indian stories, and believe them to be so many fairy tales, all purely imagination. I have lately received information, which I think is reliable, that certain men have crossed the mountains from the East, and are now prospecting up Hishu Creek. They have a small settlement at its mouth near the river. A notorious character, Siwash Bill by name, has a trading store there, and I believe him to be the ringleader of the gang who kidnapped that child. Prospectors on the Mackenzie River side of the mountains carried this news to Edmonton, which was forwarded to me only last week. I intended to send a man there shortly to investigate, but this unexpected occurrence demands immediate action."

Thus for an hour officer and subordinate sat and talked in the deepening twilight. When at length the latter rose to go, the Major reached forward and drew from a pigeon hole in the desk a small slip of paper.

"Wait a minute, Grey," he commanded. "I find that your time will be up two weeks from to-day."

"Yes, sir."

"And you intend to leave the Force then?"

"Yes, sir."

"And you don't mind being sent out on this business at the end of your time?"

"No, sir."

"Well said. I'll remember that. Good night, Grey, and God be with you."

Slowly the constable walked back across the Square toward the Canteen. His Commanding Officer's parting words touched him. He realised on this night as never before what a sympathetic heart beat beneath the Major's cold exterior. He was human after all, and cared for his men. What a change, too, he thought, to be out of the Force—to be free! And yet, why should he leave? Why should he not "take on again"? What was there for him in life? Where should he go? What was there to do? He could go home, but what was home without her? He paused, and bared his head. The evening breeze cooled his hot brow, and played with his wealth of dark hair. Above him shone the stars—their glory dimmed by the long northern twilight. There was the pole star steady as of yore. He remembered the night they had last looked at it together by the garden gate among the flowers. How beautiful she was then in all her virgin purity! That was six years ago—and where was she now? Six years, and not a trace of her since!

"Star of heaven," he murmured, "where is she to-night? Where is my long lost darling? Guide me, oh, lead me, to her side!"

The bugle sounded "Lights out," and soon all was in silence in the Big Glen Barracks. Major Sterling still sat at his desk, studying the map before him, and occasionally glancing at several closely-written papers lying near. From the stable at one corner of the Square Norman Grey led forth a jet-black horse, and stood for a minute stroking her glossy neck. There was no one to bid him farewell, no one to grip his hand and speed him on his way. A slight sarcastic laugh escaped his lips as he sprang lightly into the saddle and headed Blackbird for the open road. He was going out alone, unnoticed. But he would return—and what then? Again he smiled, settled himself firmly in the saddle, and gave one word to Blackbird. Then the ring of steel-shod hoofs sounded along the gravelled way as horse and rider sped through the night, out of the Barracks Square, out of the little straggling town, and out upon a great lone trail stretching dim and uncertain beyond the farthest bounds of civilization.

CHAPTER II
THE TERROR OF THE MOUNTAINS

The long trail wound and twisted far ahead, shimmering faintly in the light of the westering sun. Miles and miles of wild bunch grass, sage brush, and desolate sand met the eye, flanked on either side by high mountain ranges.

"Good Lord, what a trail!" muttered Norman Grey, regaining his seat with difficulty as Blackbird plunged her right foot into a concealed gopher hole. "Will this cursed valley never end? It's getting worse all the time."

Almost a week had now passed since he had swung away from Big Glen. Almost a week, and yet how much that brief period of six days contained. What desolate regions he had traversed, what streams forded, and what lonely nights he had spent upon the cold hard ground beneath the starry canopy of heaven. Thrice had he met Indians encamped along the way. Friendly were they, and had provided him with a liberal supply of tender moose meat. A mighty leveller is the northern trail. Here rank, title, creed and race fade into absurd insignificance. Here all useless appendages are swept aside. Here each stands for what he is, and his sole worth lies in himself. And here, too, in a region so vast, where the loneliness mocks and appals, the sight of a human face, though dark and uncouth, thrills the heart with a sweet gladness.

These children of the wandering foot looked with admiration upon the pale-faced stranger. They conversed with him in broken English, and slowly shook their heads when Grey pointed away to the left and mentioned the word "Hishu." As he started to leave the camp an Indian woman, old and scrawny, had laid her long, slim fingers upon the pommel of the saddle and looked up anxiously into his face.

"No, no, Hishu!" she cried, waving her left hand to and fro. "Bad, bad, ugh!"

So impressed was Grey by her earnestness and vehement manner that a foreboding chill smote his heart, and the reins dropped from his hand upon Blackbird's neck.

"Me no savvey. What you mean?" he demanded.

More emphatic now than ever did the unkempt creature become. She tried to explain herself, but her knowledge of the English language was slight, and her words developed into a torrent of unintelligible jargon. Seeing she was making but little impression upon the rider she suddenly seized the bridle with both hands, wheeled Blackbird sharply about, and headed her down the trail toward Big Glen.

"Go, go dat way," she cried. "No come back! No, no, Hishu!"

A slight smile of pity flitted across Grey's face at this woman's peculiar action. The momentary feeling of awe had vanished. He remembered how the Indians in the vicinity of Big Glen feared and shunned the Hishu region. No doubt these were of the same tribe, and believed the wild tales.

Two days had passed since then, and try as he might he could not banish that incident from his mind. It came to him now late this afternoon as Blackbird carefully picked her way among the innumerable gopher holes. The whole region was conducive to deep reflection. Sombre stood the rock-ribbed mountains. Silent throbbed the moistless air. Iron-grey stretched the sunburnt valley. To the lone rider crouched in his saddle the very atmosphere seemed to pulse with undercurrents of mystic forebodings. Hundreds of miles was he from civilisation, thousands of miles from home, a mere speck crawling over an execrable trail. What did it all amount to anyway? he asked himself time and time again. What had he gained during those five years of service in the Force? He was no nearer to her now than ever. What hopes had thrilled his heart when first he had entered upon his world-wide quest. He would find her, oh, yes. The world was large, he knew, but love would make it small. And this was the end—oblivion—merely for the sake of a child.

Presently Blackbird paused with a sharp jerk, causing Grey to look quickly up. The cause was at once apparent, for rammed across the trail was a long ragged ditch about three feet wide and four deep. With widely-extended nostrils and flashing eyes Blackbird had planted her forefeet close to the edge, and stood looking anxiously down into the excavation. On every side and far ahead stretched a chaotic maze of trenches. Some were short and narrow, while others were deep, and rods in length. This Grey knew to be the work of hungry bears in search of fat and toothsome gophers.

"Heavens, what a mess!" he exclaimed, as his eyes scanned the scene. "Grizzlies, I believe! There must be an army of them in this place. I only hope they've had their supper by this time, and will leave us alone. But if they do come they will receive a warm welcome," and he laid his hand upon the smooth dark barrel of his comforting rifle. "They will be flesh and blood, anyway, things I can see, and not those horrible unseen devils which have been torturing me the whole afternoon. Come on, you swine of the mountains!" he cried. "I fear you not. I'll send more fiery demons into your tough hides than the Master did long ago into the whole Gadarean herd." Grey was himself once more. The presence of danger affected him like a tonic. He even laughed at his morbid fears as he reined Blackbird to the left, and soothed her restless mettle with words of encouragement.

Slowly, very slowly the noble animal picked her way between the innumerable pitfalls. She was calm now. The spirit of the master was hers, and all fear was banished. For over an hour they moved steadily forward, and at length gained firmer ground where the earth was not disturbed. The sun was sinking behind a mountain peak as they left the valley and entered upon a deep ravine. The ascent was gradual, and at times the trail hung over high wooded banks. Up and up they moved through dark battalions of pine, spruce and fir. It was a weird place, and Grey breathed a sigh of relief when at length the summit was attained. Here he dismounted, tied Blackbird, and climbed far up into a large tree, towering high above its fellows. From this lofty position he was enabled to obtain an excellent view of the surrounding country. Back to the right he saw the valley over which they had lately painfully travelled, while ahead, and somewhat to the left, a river was to be seen lying like a long silver thread athwart the dusky landscape.

"It must be the Hishu," Grey muttered, as his eyes followed it away northward. "The place I'm bound for is, no doubt, somewhere over there. Should reach it to-morrow, and what then? Oh, well, I'm not going to worry about that now. It will soon be dark, and I must find a good camping spot. Down by the river is a likely place where those trees rise like millions of pointed spears. There should be grass for Blackbird down there on the level."

Leaving his lofty perch he descended the tree, unfastened Blackbird, and sprang into the saddle. Down the hill they slowly moved, the trail—if it could be called a trail—becoming more difficult all the time. At length they reached a hollow through which a little brook gurgled on its way to the river. Grey looked anxiously up and down, hoping to find a reach of wild meadow grass for the horse.

"Guess we'll have to go farther, lady," he remarked. "We must get you some supper, and there's nothing here."

Beyond the brook the trail wound up a steep incline, and curved sharply to the left around a large and almost perpendicular rock. Blackbird ascended the slope with an eager pace, for the tang of the wild meadows down by the river had drifted to her sensitive nostrils. She had just reached the flinty wall when with a terrified snort she threw high her head and reeled back upon her haunches. Instinctively Grey clutched the mane with his right hand to keep from falling and peered keenly forward. The cause of the disturbance was immediately evident, for coming slowly around the bend was a huge grizzly bear. The sudden appearance of the intruders into its domain startled the brute. Its upper lip curled, its teeth gleamed white, and an angry growl sawed the air. Blackbird was nearly frantic now. She quivered with excitement. The froth flew from her champing mouth, and her steel-shod fore hoofs beat sledge hammer blows upon the ground. With the greatest difficulty Grey managed to hold her in check with the left hand, while with the right he unslung his rifle. The bear was nearer now, coming steadily onward, still growling, and causing Blackbird to back farther and farther down the hill. It was not Grey's nature to retreat. He had never done so before the face of man, and he was determined that the first time should not be from a lumbering bear. The creature's insolence nettled him. It made him angry to be checked when he was anxious to reach the river. If it was fight the bear was looking for, it had sought the right spot. Quickly Grey brought the rifle to his shoulder, took aim and fired. The ball struck the bear a glancing blow upon the head. For an instant only the brute paused, and then with a terrific roar hurled itself forward like an avalanche. No longer could human hand control Blackbird's pent-up terror. She reared on high, and swung about with such a sudden jerk that Grey was hurled from the saddle and tossed like a ball among the underbrush. Of his scratches and bruises he thought nothing, for sterner work demanded his immediate attention. He had no time to regain his feet, for the bear was coming, and every instant was precious. Kneeling on the ground he seized the rifle, which had luckily fallen by his side, threw out the empty shell and drove a loaded one into its place. And none too soon, for the bear was almost upon him. Its rage was terrible to behold. Its eyes glowed like living coals, and the hot hissing breath poured from its gaping mouth like hell fire. With lightning rapidity Grey thrust the muzzle of his rifle between those gleaming teeth and fired. A deafening report ensued, and man and beast rolled over in one confused heap. Grey fully expected to feel the slashing rip of lance-like claws, and the sickening crunch of closing teeth. He stretched out his hand for his sheath knife; he would fight to the last; he would leave marks which would be remembered. But the keen blade was not needed; the terror of the mountains had made its final charge, had fought its last fight, and lay there upon the ground a quivering, inert mass—dead. Slowly and with difficulty Grey extricated himself and regained his feet. For a moment he stood and looked upon the fallen brute.

"Close call that," he commented. "Nearly put me out of business, hey, old chap? Good Lord, what claws and teeth! But for that lucky shot they'd've had me torn to ribbons by this time. I'd like to show them to the Major; he's a great eye for such things."

Blackbird was nowhere to be seen; the wilderness had swallowed her up. Suddenly Grey realised his position. Night was shutting down, horse gone, and the region alive with bears. He had settled the account of one, but there were hundreds more, and they might appear at any moment. He could not go back over the trail after the horse; that would be folly. He must reach the river. Picking up his rifle he wiped away the froth and moisture from the barrel and carefully reloaded it.

He was about to leave the place when he paused and looked at the bear lying before him.

"Ah, old chap," he exclaimed. "You've made me lose my grub by frightening Blackbird out of her senses. She's taken my small supply with her, and what shall I do for supper? You look fat and well liking, so I think a piece of your carcass will have to serve instead."

Drawing forth his sheath knife he deftly removed a portion of the skin and cut off a fair sized piece of meat from a part he considered the choicest. Next he sharpened a small stick, and thrust it through the flesh. This done, he threw it over his shoulder, seized the rifle and headed for the river.

CHAPTER III A CHILD IN THE MIDST

The river Hishu was swift. It raced and swirled between its clay banks. The water was cold—icy cold—for countless small streams from snow-capped mountains contributed to its volume. It was a fascinating monster, sinuous, terrible, beautiful. The most dangerous spot on the whole river was the Klikhausia Rapids. Here the current struck hidden rocks, which swirled, eddied and boiled down through a flinty channel, to leap at last foaming and spuming into the steady stream below. Skilled canoe men could bring their crafts safely through this turbulent piece of water, but woe speedily overtook the voyager who made the venture without a thorough knowledge of the place.

Norman Grey sat upon the bank a short distance below the rapids, with his eyes fixed upon the flowing stream. It held him spellbound by its mystic music and the clearness of its liquid depths. There beneath the surface, down among those polished stones, was peace—a peace and rest for which he ardently yearned. He might have been a stump for all the movement he made. A few birds twittered in the jack pines, and a noisy squirrel scolded from the branch of a nearby tree. But Grey heeded them not. His rifle was thrown carelessly on the ground by his side. His buckskin jacket and trousers were covered with dirt, and stained here and there with fresh blood. Grey was sore and weary. The long ride, the excitement of the day and the heavy fall from his horse were having their effect. His whole body ached, and through his left shoulder surged a numbing pain caused by the contact with the ground. The piece of bear meat was lying by his side. He had matches, and could soon build a fire and broil a slice of steak. But his energy had deserted him. He longed to lie down and rest—rest forever. His one blanket had gone with Blackbird. But what did it matter? He was accustomed to the open, and his buckskin jacket would do instead. Yes, he would sleep, and forget everything—bears and all.

Slowly he rose to his feet and began to climb the bank. Scarcely had he reached the level above ere he gave a start and looked quickly up-stream. What was that? A shout, a cry of terror, which winged its way to his ears. He straightened himself up, shaded his eyes with his hand, and scanned the river. The sun had been down for some time, but the long northern twilight was still struggling with night, and it was not hard to discern objects some distance away. As Grey's eyes rested upon the rapids he beheld a boat—a frail craft—go to pieces upon a sunken rock right in the centre of that swirling death. Then out from the midst of the roaring mass of tumultuous billows darted a dark object. Rapidly it was borne down the stream, and as it approached nearer Grey observed a man clinging frantically with one hand to a fragment of the boat, while with the other he was clutching the limp form of a little child. Grey was all alert now. His weariness and pain were gone. His tall gaunt figure was drawn to its full height, forming a dark silhouette against the evening sky. The clinging man looked toward the shore. His face was filled with agony, and twitched convulsively.

"Help! help!" he cried. "This icy water's killing me! I can't hold on any longer!—oh—God!" and with a wild piercing yell he threw up his hands and sank beneath the surface.

Quicker than words Grey tore off his buckskin jacket, and throwing discretion to the wind hurled himself into the racing stream. Though a powerful swimmer he was but a gnat in that terrible current. It seemed the maddest of folly to attempt a rescue in such a place. The waters were icy, and his soggy clothes impeded his progress. Why give up his own life for a vague uncertainty? Why risk all in a hazardous throw? But a little face—oh, so white—gleamed before him, and a curly head of gold appeared. The sight nerved him almost to superhuman effort. With lusty sinews and mighty strokes he clove the water like a Titan. He reached the child, he clutched it, held its head above the surface, and turned toward the shore. Fortunately the piece of broken boat floated near. This he grasped with one hand, and the child with the other. No longer now did he try to stem the stream, but simply allowed himself to drift. On and on they sped, Grey becoming more numbed all the time. Often he felt he could endure no longer, that he must give up and sink. But the sight of that little child, lying so still in his arm, caused him to grip the wreck more firmly. Only a short time before he had cherished the idea of rest and peace beneath those same cold waters. Now all was changed, and, instead of death, life was uppermost in his mind. Not life for himself alone, but for that helpless form pressed close to his breast. Oh, for a friendly voice from the shore, and a strong hand stretched out to lift them from the icy depths. Ere long his brain began to whirl. He seemed to be battling in the midst of thousands of hideous serpents. They were coiling about his legs, arms and body. They were leaping up, trying to tear away the child from his breast, and to loosen his hold upon the boards. How much longer would they torture him? Would they soon gain complete possession and bear him down never to rise again? No, he would fight them. He would conquer. He would beat them back. They were worse than the grizzly, but he would win. And even as he made another great determined struggle his feet struck something which sent a thrill of hope through his heart. Was it merely a delusion? Was it only a fond fancy of his reeling brain? No, it was true. His feet had struck a sand-bar, which put out from the shore like a long finger hidden beneath the surface. Relaxing his grip of the raft, and with the child in his arms Grey feebly and with much difficulty made his way through the swirling water. So numb was his body that his legs seemed like two lifeless sticks as he staggered forward. It was all he could do to reach the shore and climb the bank. Then his strength deserted him. He trembled and sank upon the hard ground. It was only for a few seconds, however, for the child lying there needed immediate attention. Kneeling by his side he peered into the little white face, noticed the wan, pinched features, the luxuriant curly hair dripping with water, and the soaked clothes clinging like cerements to his body. "What was such a lad doing there?" he wondered. That not more than three summers had passed over his head was quite evident. He was no poor man's child, for the garments betokened a home of means and loving care above the ordinary. At his throat a small safety pin was fastened, and as Grey peered down through the faint and uncertain light he saw engraved there the one word "Donnie." An exclamation of astonishment escaped his lips. His eyes were suddenly opened, and he beheld before him Silas Farwell's little stolen child.

"Fool—more than fool," he muttered. "To think that I didn't realise it before. And here I've been cursing my fate ever since that grizzly unhorsed me, and it was all for a purpose. I begin to see now that another Hand is having much to do with this affair."

At that instant a shiver shook the child's body. He looked up, began to cry and to call for his mother.

"Hush, hush, dear," soothed Grey, bending over him. "You shall have your mother."

Then the helplessness of his position swept upon him. In a vast wilderness, leagues from any settlement, and night shutting down. Not a shred of dry clothing did he have in which to enwrap the child, and not even a fire. He was numb and chill himself. That he could stand, but not this delicate lad. "What am I to do?" he groaned. "Is this sweet child to die here slowly after all? Better to have left him to perish in the river; it would have been quicker."

Rising to his feet he peered through the gloom, but no sign of human life could he behold, nothing but the scrubby forest, silent and grim. He lifted up his voice and called, once, twice, three times, but only a far-off echo, ghost-like and hollow, sent back its mocking response. Again he knelt by the side of the child.

"Are you cold, dear?" he asked.

"Ya, cold, cold," and the lad shivered. "I wants my mother. Why doesn't she tum to her 'ittle boy-boy?"

Grey looked at his own clothes. They were very wet; not a dry stitch upon him. Then he thought of the buckskin jacket he had thrown off ere he leaped into the river. He believed there were several dry matches in one of the pockets. Suppose they had fallen out during his tussle with the bear! They were his only hope now. The liberal supply he had brought with him, rolled up in his blanket, had gone with Blackbird. Never before had he realised the value of a few tiny matches. Now they meant life or death. He must have them if they were there, and at once.

"Are you afraid to stay here alone, little one?" he asked. "It will be only for a short time, and I shall soon come back."

A startled look came into Donnie's face, as reaching out a small hand he clutched the arm of his rescuer.

"No, no, don't go!" he cried, with tears streaming down his cheeks. "Take me home. I wants my mother."

"I won't leave you, then," was the reassuring response. "You shall go along, too."

Stooping down, he lifted the child tenderly in his arms and turned his face up-stream. Could he make the journey? That was the question. Had he the strength after his two fearful ordeals to struggle through that dusky tangled underbrush, where no trail marked the way, and with his feet stumbling at almost every step? Suppose he should fall and not be able to rise again? He banished the thought. It was too horrible to be entertained even for an instant. No, he must not fail. What would the Major, who had entrusted him with such a sacred commission think? And how would the Force regard it? "Constable N. Grey, Regiment No. —— lost; supposed to have died on the trail, somewhere between Big Glen and the river Hishu, while in search of a stolen child." How would words such as these sound in the laconic Police Report when it appeared the following year? Would their bones, bleached and white, at last be found amid those tangled bushes? And the mother, what of her? Would she ever know of the struggle he had made to save her darling child? There came to him now her white, drawn face. Did not every man in the Barracks know Mrs. Farwell? She was beautiful, cultured, and a general favourite in the little social circle of Big Glen. But she was kind to all, and greeted each constable she met with a pleasant smile. She had spoken to him once, and congratulated him upon the capture of "One-eyed" Henry, the Swede. He had never forgotten that, and her sparkling eyes and sunny face had haunted him for months. For her sake now, at least, he must not fail. He would save her child. He had taken but a few steps forward when he stopped short in his tracks. A dark form had suddenly loomed up out of the night right in front of him. It was an Indian tall and silent, leaning upon his grounded rifle. For the space of ten heart throbs neither spoke. Then,

"Who are you," Grey demanded, "and what do you want?"

"You call?" came the calm reply.

"Yes, indeed, I did call. Look you. This child is wet, cold, freezing. Got in river. See? You savvey cabin—fire, eh?"

At once the Indian took a step nearer, and peered keenly into the white man's face.

"Ah, ah," he remarked. "Me savvey. Come."

Turning abruptly he plunged into the thicket of jack pines and cotton wood trees. He had not gone far, however, ere he paused and looked back.

"Me take bah-bee," he said; "you cally gun, eh?"

But when he reached out his hands Donnie shrank back with a little sobbing cry, and threw his arms tightly around his preserver's neck.

"Don't want to leave me, little man?" Grey asked, while his heart thrilled with a new-found joy at the child's confiding action.

"Ya, me tay," whimpered the boy. "You carry baby."

"All right, dear, you shall stay with me as long as I have any strength left," and he motioned the Indian to advance.

Silently they threaded their way through the chilly night, Grey using every exertion to keep up with his dusky guide. Donnie was a considerable weight to him in his weakened condition. Once he felt he should be forced to relinquish his burden to the Indian, no matter how badly the child might feel. But the pressure of that little body and the hand laid so trustingly against his shoulder nerved him to greater action, and painfully he stumbled forward. After what seemed to Grey to be an interminable distance, although in reality it was not far, a bright light suddenly pierced the darkness. It came from a camp fire directly ahead, around which he observed someone moving. In another minute the place was reached, and gladly he laid the child down in front of the cheerful blaze.

It was only a temporary brush camp erected there in the wilderness, but to Grey no place had ever seemed half so welcome. Seated on a blanket spread over some fir boughs was an Indian woman with hair, jet black and straight, falling over not unshapely shoulders. Nearby stood a girl of fifteen years, whose eyes sparkled with curiosity as she turned them upon the stranger and the little form at his feet. One glance at the sympathetic faces before him told Grey that he was in the midst of friends. A few brief words in the rhythmical native tongue passed between the Indian man and woman, and immediately the rude camp was converted into a hive of industry. The child was stripped of his wet clothes, his cold body thoroughly rubbed and then enwrapped in a soft grey blanket which the girl had brought forth from a mysterious corner of the camp.

Donnie had no fear of the woman, but sat contentedly on her lap, alternately watching the blazing fire and the animated face of the young maiden kneeling by his side. Then, after he had taken some of the savoury ptarmigan soup which the girl had dipped from a kettle near the fire, he laid his tired little head against the Indian woman and was soon fast asleep.

All this Grey noted with much satisfaction as he lay close to the fire trying to dry his own wet garments. How his heart warmed toward these dusky waifs as he watched their care of the child. He saw the little head droop, the eyes close, and observed how gently the Indian woman laid him down upon the brush bed, and tenderly placed over him a thick warm blanket. The thoughtfulness and dignity of these people surprised him. Formerly he had very little use for the natives, and considered them with a certain degree of pity, mingled with contempt. Most of the Indians he had seen in this northern land were weak, inferior creatures, fond of hanging about towns and mining camps, and trying to imitate the ways of the whites. But these were different, and he fell asleep there on the hard ground wondering if all the Indians in the Hishu region were of this same superior class.

A cry fell upon his ears, and he awoke with a start. He sat quickly up, and looked around in a dazed manner. He glanced toward Donnie, and instantly realised the nature of the trouble. The icy water had done its work, and he saw the poor little form racked with a terrible cough. The Indian woman had the boy on her lap, and was rubbing his chest with oil which was warming near the fire. But still the child cried, stopping only as the painful, wheezing cough swept upon him.

CHAPTER IV THE SHADOWING HORSEMAN

Grey was completely surprised at himself as he leaped to his feet and hurried to Donnie's side. He could not account for the anxiety which now filled his heart. Had anyone suggested such a thing a week before he would have laughed him to scorn. Had the Major sent him in quest of a horse it would have stirred him about as much as going forth to find a stolen child. With him sentiment had no place in the undertaking. It was stern, iron duty, and nothing more. But this sudden interest was something for which he had not planned. The child sitting there before him was more than a mere pawn in this game he was playing. It appealed to his nature by its very helplessness and confiding manner. The pinched, drawn features, the frail cough-racked body and those large blue eyes looking so beseechingly up into his rough bearded face sent a peculiar thrill through his heart.

"What's wrong, old man?" he asked, placing his hand upon the little hot forehead. "Too much water, eh?"

At once Donnie stretched out his hands, and slipped from the Indian woman's lap.

"I wants my mother," he wailed. "Take me to my—" His words were cut short by another fit of coughing, and he stood trembling there, a pitiable figure of distress. At once Grey reached down, caught the child in his strong arms, and held him close to his breast.

"Can't you do anything for the boy?" he demanded, turning to the Indian woman standing near.

The latter slowly shook her head, and spoke a few quick words to her husband who was stirring the fire. Deliberately straightening himself up he confronted the constable.

"Can't you do something?" Grey repeated. "Baby sick. You savvey Injun medicine? You make him well?"

"Me no savvey," was the slow reply. "Me no ketch 'um root. Me notting here."

"But the child will die! See how he coughs."

"Me no savvey," was all the Indian would say, and Grey realised that no help could be expected from these natives.

What was he to do? Could he permit the child to die without an effort to save his life? He had suffered for him already, and would all that he had done amount to nothing? He thought of Big Glen. Oh, to have him there, in his mother's tender keeping. But that was out of the question. Next he thought of the Hishu village. Would he find assistance there? Would anyone know what to do in such a place? It was not likely, and yet it was worth trying. He turned to the Indian.

"You savvey white man over there?" and he pointed away to the left.

"Ah, ah, me savvey 'um," was the reply.

"How far?" Grey demanded.

"White man cabin over dere. Wan sleep? No."

"What, can I get there to-night?"

"Ah, ah. Sun heem come up dere, sun heem go down dere. White man cabin. You go, eh?"

"Yes, yes, I must," and Grey looked intently at the coughing child.

"You cally bah-bee, eh?"

"Certainly. What else can I do?"

"Bah-bee velly seek. Bah-bee beeg. White man no strong. Bime by stop. Soon all sam bah-bee."

Too well did Grey realise the force of these quaint words. He was feeling the effect of his experience in the icy water, and his body ached. The child, too, was large for his age, and to carry him all day long over a rough trail was utterly impossible. And yet he was willing to try even the impossible rather than stay there and see the lad die without an effort to save his life.

The Indian watched him closely, and, noting his determination, an expression of satisfaction appeared upon his tawny face.

"White man no squaw," he remarked. "White man all sam beeg chief. Me help white man."

"What, will you go with me?" and Grey looked his astonishment.

"Ah, ah. Hishu Sam help white man cally bah-bee."

The eastern sky was flushed with the radiance of the rising sun as constable and Indian started forth with the little child. The trail, worn by numerous moccasined feet, wound and twisted for weary miles through the vast wilderness. Here it skirted and crossed open plains covered with wild bunch grass and sage brush. There it dipped into deep valleys where the trees stood thick and grim. At times it circled around ragged ledges where the foothold was precarious. The sun rose and swung clear of the tallest mountain peaks. It rode high in the heavens, and poured its hot beams upon the hurrying wayfarers.

Often Grey's steps faltered as he staggered up some steep incline, and his feet were sore from contact with snags and sharp stones. Not so the Indian. He seemed tireless. Light of heel he sped forward with a rhythmical springing gait. His slightly stooping form, long and lithe from hips to shoulders, was the very embodiment of physical endurance. Such strength and grace of movement filled Grey with profound admiration. Of what avail now was his own special training? He had excelled in running, jumping and swimming. He could pull an oar with the strongest, and on the baseball field could tantalise a crack batsman with cranky balls. He had prided himself upon his prowess, and ever struggled to be first. But here was one of nature's own children, an uncouth native, putting him to the blush.

The Indian insisted upon carrying the boy, and Donnie no longer objected, but lay quietly in those great strong arms. Instinctively he felt that the powerful stranger was his friend, and would do him no harm. Hishu Sam seemed to think nothing of the lad's weight, and when Grey tried to relieve him of the burden he would always refuse with an emphatic grunt and a shake of the head. At noon they paused to rest by the side of a little babbling brook, whereupon the Indian brought forth a piece of dried salmon, and shared it with his companions. Donnie hardly touched the food, but Grey ate eagerly, for he was hungry after the long tramp. He sat on the ground with the boy on his lap, and gently stroked his curly head. Donnie was feeling somewhat better, and the cough was not so troublesome. He even smiled, a wan little smile, as Grey told him a simple story he had heard when a child. The Indian sat silently near, steadily smoking an old blackened pipe. He, too, was interested in the lad, and gave a brief grunt of satisfaction as the child smiled.

"Look here, Sam," said Grey as they were about to resume their journey and the Indian had risen to his feet, "how much do you want for helping me out to-day?"

"What you mean?" came the reply. "Me no savvey."

"How much I pay you? How much money you want?"

For a minute the native did not reply. He stood like a statue. Then he turned his piercing eyes full upon the constable's face.

"Me no tak pay," he almost fiercely rejoined. "No, no, ugh!"

"But why no take pay?" Grey insisted. "You save baby's life. You do much good."

"No, no, me no tak pay. You savvey Injun bah-bee in camp?"

Grey nodded.

"Wan, two, seex winter mebbe, Injun bah-bee velly seek. Heem no get well. Me no feex 'um. Me velly seek here," and he placed his hand over his heart. "Me t'ink bah-bee die. White man, beeg, beeg Chief, heem come 'long. Heem see bah-bee. Heem do all sam dis," and he knelt upon the ground. "Heem savvey all sam Medicine Man. Heem mak Injun bah-bee well. Heem no tak monee. Heem good man. No, no, me no tak monee. Me all sam white man."

"You savvey white man?" the constable asked.

"Ah, ah."

Grey was about to question further when the Indian gave a sudden start, and pointed to the left. Following the direction of the finger the constable noticed a man astride a cayuse on the high bank of the river about two hundred yards away. Whether a white man or an Indian Grey could not tell, but he appeared to be watching them very closely. This incident, trifling as it seemed, aroused in Grey a feeling of apprehension. So intent had he been upon the child that he had almost forgotten his fears concerning the Hishu region and the characters he knew had their abode there. Perhaps this was one of them. Anyway it was as well to hurry forward out of that desolate place before night shut down.

Hour after hour they plodded steadily forward, their eyes and ears keenly sensitive to any sound or sight of the strange horseman. Once only did he reappear. They had paused for a brief rest in a valley, and to drink of a stream whose water ran icy cold from the mountains, when he had suddenly darted out from a hill above and peered down upon them. The Indian had laid his hand upon his rifle, and whispered, "Me feex 'um." But Grey shook his head, and the native had desisted. Although he felt that the rider was following them for some sinister purpose, it would not do to enter Hishu as blood-stained travellers. And, besides, there was the strict command instilled into every new recruit not to shoot first. "Get your man," was the brief stern order. "If you don't get him, it means three months' hard, and if you shoot him it is all the same, with perhaps dismissal tacked on." No, Grey was not going to run counter to such orders. Anyway, what good would it do? Perhaps after all this was a harmless horseman, watching them out of mere curiosity.

He thought of these things through that long afternoon. Would the trail never end? It seemed like a week since they had left the camp. The child slept much of the time in those tireless dusky arms. Occasionally he awoke with a cry of fright, and the annoying cough would sweep upon him. He was becoming weaker, Grey could see that, and his heart ached as he watched the limp, pathetic figure, and the face all too white. "What must be a mother's love?" he asked himself over and over again. "If this little lad I have known such a short time appeals to me so strongly, how must she feel who suffered for his sake, and watched over him for three years?" At such times his hands would grip hard the rifle, and a scowl would furrow his brow as he inwardly cursed the villains who had torn away this sweet, innocent child from his mother's tender keeping.

The sun was swinging low in the heavens as slowly and wearily they at length toiled up a steep incline and reached the brow of a high hill. Here the Indian paused, and pointed to the opposite side of the valley lying snugly below. Grey, following the direction of the outstretched arm beheld several log buildings, nestling among the trees on the farther hillside. To the left flowed the Hishu River, glimpses of which could be easily observed from their high vantage ground.

"Hishu," the Indian quietly remarked. "Ketch 'um bime by."

Grey's heart thrilled as he shaded his eyes and scanned the little settlement. And this was Hishu, the spot toward which his face had been turned for weary days. He smiled as he thought of the wild blood-curdling Indian tales he had heard. What of the savage Indians and the monsters of the mountains? How tame and commonplace everything seemed, and Hishu was only that straggling cluster of houses over there in the distance. It was simply a mining camp, and no doubt all of the rascals who had kidnapped the child had gone down in the Klikhausia Rapids. His heart was lighter than it had been for days, and he descended the hill with a new springing gait. He began to see the end of his venture, the quiet return to Big Glen, and the child safely restored to his mother.

The trail was becoming easier now, for numerous feet had worn it smooth. On both sides of the way signs of woodsmen's axes were visible in the many stumps dotting the land. Ere long the first house burst upon their view as they emerged from the forest. It was only a rude log cabin, but how good it looked to Grey after that long desolate trail. The building was standing by itself, no other cabin being visible. Of its isolation he thought nothing then, but only of the shelter and relief he might find for the child. The door was open, though no one was to be seen. With the customary freedom of the frontier he gave a loud rap, and entered, the Indian following with Donnie in his arms. The room was not large, but clean, while a few rude benches, a couch and one table adorned the place. In a far corner were several shelves on which stood a number of black bottles. All this Grey observed at a glance, for scarcely had they entered ere a curtain was drawn quickly aside, and a woman stood before them. Grey started back in amazement, and gave vent to an ejaculation of surprise. Men he had expected to find in Hishu, but not women. His astonishment was succeeded by a feeling of joy. How fortunate, he thought, that she is here, whoever she might be. She will be able to help the boy better than men.

The woman was neatly dressed, of medium height, and at the first glance fair to look upon, although her face was somewhat pale. Her eyes were what fascinated the constable. They were cold steel grey, piercing in their intensity. They were cruel eyes, devoid of the softening grace of pity. To them tears of sorrow or sympathy seemed unknown. A faint semblance of a smile flitted across her face as she observed Grey's unaffected stare. She took a step forward, and then,

"Who are you," she demanded, "and what did you bring that brat here for?"

If Grey was surprised before he was completely dumbfounded now. He did not expect this. Presently an idea flashed through his brain. He glanced again at the bottles, and from them to the woman's face, and then he understood.

A coarse laugh greeted his embarrassment. She had divined his thoughts, and it pleased her.

"Don't like the place, greeny, eh?" she sneered. "You needn't stay; there's the door. But I guess you'll soon get used to it. All the men here have except one d— fish, and I'll have Buckskin Dan yet."

At this Grey found his tongue. He knew now what kind of a character he had to deal with. Her rough talk and heartlessness nettled him.

"I don't want to stay here," he replied, "but you might do something for this sick child. He'll die, otherwise."

"Let him die, then," came the cruel response; "he'll be better off."

"And you won't care for him?" Grey questioned.

"Oh, I'll not turn the brat out. Throw it on the couch there. What's wrong with him anyway?"

Briefly Grey related the story of the wreck in the rapids, the rescue from the icy water, and the effect upon the child.

A sudden change passed over the woman's face as she listened to the tale.

"And you say the men were drowned?" she cried when Grey had finished.

"Yes."

"My God! What will Bill say?"

"Bill who?"

"Siwash Bill. Don't you know him?"

Grey was about to reply in the negative, when he suddenly started, and stood as if transfixed. The sound of someone singing had reached his ears. It was a woman's voice, full of unutterable pathos. It sounded nearer now, and he caught the refrain:

"Somewhere, somewhere, beautiful isle of somewhere,

Land of the true where we live anew,

Beautiful isle of somewhere."

The singer by this time had reached the door, and the song ceased. She was a young woman, slight and beautiful, who crossed the threshold, carrying a sunbonnet in one hand and a bunch of wild flowers in the other. Her eyes glanced for an instant at the bearded stranger standing in the centre of the room. Then they rested upon the child lying on the couch and with a cry of surprise and delight she darted forward and knelt down by his side. Later when she looked inquiringly around Grey was nowhere to be seen. He had disappeared, and only the woman with the hard eyes was standing before her.

CHAPTER V THE FUR TRADER'S STORE

Grey stumbled rather than walked out of the log cabin. He looked about for the Indian, but he was nowhere to be seen. The evening breeze fanned and cooled his flushed face. He wished to get away somewhere. His throat was dry; he felt he would choke. His brain reeled as he staggered forward. A trail to the left caught his eye, and along this he tottered. Madeline there! Madeline in such a den as that! What did it all mean? Was it only a horrible dream, or was he going mad? Had he been mistaken? Perhaps it was someone else. No, it was all too real. It was she without any doubt! Could he ever forget that face, those eyes, that wealth of dark-brown hair, and the slight girlish figure? It was Madeline, his long-lost Madeline. He had expected to find her some day, somewhere, but not here.

He had reached the forest now, and sat down on a log by the side of the trail. He wished to think, to solve the mystery. Madeline there! Was it possible? Then thoughts, terrible spectres, surged through his brain. Why was she there? How could he associate the pure-souled woman as he had known her with such a life as that? That song, full of intense pathos, that face, that cry of surprise and joy; they came to him again. Madeline was there—only a few rods away, beneath that roof! A great longing filled his heart. Oh, to go to her, to look into those eyes and listen to her voice! He rose from the log, and took a step forward. He would go. He would know the worst at once. But he hesitated. His hand sought his brow in perplexity. He tried to think, to reason. No, not to-night. He would rest first, and in the morning, perhaps, it would be better to go to her.

The bark of a dog aroused him. It made him realise that night was upon him, and he must have food and shelter. Following the direction of the sound, ere long he reached a clearing of several acres in extent. All around he beheld log cabins and frames of numerous tents. Through the midst of these the trail wound, and along this he moved, watching for some sign of life. At length he reached a building larger than the rest, where stood a lean Indian dog which sidled angrily away as Grey approached. In answer to his knock a gruff voice commanded him to enter. Pushing open the door he beheld two men seated before a rough deal table, playing cards. In a corner nearby sat a powerfully-built man, with a long beard, and wavy hair well streaked with grey. He was calmly smoking, and watching the game with much interest.

Across one side of the room ran a rough counter, formed of whipsawn boards, which evidently knew nothing of soap and water. Behind this and arranged along the wall were all sorts of articles from cheap prints to tea, tobacco, beads and candy.

The opposite side of the room was lined with goods, useful in bartering with Indians. Rifles and shot-guns were lying on stands. Sacks of flour, rice and beans were piled in one corner, while slabs of bacon hung from the huge ridge-pole overhead. All this Grey intuitively observed as he stood for an instant near the door.

The players paused in their game, and stared hard at the new-comer, while the man in the corner forgot to take three regular and deliberate puffs of his blackened pipe. A visitor was evidently a curiosity at Hishu.

"Chair, stranger?" remarked one of the players, shoving forward a three-legged stool with his foot.

"Do you own this cabin?" Grey asked as he accepted the proffered seat.

"Reckon so," was the reply. "Paid, and d—high, too, for everything here. Anything I can do for ye, stranger?"

"Yes. I'm dead beat, and almost starved. So if you'll give me a snack of food and a shake-down for the night it will make a new man of me."

"Sure thing," was the response. "You're welcome to the grub, such as 'tis, but can't say about a shake-down. We're mighty cramped for room just now. Anyway, we'll see later how things pan out, and maybe we can do something for ye."

Saying which he turned toward a door at the back of the room, and gave a short, sharp command in the native tongue.

What he said Grey did not know, but almost immediately an Indian woman appeared in the doorway. It was not her sudden appearance which arrested Grey's attention, so much as her strange attitude. Her eyes glowed with defiance, mingled with fear, while a surly expression shrouded her face, which exhibited marks of much natural beauty. A glance was sufficient to show Grey that this was no ordinary, submissive Indian woman standing before him. Combined with her defiance and fear was a haughtiness which could not be concealed. Although partially cowed and curbed, she had evidently known the exhilarating joy of unrestrained freedom. And that same spirit still animated her heaving breast, but in a more terrible form. It was pent up, and liable at any moment to break forth in the wildest fury like a checked mountain stream or the boiling lava of some hidden volcano. But now she listened attentively to the words of command hurled forth, and at once disappeared within the back room.

"Fine squaw, that," remarked the other player, gazing with admiration upon the retreating form. "How in h— do you manage to curb such a spirit? Your deal, Bill," and he shoved the cards across the table.

Mechanically his partner shuffled and dealt the cards. But his thoughts were elsewhere, and as the game proceeded he shot an occasional furtive glance at the stranger sitting near.

An uncomfortable feeling stole into Grey's heart as he felt those piercing eyes fixed upon him. Once he looked full into their cold depths, and involuntarily recoiled at the sinister expression he beheld lurking there. The player noticed the start, and an oath escaped his lips as he flung his last card down upon the table. Then swinging on his stool he hurled a torrent of Indian words across the room.

In a moment or two the woman reappeared with a rough wooden tray containing some beans, thick bread and a cup of black tea.

"Put it here," demanded her imperious lord, shoving forward the small table. "We're done with our game for the present."

Grey was hungry, and he did good justice to the food set before him. But his mind was not easy. Why had that man given him those keen lightning glances? Did he surmise who he was and the purpose of the visit? Then his thoughts drifted away to that lone house down the trail, to the child and to Madeline. He forgot for a time his surroundings and the sinister-eyed man. He was with her, sitting by her side, looking into her face, and listening to her words of love.

At length he roused from his reverie and looked quickly about the room. The two card players were nowhere to be seen. Only the man in the buckskin jacket was sitting in the corner, pulling away at his old pipe. Their eyes met, and instinctively Grey felt that here was one to be trusted.

"Do you live in this place?" he asked, pushing back the table a little, and turning around on his stool.

Instead of replying the man took the pipe from his mouth, knocked it against the bench on which he was sitting, and examined it carefully. Then from a deep capacious pocket he drew forth a large clasp-knife and a plug of tobacco, and began deliberately to whittle away at the latter.

Grey was surprised at this action, and believed that his question had not been heard. Perhaps the man was somewhat deaf, and it was necessary to speak louder. He was about to repeat his words, when the man suddenly paused, looked carefully around the room, and jerked his bench closer to Grey's side.

"Young man, what are ye adoin' here?" he asked.

So low and full of meaning was the voice that Grey's eyes opened wide with astonishment.

"Just travelling," he replied.

"H'm," ejaculated the questioner, as he carefully rolled the tobacco between his hands. "Prospectin' or trappin'?"

"Oh, anything that turns up. I'm not particular."

Creak, creak. It was the back door, which moved as if shaken by the wind. The buckskinned man gave a slight start and glanced to the left.

"Doin' anything that turns up, eh?" he remarked. "Isn't it rather unsartin bizness? How d'ye expect to live?"

Creak, creak, went the door again. The creaking of a door generally disturbs one's nerves. There seems to be something uncanny about it, as if unseen evil spirits were outside trying to force an entrance. But when one suspects that men are standing there, with ears close to the crack, listening with sinister intent to every word which falls from the lips of those in the room, the tension becomes almost unbearable. Grey was all alert now. The whole place was conducive to suspicion. The sudden disappearance of the two card players, the low warning voice of the quiet smoker, and that creaking door. There was no breeze to cause it to move, for the evening was still, with not a leaf aquiver.

"An' whar will ye stay to-night?"

The question was kindly asked, and the eyes which looked straight into Grey's spoke of trust.

"Don't know," was the reply. "Under the trees maybe, unless the owner of this cabin will give me a shake-down here."

"No, that won't do," came the response. "I've a snug cabin over yon, so if ye'll put up with the accommodation ye're welcome to it, sich as 'tis."

Grey at once rose to his feet, and followed his companion, who was already starting toward the door. They had advanced but a few rods from the cabin when the clatter of hoofs sounded along the trail. In a few moments a horseman appeared, astride a raw lanky cayuse, and drew up before the store. Grey had paused, and was looking back, but his companion clutched him fiercely by the arm, and hurried him along.

"Come, lad," he whispered, "it's no time fer starin' now. Let's git under shelter."

CHAPTER VI THE DEN OF PLOTTERS

The horseman quickly made the cayuse fast to a post. He then turned and watched the retreating forms of Grey and Buckskin Dan. He stood there for several minutes after the two had disappeared within a small log cabin up the trail. He was a lean, lank, Cassius-type of man, with furtive, restless eyes, which had won for him the sobriquet of "Shifty" Nick. An old, dirty, weather-beaten slouch hat had been drawn over his low receding forehead until the broad brim was on a dead level with his piercing eyes. Presently his lips curled in an angry snarl, and a row of white teeth showed for an instant beneath a heavy dark moustache. Thrusting his hands deep into his pockets he moved toward the store, gave the dog lying by the door a savage kick, and entered the building. Seeing no one there he strode swiftly forward to the door at the rear of the room. Here he paused and listened. Hearing voices within he gave the door a push, and entered. Seated on stools were the two card players, Siwash Bill and Windy Pete, while sitting on the floor in one corner was the Indian woman. Her fingers were busy stringing beads for a buckskin jacket lying near. She seemed to be engrossed solely with her work, and her head was bent low. But not a sound in that room escaped her acute ears. Occasionally she lifted her eyes and gave a lightning glance toward the two men. Then in that brief instant her dusky face revealed a world of meaning. A passion deep and intense was consuming that quiet form. Love, fear and hate were raging there, contending with one another in fierce conflict.

Shifty Nick looked contemptuously at the two men before him.

"So this is how yer spendin' yer time," he snarled. "Great lot you are. Are yez scart of somethin'? What's happened to the d— place? Scarce a soul around, an' you hidin' here with the squaw."

"What's wrong, Shifty?" returned Bill. "Ye seem to be outer sorts. What's the news? Where's the gang an' the kid?"

Deigning no reply Nick flung himself upon a stool, and eyed the two. His bronze face was paler than usual, and his face twitched in an agitated manner.

"Where did that cub come from?" he at length demanded.

"What cub?"

"Oh, you know. That young cuss with old Dan. What's he doin' here?"

"How in h— do I know," replied Bill, somewhat nettled at the other's surly manner.

"But ye ought to know. It's yer bizness to know. Here I've been out in the blazin' sun all day watchin' the trail, while you've been skulkin' here in this hole."

"Well, suppose we have, ye needn't git so tarnal ugly. We've been doin' nothin', 'bout same as you. There was nothin' fer us to do but wait."

Nick tapped the floor with his boots for a minute or two lost in thought.

"Boys," he at length began. "I'm sore upset to-night. I've brought yez bad news—the gang's gone down in the Rapids."

The effect of this message was most startling. With a muttered oath Siwash Bill leaped to his feet and confronted the horseman. Pete sat on the stool like a statue. His lower jaw dropped and his eyes bulged big with astonishment. Even the Indian woman paused in her work and looked up. Her eyes glowed with a strange light, whether of sorrow or fierce joy she alone knew.

"Speak, speak, man, fer God's sake!" shouted Pete, "an' tell us what ye mean."

"Haven't I told ye?"

"Yes, yes. But don't stop there. Tell us all. When did it happen, an' where's the kid?"

"Damn if I know where the brat is. I thought you knew. Why didn't ye ask that stranger?"

"The stranger. What has he to do with the kid? What are ye drivin' at?"

"Nuthin' much, 'cept he had 'im."

"Had 'im?"

"Sure thing."

"Not when he was here."

"No, so I understand."

"But when? What's wrong with ye? Why don't ye spit it out?"

"I will if ye'll sit down an' give me time. There, that's better," he continued, as Bill with a growl dropped back upon his stool. "Now I kin spin it off. Well, fer two days I watched yon trail an' river, not knowin' by which the gang 'ud come. I knew it 'ud be by one or t'other unless they got pinched. Early this mornin' as I happened by chance along a high bluff this side of the rapids I spotted two men hikin' along the trail headin' fer Hishu. At first I thought they were the gang, but watchin' closer I saw that one was an Injun carry in' somethin' large in his arms."

"The devil!" ejaculated Pete, and the Indian woman again looked suddenly up.

"They didn't see me, though," continued Shifty, "fer I smelled a rat, an' scuttled. Then I did some tall thinkin', an' made up my mind to see what was behind, fer I knew they hadn't come fer at that time of the day. Hittin' the trail some distance up, an' follow-in' it fer a piece I found a huge grizzly lyin' dead at the foot of a little knoll. There were signs of a lively skirmish, an' the man wot pumped lead into that critter ain't to be fooled with, let me tell ye that."

"Good Lord, no!" gasped Pete; "guess not."

"Continuin' my way I reached the river, an' there jist at the ford I found some things which set me thinkin' some more."

"What?" was the excited question.

"A rifle an' a buckskin jacket."

"Whew, ye don't tell!"

"Yes, there they were, thrown down upon the bank. Lookin' up an' down the river my eyes caught sight of a piece of a canoe floatin' in a little eddy along the shore. Examinin' it closely I found it was the one Shorty kep' above the rapids. Goin' down-stream a bit I found another big chunk on a sand-bar, which made me sartin that somethin' had happened to the gang. Comin' back I struck an Injun camp, where there was an old squaw an' a young 'un. They told me the hull yarn an' a d— sight more, too. That afternoon I skirted the river an' caught up with the travellers. Twice they spotted me, which made 'em hike like h—"

"But what did they do with the kid?" questioned Pete.

"Took it to Old Meg's, so the squaw told me. Guess it's there yit."

"Good," exclaimed Bill, "we'll not lose it. If Meg's got it, we're all right."

"Don't be too sure of that," replied Shifty. "What about that young cub with Buckskin Dan?"

"An' ye say that he had the kid?"

"Sartin. Didn't I tell ye?"

"But how in h— did he git hold of it?"

"Jumped in the river an' saved its life, so the squaw said."

"The devil! Ye don't say so! But how did he happen to be there jist in the nick of time?"

"Bah," and Shifty spat contemptuously upon the floor. "How did he happen to be there! How does he happen to be here? How does he happen to be everywhere? Don't ye know he's one of them d—Yellow-legs from Big Glen?"

His companions started at these words, and glanced anxiously toward the door. Shifty gave a sarcastic laugh, drew a pipe from his pocket and stuck it between his teeth.

"Scart are ye?" he asked. "I thought y'd scent 'im five miles off."

"To tell ye the truth," Pete replied, "we didn't like the looks of 'im from the first, so we came back here to talk it over. Thought mebbe he'd tell Old Dan if left alone. So we listened."

"An' what did ye learn?"

"Nuthin', only we concluded he wasn't a Yellow-leg."

"How's that?"

"Why if he was after the ones wot pinched the kid he couldn't git here so soon, an' anyway he wouldn't come alone."

"An' so that's yer conclusion, was it? I thought yez had more sense than that. 'Couldn't git here so soon,' an' 'wouldn't come alone,'" he mocked. "Don't ye know that them Mounted Devils are everywhere? Ye may think there isn't one within two hundred miles. But let somethin' happen an' he's at yer heels like greased lightnin'. As fer comin' alone he doesn't mind that. He's used to it. He'll stroll into a gang of cutthroats as cool as ye please, pick his man, snap on the irons, an' walk out. Why haven't I seen it done time an time ag'in?"

"It takes nerve to do that," suggested Pete.

"Sartin. That's what made the Force what it is to-day. Only the man with nerves like steel is picked to do an ugly job, an' he knows that the hull damn Force is back of 'im, an' back of that the British Empire, Army an' Navy combined. Touch 'im an' ye touch the hull consarn. So ye may be sure it's no weak-kneed, wobbly-spine chap wot's been sent here, let me tell ye that."

"But how are ye so sure that he *is* a Yellow-leg?" questioned Siwash Bill.

"Know?" retorted Shifty. "Who else would be hikin' about Hishu without any object? Besides what about that Police rifle out there on that measly cayuse, an' the buckskin jacket? There's not a shadow of a doubt about it, so ye needn't worry over that. He's here fer bizness, an' the sooner we git a move on, the better."

"Oh, if he's as ye say," replied Bill, rising and stretching himself, "we kin soon fix 'im. He hasn't struck a bunch of kids an' babies here in Hishu."

"What's yer plan?" asked Shifty.

Bill glanced significantly at a revolver at his hip.

"Now, look here, Bill. Don't make a fool of yerself. D'ye want to bring down the hull Force upon us? We've done enough already. But lay hands upon yon chap, an' they'll be about us like hornets."

"What else kin we do, then?"

Shifty sat for some time in silence, while his face twitched more than ever, as it always did when his mind was working keenly. At length he brought his hand down upon his knee with a resounding whack.

"I've got it!" he exclaimed. "Ho, ho. It'll be all right. *We* won't touch 'im. But what about that pious-tongued hypocrite, Dan? Mebbe he'll have a finger in this little affair which he didn't expect. Ho, ho, me an' Pete'll help the Police to find the villain; oh, yes."

"How?" questioned Bill.

"How? Never ye mind that. We'll tend to the tail if you'll look after the head, an' that's the kid over yon. You keep an eye on it, and we'll look after the spyin' cub. Is it a go?"

"Sure," Bill assented somewhat dubiously, "but I'll be alone in my game, though."

"What about that gal with old Meg?" and Shifty tipped a wink to Pete. "She's a shy 'un, an' hasn't been broken in yit, but I guess you kin do it. I'd like to try meself, but haven't a ghost of a chance with you. She'll help ye if ye work her right."

"Think so?"

"Sartin. That kid's got to be moved. It's no place fer it here. So you've got yer job cut out. Git the kid, an' don't fergit the gal. She's a trim one that, an' I can't see how old Meg cinched her. She's the pardner fer ye. None better. If ye had her here she'd bambozzle every miner an' Injun wot comes to Hishu. They'd crowd in jist to see her, an' ye'd sell yer stuff like hot cakes."

"But they kin see her over there," replied Bill.

"No. Didn't I tell ye she's too d— shy? I can't savvey it nohow. An' ye better git a hustle on, too, fer in a short time the Injuns'll be pilin' in here like mad."

"Why, what d'ye mean, man? They won't be back fer two months yit."

"Won't they, hey? Jist you wait. I learned somethin' to-day which makes me say they will."

"Wot's that?"

"The Big Lake Injuns are on the warpath. The Hishus have trespassed on their ancestral huntin' grounds, an' won't take back water. The trouble's been brewin' fer years, an' has at last come to a head. It'll be either a big potlatch or war. But I fear the latter."

"Good Lord, man!" exclaimed Bill, "how did ye learn all this? Surely yer only foolin'."

"Not a bit of it. That old squaw I met on the trail let the cat out of the bag, an' the big Injun wot toted the kid is her husband, Hishu Sam. So ye know wot that means."

During the latter part of this conversation the Indian woman's eyes glowed with an intense light. She kept them fixed full upon Siwash Bill's face. Jealousy mingled with a deep hatred was expressed there. Occasionally her right hand slipped into a bundle by her side until it rested upon the haft of a keen sheath knife. But when Shifty told about the threatened war between the Indians, and mentioned the name of Hishu Sam, jealousy and hatred gave place to fear. It was expressed both in her eyes and in her face. She sat perfectly rigid, however, until the conversation had ceased and the men had passed out into the other room.

CHAPTER VII BUCKSKIN DAN

"What are ye doin' here, young man?"

The words startled Grey, and caused him to look quickly around. Twice had this man asked that same question, and each time there was a peculiar warning note in his voice.

They had entered a small cabin, and were seated upon rough stools. The place was clean and neat, a striking contrast to the disorderly room they had just left. Two narrow bunks, one above the other, stretched part way across the south end of the room, while on the opposite side, and near the door, stood a small sheet-iron camping stove. Nearby was a rough table of whipsawn boards, over which, fastened to the wall, was a rude cupboard, containing a few iron plates, cups, saucers and knives. On the floor in the centre of the room a large bearskin was spread, while the principal adornments of the walls were snowshoes, rifles and traps, suspended on wooden pegs driven into the logs. Not until the owner of the cabin had started a fire in the stove, for the evening was cool, did he blurt forth his question, "What are ye doin' here, young man?"

"Just travelling," Grey replied.

"Travellin'; jist travellin', are ye? But isn't it rather risky bizness?"

"In what way? What do you mean?"

"Oh, nuthin' much. It only depends upon what yer travellin' fer that makes the difference."

"I don't understand. Will you please explain?"

"Wall, some people travel fer their health, some fer pleasure, an' some fer bizness. Now you ain't out fer yer health, that's sartin, fer ye've got more'n yer share, it seems to me. As fer pleasure—wall, folks don't ginerally come to a place like this. Tharfere ye must be out fer bizness, an' I reckon it's mighty delicate bizness at that."

"What makes you think so?" questioned Grey, somewhat amused at these shrewd remarks.

"I dunno exactly," and the old man scratched his head. "But somehow I feel ye're here in kernection with that gang over yon. If so I say ag'in that it's mighty delicate bizness."

"What makes you think so?" and Grey looked keenly into the calm eyes before him.

"Yer one of them Reds from Big Glen, are ye not?" and the old man jerked his stool a little nearer. "Thar now ye needn't git excited," he continued, noticing Grey about to interrupt him. "Buckskin Dan hasn't studied the gentle art of observation all these years fer nuthin'. In towns, cities an' sich places yer nat'ral senses peter out. Ye don't have to look much, fer yer streets are nuthin' but grooves, like a hull bunch of sluice boxes, an' ye jist foller yer nose. Somethin' gits wrong, too, with yer hearin' gear, fer I've had men tell me that right down thar in New York on Broadway, they never hear a sound, they're so used to the noise. As fer the smell, it almost drives me mad, an' yit folks wot live thar never smell anythin'. Now that ain't nat'ral. The good Lord when he gave me my senses meant me to use 'em. Fer some time past I've been seein' an' hearin' things over in yon store which made me sorter suspicious. Now, when I see a chap like yerself wanderin' about here in a vague sort of a way I begin t' see more things, an' surmise that thar's somethin' crooked afloat. I may be wrong, but guess not. So if ye'll take a word of caution ye'll go keerful, an' if I kin help ye a leetle, don't be afeered to ax me."

At first Grey was somewhat annoyed at Dan's words, and felt like rebuking him for his interference. This resentment, however, was quickly replaced by a very different feeling. It was impossible not to be impressed by this quiet man. He realised the truth of his words, and knew how serious was his own position, and how important it was to have such a sturdy ally in Buckskin Dan.

"You've lived some time in the North, I suppose?" he at length remarked.

"Nigh onto fifteen years," was the reply.

"And you know most of the people here?"

"Sartin. Know 'em all, an' some too well fer convenience."

"Do many miners live here?"

"'Bout fifty. But they're all out in the hills now prospectin'. They're comin' and goin' most of the time. Mark my word, thar'll be a big strike made about here one of these days. The gold's thar jist waitin' fer some lucky chap to find it."

"I suppose you know Siwash Bill and his gang," remarked Grey.

"Y' bet. Remember the fust time they struck this place, an' they've been raisin' Cain ever since, especially with the Injuns."

"How many are there in the gang?"

"Five, an' they stick together like tarred feathers."

"Are you sure there are five?"

"Sartin. Never more so."

"Well, I think you'll find there are only three now."

"Three! Only three! What d'ye mean?"

"That two of them went down last night in Klikhausia Rapids, when their canoe struck a sunken rock."

At this Dan sprang to his feet, and laid his hand heavily upon Grey's shoulder.

"What! What!" he whispered in a hoarse voice. "Say that over ag'in. Mebbe I didn't hear ye aright. D'ye tell me that two of 'em have gone down?"

"I believe so."

"What! Shorty an' Tim?"

"I don't know their names, but if you sit down I'll tell you all about it."

And there in that little cabin Grey told about the stolen child, the fight with the grizzly, the wreck in the rapids, and the rescue of the boy. To all this Dan listened with wide open eyes, at times interjecting a word of surprise.

"My God!" he exclaimed, when Grey had finished. "So them poor divils have gone down! Yes, I'm sartin it's them, fer I savvey things now which I couldn't afore. It's all clear to me as day. I see through their game—to steal the poor lad from his mother's arms, an' make the old man cough up the dough. Oh, them villains! It jist sarved 'em right, fer they war mean skunks. But I do pity the ones who'll have to look after 'em in t'other world. Parsons an' sich like may talk about goin' to hell, but Shorty an' Tim have taken their own hell fire along with 'em, an' don't ye fergit that."

"I wonder if the rest of the gang know about the accident," Grey remarked, gazing thoughtfully at the little stove, which was sending out its genial heat.

"Can't tell fer sartin," was the reply. "But they'll savvey about the lad at Old Meg's over yon, an' that'll be enough fer them."

"Will they try to do anything now, do you think?"

"Do? They'll never stop doin' as long as life's in their nasty bodies. Ye don't know them varmints. They're after money, an' they're bound to git it."

"And so you think the child's in danger yet?"

"Think it? I don't think anything about it. I know it."

"And what is to be done?"

"Git that youngster out of this as soon as he's able to be moved."

"But will they let us?"

"Not if they kin help it. But thar are always ways, don't ye fergit that. Thar are ways. But come, lad, ye're dead beat an' need some rest. So curl up in yon bunk while I stroll around outside a bit."

Grey was tired, very tired, and the bed soft and comfortable. For some time, however, he lay there thinking over the events of the day. His principal thoughts were of Madeline. How strange that after such a long separation he should find her in such a desolate region—and in that house! The sight of her had brought back the old memories of happy days, when they had strolled together, talked, and loved. Thinking thus he drifted into a restless sleep in which he was besieged by wild dreams. He was surrounded by the "gang." They were trying to throttle him. Then he saw Madeline, with face as white as death, struggling in the grasp of Siwash Bill. Her eyes were full of terror as she reached out to him appealing hands for help. For an instant he had not the power to assist her. He was bound by chains which held him fast. With a great cry he made one mighty effort. The chains snapped and he was free. At once the scene faded and he awoke. The room was fairly light, for the bright moon was shining in through the little window. How late it was he could not tell. Overhead he could hear Buckskin Dan's deep breathing. For some time he lay quietly in the bunk, hoping that he would soon drop off to sleep again. But try as he might his eyes would not close. The dream had been too real, and ever before his mind rose Madeline's tearful face, while her cry of fear rang incessantly in his ears.

At length he could bear it no longer. The bunk seemed like a prison. Slipping quietly to the floor, he softly opened the door, and left the building. It was a glorious night, and the moon, almost full, was drifting through masses of fleecy clouds. The air was cool and a long, filmy fog hung over the trees down by the river. Grey stood for a while outside the door, and looked around. Not a sound broke the intense stillness of the night. The chill air cooled his flushed face. He looked toward Old Meg's house, and moved by a sudden impulse started down the trail. A walk, he thought, would do him no harm; he would sleep the better after it. He wished to look again upon the cabin which sheltered Madeline. It did not take him long to reach the little clearing in which the dwelling stood, and, not wishing to pass out into the open, he stepped aside from the trail a short distance.

Seating himself upon a fallen tree at the edge of the forest he could obtain a good view of the house, while he himself was hidden. He was somewhat surprised to see a light shining in one of the windows facing him. Then he thought of the child. Perhaps someone was watching by its side. Was it Madeline? Was she sitting there in that room keeping faithful ward over the little one? It was just like her, he knew that, to give up her own comfort for others, especially for children. He looked carefully around. Not a living thing could he see. Suppose he stepped across to the house and peered in through the window. It could do no harm, and he did so long to see her face again.

He was about to step out into the open, when an object arrested his attention, which caused him to shrink back behind a small fir tree. The object soon proved to be a man, creeping guardedly toward the house from the right. Although he kept somewhat in the shade of the trees he was exposed to full view. Almost breathlessly Grey watched him as he proceeded slowly by the side of the building until he came to the window from which the light shone. Here he paused, and looked cautiously into the room. What he beheld Grey could not tell, but presently he went to the door and gave a gentle tap. Ere long it was slowly opened, and someone appeared. At that distance he could not hear what was being said, although several minutes elapsed as Grey stood there straining his ears in an effort to distinguish the words. Then the sounds grew louder, and occasionally an intelligent word drifted toward him. It was a woman's voice he heard, and now there was no doubt about it—it was Madeline's. What was she doing there at that time of the night? He recognised the man by his voice. It was Siwash Bill—and what was Madeline doing there with him? Was it his custom to meet her thus? These thoughts and others of a similar nature surged through Grey's brain.

"I tell you no! It can never be!"

How decisive were the words which now reached him clear and distinct. Then they sank lower, and listen as he might he could not distinguish their meaning.

"Leave me, and never come here again!"

Ah, he could hear these, and they thrilled the heart of the concealed listener. She did not wish him to come. A weight was lifted from his mind, and he breathed more freely. It was only for an instant, however, for at once a cry fell upon his ears—a cry for help—and it was Madeline's! No longer now did he hesitate. She was in danger, and needed him. He sprang from his hiding place, and bounded across the open, straight toward the spot where the two were standing.

CHAPTER VIII THE INTRUDER

Madeline's joy at beholding the child lying on the couch soon gave place to surprise. In her first intense delight at seeing the little one with the white face and curly hair, she had thought of nothing else. The child was enough, and she had rushed forward and bent over the frail form. That sight was sufficient to stir within her memories which she believed had long since been dead. Gradually wonder took possession of her. Where had the boy come from? What was he doing in such a place as Hishu, and especially at this house above all others? Then she thought of the tall silent form she had noticed standing in the centre of the room. She had given but one fleeting glance, and yet how that figure stood out in her mind clear and distinct. There was something familiar about those broad shoulders and the poise of that head which set her heart beating fast and brought the blood surging to her cheeks. Could it be possible that it was—? She caught her breath at the mere thought. No, such an idea was ridiculous. And yet something seemed to whisper it to her, and tell her that there was no mistake, that it was Norman and none other. A peace such as she had not known for years filled her heart. A subtle influence seemed to surround her and pervade the room. For a brief space of time she kept her face close to the child. How could she look upon him? What would he say? How would he greet her? She felt that his eyes were fixed upon her. Were they filled with sorrow or reproach? Would he scorn her? At length she raised her head and looked around for one quick glance, but he was gone. Then a sharp revulsion of feeling swept over her. The crimson left her cheeks, leaving them as pallid as death. Her bloodless lips were compressed. He was gone, and she knew why! He had recognised her, had understood, and had fled!

Madeline rose to her feet, and stared straight before her toward the door, and out into the yard beyond. She saw no one; she heard nothing but the beating of her own tumultuous heart. She presented a beautiful pathetic scene standing there. But the woman watching her thought nothing of this. Her cynical eyes were fixed upon Madeline's face, and her lips parted in a cold smile.

"Don't worry. He'll come back."

Madeline started at these words.

"Who is he?" and her voice was hoarse as she whispered the question.

"You'll learn in time, so don't be uneasy," replied the woman. "But, come, you had better look after that brat. I don't want to be bothered with it, and as you think so much of it you'd better tend to it at once. You must get the thing fixed up as soon as possible, for I don't want it kicking about here when the men come back from the hills. You won't have any time to look after it then, mark my words."

Madeline turned from the cruel creature toward the child. A great weight pressed upon her heart, and she felt she must cry out. Had Old Meg spoken such words that morning or the day before she would have thought little of them. Was she not accustomed to the life—hideous though it was—and this woman's sharp, pitiless tongue? Madeline imagined that she, too, was hardened and indifferent herself. But now she realised that a change had taken place. That subtle influence which surrounded her and the presence of that sweet-faced boy sleeping there on the couch made a great difference. The men would come from the hills, they would crowd into the house, and then hell would be let loose. She shuddered as she thought of it.

A cough from Donnie brought Madeline quickly to his side. He opened his eyes, and looked up into her face.

"Mother. I wants my mother," he wailed. "Why don't she tum to her 'ittle boy-boy?"

Madeline was all alert now. Soothing the child and winning his confidence she carried him off to her own small room at the side of the house, and laid him upon her rude cot. Quickly and deftly she undressed him and tucked the blanket carefully about his little body. Donnie was restless and feverish, and the rasping cough still shook the delicate frame. For a while Madeline stood in doubt. She hardly knew what course to pursue to relieve the suffering. At length a simple remedy came to her mind. Crossing the room she drew back a curtain and brought down from a nail a much worn flannel skirt. Only for a moment did she hesitate as she looked upon it. Then seizing a pair of scissors lying on a table near by she cut off a large portion from the bottom of the garment. Telling Donnie not to be afraid, that she would return soon, she went at once to a small cooking stove at the back of the building, lighted a fire, and placed the flannel near to warm. Then going to a corner of the room she poured some coal oil from a tin can into a saucer and placed it on the stove to heat. When this had been accomplished to her satisfaction she carried Donnie to the kitchen, placed him on her lap near the fire, and thoroughly rubbed his little chest with the oil, and then applied the warm flannel. It was only a simple remedy, she was well aware, but it was all she knew, and she was willing to do what she could. This she kept up for some time, and then once more placed the little fellow back into bed. Soon she had the satisfaction of seeing his eyes close in a peaceful sleep. But not for a moment did Madeline relax her watchfulness.

Hour after hour she remained faithfully on guard, keeping the fire in the stove and the flannels warm upon the chest. How thankful Madeline was for the presence of the child! Sleep fled her eyes as she sat there watching. No sound broke the intense stillness which reigned. The house was unusually quiet, for often sounds of revelry continued throughout the night. Her mind was greatly agitated. Where had this child come from, and why was such a delicate lad so far in the wilderness away from civilisation? Carefully she examined his clothes, studying well each little garment, the fine quality of the material of which it was made, and the signs of a loving hand in each tiny stitch. And why should *he* have the boy? No longer did she doubt that the man was Norman. But what was he doing there? Then a question stinging in its intensity pierced her heart. Was this his child? Had he a wife living somewhere in the North? Was she beautiful? Did her hands fashion the little garments lying before her? Was this the reason why Norman had fled so hurriedly from the house? Had he recognised her, and did not want to speak to her because he was married? She could not rid her mind of the thought. Dry-eyed and motionless she sat there, staring straight at the sleeping lad. She did not blame Norman. How could she expect that he would wait six long years for her, whom the world believed dead? How strange it was that she should be watching by the side of his boy! What circumstance, she wondered, had brought such a thing to pass? Though now a gulf yawned between them his child was with her, and she could love it for his sake. Bending suddenly forward she pressed her hot lips to Donnie's cheek. How soft was the little face, and what a strange new thrill that simple touch brought to her heart.

A knock upon the door at the side of the house startled her. She drew back abashed. Was it Norman, and had he been watching her through the window? It was but natural that he should come to see about his sick boy. How could she meet him? Rising to her feet she stood irresolute by the foot of the bed. What should she do? What could she say?

Again the knock sounded, louder than before. Madeline no longer hesitated. She crossed the room, turned the wooden button, and cautiously opened the door. As she did so she started back, and a slight cry of fear escaped her lips. Standing on the step with his left hand upon the side of the door was Siwash Bill. His swinish eyes leered in upon her, and a frown wrinkled his brow as he noted how she recoiled from his presence.

For some time past Madeline had noted how the squaw man had sought her company. He had come to the house, and often met her as she took her lonely walk along the trail leading to the river. He followed her like a shadow, and lost no opportunity of ingratiating himself in her good will. The more she repulsed him, the more determined he became. Rough, uncouth men frequented the house when they were in Hishu. Them she could tolerate, or had to tolerate. But this creature filled her heart with a loathsome repugnance, like the presence of a slimy, crawling viper.

"Frightened are ye, miss?" Again Bill smiled—the smile of the evil one. "Didn't know I was sich a monster."

"What do you want?" and Madeline spoke sharply. "Why do you disturb me at this time of the night?"

"Saw a light in the window, an' thought mebbe ye'd like company," was the reply.

"No, I prefer to be alone—with the child. So you might have spared yourself the trouble."

"Now don't git heady, miss. It's partly on account of that little chap that I've come here to-night. He means a pile of money to me. I've run a big risk consarnin' him, an' I can't afford to take chances."

"Run a big risk? What do you mean?"

"Listen," and the squaw man moved closer and whispered something into Madeline's ear, which caused her to start. "Thar now, ye needn't take on," Bill continued. "All ye've got to do is to hand over that kid to me when he gits better, an' part of the chink's yours."

"Never!" Madeline's determined negative rang out distinctly through the night, and thrilled a silent listener concealed not far away. "I can't do that, so God help me!"

"Can't? Think ag'in. Money's a god; it works miracles."

Madeline did not reply. How could she answer this villain? What was the use of speech? She would leave him; close the door in his face. Siwash Bill mistook her silence for acquiescence. He drew nearer, and she shrank back.

"Yes," he continued, "money's a god; it'll do anything. An' look you; there's money in it, twenty thousand dollars! A man with that kin leave the North, go outside, an' be rich. Miss, I want that chink, an' you in the bargain. D'ye suppose I've been watchin' ye all these weeks fer nuthin'? D'ye suppose I'd a taken all yer rebuffs in silence if I didn't love ye? Not a bit of it. Come, say ye'll have me, an' we'll cut this d—place ferever. We'll cinch that twenty thousand dollars an' git out."

Madeline, though pale before, was white as death now. She clutched at the door post for support. She knew something of the determined nature of the man standing before her.

"You scoundrel!" she cried. "How dare you say such words! Leave me, and never show your face here again!"

"An' ye won't have me?"

"No; a thousand times no!"

"Then I won't ask ye. This is the land whar strength rules. If ye won't be mine one way ye will another."

Saying which the brute took a quick step forward, and placed his arm suddenly about her waist.

With a cry Madeline strove to wrench herself from his grip. But the more she strove the firmer he held her fast, and drew her closer to his breast. A faintness swept over her as she felt his hot breath upon her face, and she gave one wild piercing cry for help.

And even as she ceased to struggle, and a fearful blackness blinded her eyes, she heard the sound of rapid steps, and felt the squaw man's arms suddenly relax. Grey had arrived none too soon, and words of explanation were unnecessary. One long arm reached out, and tense knuckles caught Siwash Bill full under the left ear. Unheeding the wretch sprawling on the ground he caught Madeline in his arms and entered the building. It took but a minute for him to cross the room and lay her upon the couch. But in that brief space of time as he clasped her unconscious form to his breast an overmastering yearning took possession of him. He looked into that dear white face; his breath fanned her wavy hair, and with the greatest effort he restrained himself from pressing his lips to those slightly parted ones so close to his. But no, he must not allow his feeling to get the better of him. It would be better to wait awhile. He turned and saw Old Meg standing in the middle of the room, with a questioning look upon her face.

"What's the matter with her?" she growled. "Why all such yelling and fuss at this time of the night?"

Grey was about to express himself freely to this woman. With an effort, however, he restrained himself, knowing that angry words would do no good.

"Ask Siwash Bill," he replied. "Perhaps he'll tell you, for I don't know. But look you well after her," and he pointed to Madeline. "She's somewhat knocked out. Get a basin and some water, quick. You attend to her; I must see to someone outside."

With one deep longing glance toward Madeline he turned and left the building, leaving Old Meg staring in profound wonder after his tall retreating form.

CHAPTER IX UNDERCURRENTS

For some time after the plotters had left the room Nadu, the Indian woman, sat quietly in the corner. No longer were her fingers busy, for the buckskin jacket had been laid aside. Other things occupied her mind. She could hear the murmur of voices in the adjoining store, and recognised the men. It was quite dark now, for the moon had not risen. Presently Nadu thrust her hand beneath her blanket, and clutched the handle of the sharp knife concealed there. Running her fingers across the blade she noted with satisfaction the keenness of the edge and the sharp needle-like point. Drawing the weapon forth she hid it deftly within the folds of a blanket wrapped about her shoulders. Rising to her feet she moved softly across the room, quietly opened the door, and slipped out into the night.

To the right flowed the river, its banks lined with cottonwood trees and jack pines. Through these she glided like some weird spectre. Occasionally she stayed her steps to listen, but all was silent. After a while she paused, and crept to the edge of the clearing. There before her was the dim form of a house, with a light shining from one of the windows. For some time Nadu remained crouched upon the ground. The light seemed to fascinate her, and when once it disappeared she started to her feet, and crept forward like a tiger ready to spring, but slunk back again when the light reappeared.

At length her eyes sought the East, where a faint glow was visible in the sky close to the horizon. It was the first signal of the moon, which soon would be rising full and bright over the land. This Nadu well knew, so creeping from her place of concealment she sped across the open, and moved warily around the log building until she came near to the window from which the light was streaming. Then standing a little to one side she peered in through the small panes of glass, until her eyes rested upon a slight form bending lovingly over a little child lying asleep upon the bed.

No feeling of tenderness smote Nadu's breast at the scene which met her gaze. Jealousy and hatred held her in thrall. Before her was the woman who was making her life a hell; the one who had crossed her path, and who was alienating the affections of her husband, the squaw man. Had she not noticed it for days, nay, weeks now? Did not all the pride of her race rebel at the neglect and ignominy which were bestowed upon her? But him she blamed not. The woman alone was the cause, and now her eyes dilated as she looked through the curtainless window. Once Madeline turned half around as if she intuitively knew of that lowering face. Then Nadu had shrunk back, fearful lest she should be observed.

During the whole of this time the Indian woman firmly clutched the knife beneath her blanket. Its touch gave her a degree of satisfaction, and often her fingers caressed the keen blade as her eyes gloated over the pale-faced woman in the room.

The moon had now risen, and was flooding the whole landscape with its silver beams. To the left the trees of the forest threw out their long trailing shadows. Nadu glanced uneasily in their direction. How sombre and gruesome they appeared! The whole air seemed to pulsate with strange forebodings. Nadu was no coward. She belonged to a tribe which knew not fear. The Big Lake Indians had never retreated from a foe. They could die with a smile and a song, but knew not how to yield. And Nadu was a child of the bravest. Had not her mother often related to her the story of that terrible night when her father had led forth the Big Lake warriors and had driven back a band of Dog Rib Indians from beyond the mountains? The fighting had been fierce, and several had been slain, her father among the number. How Nadu's heart had thrilled as she dreamed of that scene, until the spirit of her father was hers. But on this night it was detection she feared. She had a purpose in view, and until that was accomplished she must be wary.

With one long lingering look through the window she moved away from the house, and glided across the open to the edge of the forest, until her form was hidden by the dark shadows. Here she paused, and squatting upon the ground kept her eyes fixed upon the light pouring from the house.

And not many minutes did she have to wait ere Siwash Bill came creeping along. She saw him peering in through the window, and approach the door. Then when she beheld Madeline standing there, and noticed the two talking together, the fire of rage and jealousy leaped to a white heat. Formerly she had believed that the pale-faced woman was entirely at fault. Now she knew that Bill was much to blame. He had come to the place to see this woman. She had loved the squaw man with all the affection of her passionate nature. She had waited upon him like a slave, and his curses she had received without a murmur. All this she could endure, for he was hers, and her love was deep. But now—She clutched the knife more firmly, and, waiting no longer, sped through the shadows, plunged into the forest, and reached the river. A trail, worn smooth, wound along the bank. This she followed up-stream for the space of fifty yards. Then she paused and listened. Hearing nothing but the rapid beating of her own heart she was about to continue on her way, when a faint sound fell upon her ears. She glanced quickly toward the river, but only the silver sheen of the ripple-less surface met her eyes. She believed she had been mistaken, and was about to proceed when again the sound was heard, much more distinct now. Something was down there along the shore within the shadows of the trees, she felt sure of that. At first she thought it might be only a wild duck, or a muskrat besporting itself in the water. This idea was soon dispelled, however, for presently she was able to detect the soft rhythmical dip of paddles. Moving behind a small jack pine, she crouched upon the ground and waited. Who could it be, she wondered, approaching at such an hour of the night? Was it friend or foe? It could not be any of the Hishus, for they had all gone up-stream. Could it be the Big Lake Indians? She thought of the conversation in the house, and of what Shifty had said about the trouble between the tribes, and of Hishu Sam's return. Were the Big Lakes coming in force to attack the settlement, to murder the inhabitants, seize the supplies in the store, and then sweep on to surprise the Hishus in their camping grounds! Well did she know the remorselessness and tiger-like swiftness of the Big Lakes when once aroused to action.

A sudden impulse seized her to dart forward and give warning of the invaders. She rose partly to her feet, but immediately sank back again. Why should she go? The Hishus were nothing to her, and the white men—ugh! What did she care for them now? Had they not treated her like a dog, and Bill worst of all? Let him go to the white woman; of what avail would she be to him if the Big Lakes came?

Such were the thoughts which beat through her brain as she crouched there with her straining eyes fixed upon the river. The sounds were becoming more distinct, and ere long she was able to discern the dim outline of something moving slowly over the water. Nearer and nearer it approached until the faint shape of a canoe could be discerned, with two forms seated therein. Stealthily and shadowy it glided forward, and passed the place where she was crouched.

Nadu arose, and crept silently along the trail. On and on the canoe moved until it came opposite the store. Here it drew into shore at a little opening which led to the water's edge. Nadu watched the strangers while they made the craft fast to an old root. Then they crept warily through the trees toward the settlement. Her first thought was to follow after, and ascertain the object of their visit. But the sight of the canoe brought to her mind a new idea. With Nadu to think was to act, and when sure that the men were some distance away she moved quickly from her hiding place, unfastened the canoe, gave it a gentle push, and sprang in. Seizing one of the paddles lying in the bottom, with a few vigorous strokes she headed the canoe up-stream, keeping well within the shadows. When she had gone about one hundred yards she ran into shore in a sheltered nook, and made the craft fast to a tree. Having accomplished this she hurried down the trail, and once more took up her position close to the spot where the Indians had landed.

Here she waited for some time ere the sound of returning steps rewarded her patience. Swiftly and softly the two strangers sped down the trail. Reaching the river they looked in surprise at the place where they had left the canoe. Then a whispered conversation ensued. That they were much concerned Nadu could easily tell. Closely she watched them as well as the shadows would permit. One she recognised, and the sight of his figure brought a thrill to her heart. It brought back memories of by-gone years. It was Tonda, the sturdy brave, who had sought her love ere the advent of Siwash Bill, his successful rival. She had given him up for the white man, and what had she gained? The roving life, the fascination of forest, river and lake all had been relinquished. And now she was a slave, confined to a hateful cabin, to wait upon her brutish lord and master.

The sight of Tonda stirred Nadu more than was her wont. Would he care to see her? she wondered. Would he have anything to do with her? Would her people have her back again after years of absence? The old life was drawing, appealing, calling her by numerous mystic charms.

As the Indians continued to converse, Nadu stepped quickly forward and stood by their side. Startled by her sudden appearance, the men raised their rifles. But Nadu lifted her hand, and motioned them not to fear.

"Tonda," she said in a low voice, in the language of the Big Lakes; "Tonda afraid of a squaw? Why does he tremble? Why does he wish to shoot? Is Tonda's heart weak?"

"Who speaks?" replied the latter, bending forward to obtain a better look.

"Has Tonda forgotten? Does he not remember the voice which once was music to his ears?"

"Nadu! Is it Nadu?" and the man straightened himself up. "What does Nadu care about Tonda? Nadu has left her people. She has joined the pale face intruders. She lives now among the Hishu 'dogs.'"

"Ah, ah!" Nadu replied. "Tonda speaks true. The Hishus are dogs, but they are swift-footed dogs, and do not bark before they bite. Let the Big Lakes beware, for the Hishu dogs are roused, and their fangs are long and keen."

"Why does Nadu say all this?" Tonda replied. "Does she not live among the Hishus, and knows her own people no longer?"

"Nadu is a child of Wabanda. His blood flows in her veins. His spirit is hers. Nadu has not forgotten her people; she would go back to them. She would go with Tonda."

"And did Nadu take the canoe?" questioned the latter, as a suspicion of what had happened to the craft floated into his mind.

"Ah, ah; Nadu knows," was the low reply.

"And will Nadu come to-night?"

Tonda was eager now. This woman was fascinating him as of yore. He forgot how she had repulsed him for the white man. In her presence he was as a child.

"Nadu will not go to-night. Two sleeps and Nadu will be ready."

"But why wait so long? Tonda cannot stay."

"Is Tonda afraid of the Hishus? Does he fear their fangs?"

"No, no; Tonda knows not fear. But the Big Lakes are waiting."

"Let them wait," answered the woman. "What does Tonda know about the Hishus? What has he learned to-night? Nothing. Two sleeps and Nadu will be here. She knows much."

"And the canoe?" breathed the warrior.

"Let Tonda wait, and he shall have the canoe. He shall have it to-night."

For a few minutes the two men moved aside and conversed with each other in low tones. At length Tonda turned toward the woman.

"The Big Lake warriors will trust Nadu," he said. "Let her show them the canoe, and after two sleeps they will be here."

"Tonda speaks well" was the reply. "Nadu is pleased. She will find the canoe. Come."

CHAPTER X SUBTLE WAYS

When Siwash Bill staggered to his feet he was still dazed by the furious blow which had sent him reeling to the ground. A burning rage filled his heart, mingled with a sense of fear. Who was this man who had so suddenly leaped out of the night with that sledge-hammer fist? His face he had not seen, for there had been no time for that. He looked toward the door, and saw a dark, tall form bearing the unconscious woman in its arms. Then the door closed and he was alone. His first impulse was to rush forward, smash down that wooden barrier and hurl himself upon his assailant. He advanced a few steps, and then hesitated. No, he would wait. He would learn more. And besides, the woman did not want him. She had repelled him. He had made her a liberal offer, and she had scorned him to his face. Slowly he moved away from the building toward the store. He reached the edge of the forest, and, stepping aside a few yards from the trail, sat down upon an old log. He could see the house, and anyone who came out would be quite visible. His small eyes peered forth from among the trees as he sat and watched.

He had not long to wait ere Grey emerged from the building and hurried across the open. The squaw man half rose to his feet as he recognised the constable. His hand slipped to his hip pocket and rested upon the butt of a revolver concealed there. Here was his chance. He would get more than even for the assault which had been made. His face was sore and swollen where the blow had fallen. That insult would soon be wiped out. Grey was near now, almost opposite, and Bill held the weapon in his hand. Another step or two and all would be over. But even as his finger rested upon the curve of the trigger his arm weakened and his hand trembled. A vision flashed before his mind.

With his outward eyes he beheld only one lone man striding forward through the night. He was unaware of danger, and how easy to strike him down. But the squaw man saw more than this. He knew full well that the figure before him represented a power which would scour every valley, hill and region in the whole land to avenge his death. The work of the Mounted Police was well known to him. Years before he had reason to dread their marvellous vigilance. Here in the far North, beyond the bounds of civilisation, he had fondly believed he would be free from their rule. But no, they were following him still. The awe for this body of men which had been instilled into his heart years ago gripped him now as strongly as ever. He thought of the dire consequences should he shoot this lone constable. The idea unnerved him, and caused his arm to drop by his side, while Grey strode forward unconscious of the danger which threatened him among the trees.

A low curse breathed from Siwash Bill's lips as he watched his enemy until he disappeared from view.

"I'm a d— fool, an' a coward!" he muttered as he stepped out upon the trail. "To think that I have let that cur escape! An' yet—" He paused, and his face wrinkled into an ugly scowl. "By G—, he won't git off always as he did this time! He's after me, I know. But maybe he'll git more than he's bargained fer. Oh, yes, my beauty. You got clear to-night with your whole skin. But there are ways, an' I'll defy the whole d— Force!"

Thinking thus he reached his own house, pushed open the door and entered. The place was in darkness. He called for Nadu, but received no reply.

"Where in h— are ye?" he shouted. "Why don't ye answer? Are ye asleep?"

But still no reply.

Fumbling in his pocket he produced a match, struck it and lighted a candle lying near. Holding this in his hand he examined the room. To his surprise the place was empty. Sticking the candle into a hole in the table, he sat down upon a bench and began to collect his thoughts. Where had Nadu gone? It was seldom she left the building at night. He took good care of that. He did not wish her to be wandering around, especially when the Indians arrived from their hunting grounds. Why had she gone during his absence? he wondered. Anyway, she would come back, there was no doubt of that, and he would wait for her. She would not do such a thing again.

Throwing himself upon a rude bunk fastened to the wall, he began to think about the events of the afternoon and night. Ere long he became drowsy, for it was late. He tried hard for some time to keep awake, but his efforts were all in vain, for sleep at length gained the mastery. He did not hear the door open, nor the soft movement of moccasined feet across the room. Neither did he see a lithe form standing by his side, while a pair of piercing eyes, full of a triumphant gleam, gazed down upon his face.

The morning light was stealing in through the little window on the left when Siwash Bill opened his eyes and looked about the room. Realising that he had overslept himself he sprang quickly out of the bunk, and stood over Nadu who was lying on the floor, rolled up in her blanket.

"Get up!" he growled in Indian, at the same time touching her with the toe of his boot in no gentle manner.

Thus rudely aroused Nadu threw aside the blanket, rose to a squatting posture, and eyed her imperious master. The look she bestowed upon him was one of scorn and contempt.

"Where were you last night?" he demanded. "What did you mean by staying out so late? I waited a d— long time for you. See that it doesn't happen again. You don't leave this place at night for a month, so understand that. If you do I'll break every bone in your black body."

At these words Nadu's lips parted in a sarcastic smile. Her teeth gleamed like polished ivory, and her eyes bespoke danger. She was no longer afraid of this man. Her days of slavery were about over.

"Did Bill wait up long?" she queried. "Then Nadu is not happy. But Bill sleeps well."

"Sleep well! Certainly. It was late enough for anyone to sleep well. I want to know where you were, and what kept you out so late. Have any of the Injun bucks come back? If I catch you with any of them, or if you go to their tents, it won't be well for you."

"And was not Bill afraid to sleep well?" the woman answered in her sweetest native tones.

"Afraid? Afraid of what?"

"Does not Bill fear the Big Lakes?"

"The Big Lakes? What are you talking about?" and the squaw man's eyes opened with surprise.

"But does not Bill know that the Big Lakes are all same wolves and foxes? They come up the river; they paddle soft; they wait till night. They come to Hishu; they creep along trail; they go among the cabins; they see much. Is not Bill afraid?"

A slight expression of concern swept across the squaw man's face at these words. He knew of the trouble which existed between the two Indian tribes, and realised what a sudden attack of the wily Big Lakes would mean to his fur-trading business.

"Nadu," he demanded after a minute's thought, "have you seen any of the Big Lakes near Hishu lately?"

"Ah, ah," was the reply.

"When?"

"They came in the night, when Bill was asleep. They paddle soft up the river; they creep up the trail; they see the cabins empty; they laugh. 'Hishu is not strong,' they say. 'Hishu is like a gopher, easy to catch.'"

"And how many of the Big Lakes came?" Bill questioned.

Nadu held up two fingers.

"Bah! Is that all?"

"Ah, ah; all now, but not all by and by."

"And you think more will come later?"

"Ah, ah."

"Did you see the Injuns? Did you speak to them?"

"Ah, ah."

"And are they near Hishu now?"

"Ah, ah."

At any other time Bill would have been furious had Nadu confessed that she had been talking with two Indians from her own tribe, especially at night. But now he was thinking of other things. Although the thought of those Big Lake spies filled him with apprehension, yet they brought to his mind a new idea. They would go back to their own people. Nadu was one of them. She knew their ways and dialect. Why should she not take that boy and go back with the Big Lakes? He had been racking his brain for some plan to get him out of Hishu, and away from that meddlesome stranger. Here was an opportunity which must not be missed. And for Nadu to go, too, would suit his purpose well. She was in his way now. He had made up his mind to win that white woman, and a repulse or two only made him the more determined. He had no doubt about the final outcome of it all, for mingled with Siwash Bill's craftiness and vileness was much personal vanity. He had won Nadu, the choicest flower of the Big Lake maidens, against numerous rivals, and who was this white woman living with Old Meg who could withstand him for any length of time? And when he had won her Nadu would be in the way. She would not endure a pale face rival in the same house. No. Nadu must go—and here was the favourable chance. He need not have her back again, and not likely would she wish to come.

A smile of satisfaction crossed Bill's face as he thought of this scheme, and the solution of two difficult questions.

"Where are the Big Lakes now?" he asked, turning toward Nadu.

"Down the river."

"And will they come back again?"

"Ah, ah, maybe so."

"Will you see them?"

"How can Nadu see them?" was the low reply. "Has not Bill spoken? Has he not said that Nadu must not go out at night?"

"Yes, yes, I know I said that. But I have changed my mind. I want you to meet those Injuns when they come back, and tell them something."

At this Bill looked cautiously around, lowered his voice, and whispered a few words into her ear.

Nadu started slightly, and looked up keenly into the squaw man's face as if to read his inmost thoughts.

"Is not Bill afraid to let Nadu go with the Big Lake braves?" she queried.

"Why should I be afraid?" he parried. "You will be among your own people, and think of the money you will get. You look after that brat until I want him, and you will get the chink."

"How soon?"

"Can't tell for certain. Shifty leaves to-day for Big Glen. It may take a little time."

"Maybe Shifty doesn't get money," suggested the woman.

"No fear of that," was the response. "When that old cuss knows it's either the money or his child's life he'll cough up the dough quicker than h—."

"But maybe Shifty get caught," persisted Nadu.

"No fear of that, either. If hands are laid upon Shifty it's all up with the kid. Old Si knows that. He's had his instructions all in black and white. He's put that d— Yellow-leg upon us, but that doesn't matter. Now will you do as I wish; see those Big Lake spies, pinch the kid and get out?"

Nadu did not reply at once, but sat very still with her head bent, and eyes fixed upon the floor. Of what was she thinking? Had she read Siwash Bill's heart, and the reason which prompted him to send her away with the child? Did any feeling of jealousy mingle with the joy of escaping from the life of bondage, and returning to her own people? Whatever were the emotions contending within her breast she betrayed not a sign as she lifted up her calm, passive face to the man standing before her.

"Nadu will go," she quietly remarked. "She will meet the Big Lake braves. She will go to her own people, and the pale face baby will go with her."

"Good!" responded Bill, and at once he turned to leave the room. "See that you don't fail, or it won't be well with you."

Nadu waited until the door had closed, and she was sure that Bill was some distance away. Then the expression on her face underwent a marvellous change. The softness and the light faded like the beauty of an evening sky before thick threatening clouds, leaving in their stead fierceness and strange forebodings. Could the scheming squaw man have seen her then he would not have felt so confident of the success of his venture.

CHAPTER XI THE CAPTURE

When Madeline opened her eyes after Grey had left she imagined it was all a horrible dream. But the sight of Old Meg standing by her side and her own great weakness of body told her that it was too terribly true. A shiver shook her form as she thought of Siwash Bill, his impudence, and insulting request. She longed to inquire about the man who had rescued her and carried her into the house. What had become of him? she wondered. She was tempted to ask Old Meg to tell her what she knew. But each time she hesitated, and found herself unable to form the words which were trembling upon her lips.

Meg asked no questions about the occurrence of the night. That something more than usual had taken place she was well assured. But Madeline's reserved manner restrained even this woman, noted for her boldness and curiosity. There was some mystery, she believed, concerning this stranger who had arrived so unexpectedly in Hishu. Did Madeline know anything about him? Had she seen him before? These thoughts puzzled and worried her throughout the day. Often she would pause in the midst of her work and gaze for some time out of the open door.

Most of the day Madeline spent with Donnie. He had awakened feeling much better, and the wheezing cough had disappeared. He soon became quite friendly with the woman sitting by his side, who looked upon him with such big pathetic eyes. Madeline told him simple childish stories, at which he would often clap his hands with delight. When night arrived Donnie was much like his former self. Madeline rejoiced to have the child near her. She knew that Hishu was no place for a boy like this, and her heart ached to think that such a delicate lad should be so far away from his parents' tender care. As the darkness deepened, and Donnie sat in her lap he asked for his mother.

"Why doesn't she tum to me, Malin?" he said. "Why does she 'tay away so long?"

Such a question Madeline could not answer. She endeavoured to soothe him, and gently stroked his curly silken hair. Long after he had fallen asleep she sat by his side and gazed upon the little face. And so the boy was stolen away, too, she thought. Why should an innocent child be made to suffer by reason of cruel, wicked men? She recalled Siwash Bill's vile proposition, and shuddered. She knew something of his persistency, and of the length he would go to carry out his base designs. Money and revenge the man wanted. She was sure of that, and had torn away the lamb from the fold to further his object. What could she do to save the boy? She longed to seize him in her arms, and hurry off into the forest; anywhere would be better than Hishu. But this she realised would be futile. Her face darkened, and her tense hands gripped each other in her lap as she thought of her own fruitless attempts in the past. She could not escape from the Argus-eyed Meg, and what could she do with a little lad in a dreary wilderness, with Siwash Bill and his gang in pursuit? She thought of Norman, and a flush mantled her face. Would not he help her? But why should she go to him? He had kept clear of her; had not even come to inquire after the lad. And yet she felt it was Norman and no one else who had saved her from Siwash Bill. Why did he leave so soon? What was the meaning of his strange behaviour? Was it because he believed her to be—? The words would not come to Madeline's lips. Would Norman think such things of her, of Madeline whom he had known and loved in the happy days of old, which now seemed so far away?

The next day Donnie was well enough to run about the house. Everything interested him, and his cheery laugh caused even Old Meg's face to soften with a new light.

"Donnie," said Madeline that evening, "how would you like to walk to the river with me? I go there sometimes by myself, but would like to have you this time to take care of me."

Donnie clapped his hands with delight, and chatted incessantly while Madeline wrapped a small shawl about his body, and tied a hood, much too large for him, upon his curly head.

Together they soon set off down the trail, Donnie holding Madeline's hand, and plying her with all sorts of questions.

"Will ou take me home some day, Malin?" he asked.

"I should like to do so, dear," was the reply. "I know your father and mother must be anxious about you. But what will Madeline do without her little boy?"

"Oh, ou will tum, too. Ou *must* tum, and live right wif me. We have a big, big house. I will let ou sleep in my room, play wif my horse and tin soldiers. Wouldn't ou like to tum?"

"Very much, dearie," and tears stood in Madeline's eyes at the child's innocent prattle.

"Is this your home, Malin?" and the lad looked up inquiringly into her face.

"Why do you ask that, Donnie? Don't you think this is my home?"

"I don't know. But it seems such a funny home. Is dat woman your mother? And where is your daddy?"

A lump came into Madeline's throat, and she pressed Donnie's hand more firmly.

"I haven't any father and mother now, Donnie. But I have a home, far, far away, oh, so beautiful, which I have not seen for a long time."

"Tell me about it, Malin," and the child perched himself upon an old fallen log which stretched itself along the trail.

By this time they had drawn very close to the river, where the bank was steep. All around stood the silent forest of firs and jack pines, with the cold, dark stream drifting noiselessly by. No sense of fear came into Madeline's heart as she obeyed Donnie's behest. So often had she come to this place that it was like an old friend, full of understanding and sympathy.

Seating herself by the lad's side she told about her old home, the house among the trees, the garden with the many beautiful flowers, where the birds sang and the bees hummed.

To all this Donnie listened with wide-eyed pleasure, occasionally interrupting with a question about the birds and flowers.

So engrossed did Madeline become with her story that she forgot how the time had flown and how late was the hour. Neither did she notice a dark form gliding silently toward her through the shadowy forest, nor a trim canoe which had dropped down-stream and was now lying below the bank not far away.

"Come, Donnie!" she exclaimed; "it's getting dark, and we must hurry home."

And even as she spoke and rose to her feet, a powerful Indian leaped from a thicket of trees a few yards away, and arrested her further movement. Too startled to cry Madeline gave one lightning glance at the intruder, and then caught Donnie in her arms. At once the child was torn from her grasp, and borne swiftly to the river by the native.

Forgetting her own danger, and thinking only of the lad, with a cry Madeline sprang forward. She leaped down the bank toward the canoe, which was lying near, held close to the shore by a swarthy Indian. Him she saw not, neither did she notice a figure crouched in the bow, with a shawl wrapped about her shoulders, watching everything with cruel, sparkling eyes. Donnie was in the canoe! He was to be taken away, and she must save him! That was all she could think about. She saw him struggling in the arms of his captor, and reaching out appealing hands to her. She beheld the look of terror blanching his little face, and heard his piercing cry of "Malin! Malin!" ere he was silenced by a dark hand placed suddenly and roughly across his mouth.

Throwing discretion to the wind Madeline sprang into the canoe, nearly capsizing it as she did so, and snatched Donnie out of the Indian's arms. That the latter relinquished the child so readily was at first somewhat of a surprise. It was soon explained, however, for, upon turning to step ashore she found that the craft was several yards from the bank, and drifting down-stream. The Indians had seized their paddles, and the canoe was now cleaving the rippling water in its onward sweep.

Madeline at once realised her desperate situation. What did it all mean? Why was she being taken away? Had some cruel plot been formed against her?

She looked at her captors. They were calm and alert, swinging their paddles with a steady rhythmical motion. She glanced around, and the figure crouched in the bow arrested her attention. A shiver shook her form as she noted the fierce malicious gleam of the eyes which met her own. What did that woman mean by glaring at her in such a manner, and what did that look signify? What had she done to merit such action, and what lay ahead of her? That great silent river flowed on down into the vast unknown wilderness—and what then? The thought was more than she could endure. She looked wildly toward the shore. She clutched Donnie close to her breast. She scanned the banks for signs of life, some human being who would come to their rescue. The helplessness of her position overwhelmed her. Lifting up her voice she gave several wild, piercing cries for aid, and then sank to the bottom of the canoe, forced down by strong, rough hands laid fiercely upon her. This insult sent the blood surging tumultuously through her veins. But what could she do? What power had she, a woman, against these uncouth natives? She crouched there in the bottom of the craft, her hands clinched together, and her dry, clear eyes staring out over the water through the deepening gloom.

She was presently aroused by a movement near her side, and then a little soft hand stole timidly into her own. Glancing quickly down she noticed Donnie nestling close to her, and looking up appealingly into her face.

"Malin, I'm cold," he whimpered, and a slight shiver shook his frame. "I want my mother. Oh, please take me home."

A throb of compunction smote Madeline's heart as she looked upon the lad. Thinking of her own trouble she had forgotten him.

Drawing the warm shawl from her shoulders she wrapped it carefully about the lad's body. Nearer and nearer he nestled until he felt quite comfortable, and leaned his head against her side.

"Tell me a 'tory, Malin," he requested. "I'm very sleepy."

Tell a story! What story could she tell at a time like this, with so many thoughts surging madly through her brain? And yet here was this child lying so trustingly by her side, and looking up to her for comfort.

"What story do you want, dearie?" she asked after a brief pause.

"Tell me 'bout the baby Moses in the ark of bulwushes," replied Donnie, as he snuggled up closer than ever.

With an effort Madeline forced herself to the task, and there in that great wilderness, in the midst of fears and unknown dangers, she told gently and softly the old, old story, which in all ages has thrilled the hearts of countless children. And as she talked the little head at her side drooped lower until it touched her lap. The big blue eyes winked hard in an effort to remain open. But nature was too strong, and ere long the lad was wrapped in slumber, far beyond all worldly care. As Madeline looked down upon the sleeping boy, and watched him lying there, with one little dimpled hand clutching at her dress, a deep, wonderful love for the child stole into her heart. In the telling of the story she had been much strengthened. In ministering to another she herself had been comforted. She knew that the same loving Father who had shielded Moses so long ago from his enemies was as able and willing to save now as then. "Oh, Father in Heaven," she prayed, "guard us to-night. Give me strength to defend this little child, and to restore him safely to his parents."

Thus all through the long, lonely hours of darkness she remained crouched in the bottom of the canoe. At times her cramped position was almost unbearable. But she must not disturb that child lying so calmly with his head resting upon her lap. But no sleep came to her own eyes. Her brain was too active for that. The swish of the water as the canoe sped forward almost maddened her. Occasionally the natives spoke to one another in their strange guttural language. But Madeline understood not what was said, and each word rasped forth only tended to increase her watchfulness and loneliness.

After hours of steady paddling a sharp word of command rang out. Immediately the canoe was turned toward the shore, and soon the keel was grating upon the pebbly beach. It was very early in the morning, what time Madeline could not guess.

Almost mechanically she watched the natives as they left the canoe and proceeded to build a small fire upon the bank. This accomplished they proceeded to cook some moose steak they had brought with them.

No one seemed to take any notice of Madeline, and for a while she remained in the canoe. At length, arousing Donnie, she attempted to rise to her feet, but sank down again with a slight cry, so numb was her body from her cramped position. The boy opened his eyes and looked around in a startled manner.

"What's the matter, Malin?" he asked. "Are you hurt?"

"No, dearie," was the reply. "I shall be better soon. Will you help me out of the canoe?"

At once the little fellow sprang to his feet, took her hand in his, and proudly led her ashore, and up the steep bank. With difficulty Madeline made her way by his side, pretending to lean upon him for support. Ere long the numbing sensation passed away, and she walked slowly around, watching the men preparing their breakfast.

The Indian woman took no part in their proceedings, but sat upon a stone a short distance away. She appeared to be gazing far off into space. But her sharp eyes noted Madeline's every movement.

The latter was strangely fascinated by that silent figure. At times she was seized with a nameless fear at the thought of what this woman might be planning down deep in her heart. Of the men, wild and uncouth though they were, she had little anxiety. Their faces at any rate were not crafty or cruel. But this woman with that strange light in her eyes made her tremble with apprehension.

When the breakfast had been prepared Madeline was offered some meat, and black tea in an old filthy tin can. The sight of the latter almost sickened her, and she turned away her head in disgust. The meat she took, ate some, and gave a little to Donnie, who was hungry, and enjoyed it thoroughly. It did not take them long to complete their frugal meal, and soon they were all again in the canoe, moving once more down that sombre stream.

Before long they entered upon a large, broad lake, and, instead of skirting the shore, the Indians struck straight away to a point of land dimly seen in the distance. This body of water, some thirty miles long, by three to five wide, was dotted here and there with small wooded islands. It was almost completely surrounded by towering, rock-ribbed mountains, whose peaks, devoid of life, were covered with snow for the greater part of the year.

Away to the left appeared a huge draw, well known for the violent gales it frequently vomited forth. Many were the native legends concerning this place; of the monster of the mountains who made his abode there, and who when angry would hurl forth his overwhelming spleen upon unwary navigators.

Often Tonda and his companions cast furtive glances toward the yawning draw, and drove their paddles with greater energy than ever. On and on they sped. They reached the mouth of the gap. They came opposite the place. They were almost past, and the Indians breathed more freely. The monster was not angry, or had not noticed them. Perhaps he was asleep at that time of the morning. But, alas! they were doomed to disappointment. Without one warning sign a gale ripped down the draw with a wild concentrated fury, and spreading over the lake lashed the water into a yeasty foam.

With dismay the Indians beheld the onrushing storm, and headed the canoe for shore. How they did work, and the craft leaped on her way like a thing of life.

Nearer and nearer they approached the beach. Would they win? Yes. No, for the tempest struck them full abeam. It whirled and roared about them in mad glee. It tossed the canoe like a cork, and dashed the water over the crouching forms.

Madeline clutched Donnie in her arms, and drew him close to her breast. His white, scared face looked up appealingly into hers, though he uttered not a word, nor did a cry escape his lips.

Steadily and calmly the natives plied their paddles, and managed the canoe with considerable skill. But as they neared the shore the large ground swells formed a menace to their advance. Into them they ran, for there was no other course to pursue. From crest to crest they were hurried, each growing larger as they surged forward. When only a short distance from land, a wave larger than usual curled angrily right astern, broke over the canoe, completely submerging everything. Instantly the craft was caught by another roller, which tossed it forward, and, retreating, left it stranded upon the beach. At once a rush ensued. Madeline with Donnie in her arms sped up the bank, with Nadu in advance. The Indians seized the canoe, dragged it after them just in time to escape the next breaker which broke, grinning upon the shore.

CHAPTER XII LINKS OF STEEL

When Norman Grey flung himself out of Old Meg's house his one burning idea was to seek the man who had insulted Madeline. He half expected to find him where he had left him, and was more than disappointed when no sign of the rascal was to be seen. He hurried along the trail desirous of reaching the store as quickly as possible, and meeting Siwash Bill face to face. Although unarmed the thought of fear or of the possible outcome of a personal affray with such a man never entered his head. But as he walked swiftly forward and the cool night air fanned his hot brow, he realised how unwise would be such a line of action at the present critical condition of affairs. Nothing would be gained, he felt sure, and much harm might be done by indiscreet hastiness. He would wait for a while. Too many things were at stake. He knew how the squaw man would be incensed by the blow he had received, and that he would, no doubt, seek speedy revenge in some underhanded manner.

Thinking thus he reached the forest, and passed by the spot where crouched his enemy with his forefinger slightly pressing the nimble trigger of his revolver. No sense of danger from that quarter came into Grey's mind, and he strode swiftly onward, unaware of the imminent peril which had been so narrowly averted.

The moon was now rising full and broad. A few fleecy clouds were drifting slowly overhead. The land lay silent and sombre. Nature was hushed in a dreamy, mystic repose. Grey paused and gazed upon the scene. His mind cleared, while a new strength and quietness entered his heart. He thought of Madeline. The sight of that slight form and fair face had awakened the vibrant chords of memory. His face had been close to hers as she lay in his arms while he bore her into the house. A great desire had seized him to press his lips firmly to hers, no matter what she might be. How he longed to seize her and bear her away from such a place. But, no, he would not do it against her will. What was she doing here, anyway? Why should she leave a home of comfort for such a desolate region? "Madeline! Madeline!" he breathed. "What does it all mean? Oh, to feel that you are as I left you by that garden gate; that you are the same pure-souled woman as of old!"

He entered the cabin, threw himself into the bunk, and soon fell into a fitful sleep. He was awakened by the rattle of dishes, and a peculiar sizzling sound. Opening his eyes he beheld Buckskin Dan standing before the little sheet-iron stove frying some moose meat. The appetising smell filled the room, making Grey realise that he was very hungry. For a while he lay still and watched Dan as he worked. What an ideal life, he thought, as his eyes roved about the cosy cabin. What did such a man need with the luxuries of civilisation? Here in the wilderness he is free to come and go at will. The land teeming with game, and this quiet abode as a place of retreat. Yet he must be lonely at times, he mused. Now a pleasant companion, a woman for instance, would prove an additional charm. She would have to be pretty and genial, or the situation might not be so fascinating. But, then, such cramped quarters might not suit her. She would need more rooms, and that would necessitate extra furniture. And suppose there should not be always two? That would certainly complicate matters, and affairs at times might not be so congenial.

A slight laugh unconsciously broke from Grey's lips, which caused Dan to turn quickly about. A smile spread over his furrowed face as he noticed that his companion was awake.

"Thought ye was asleep," he remarked, "an' here I've been tiptoein' around the room like a thief fer the last half hour."

"Oh, I've been quietly musing in this comfortable place for a few minutes," Grey replied.

"Wall, is that so? Yer musin' must have been very amusin' from the chuckles ye jist let out."

"It was," Grey replied as he sat up in the bunk. "I was thinking what a change it would make here if you had a wife. I was wondering if it would be as agreeable to you as living alone."

To these words Buckskin Dan made no immediate reply. He seemed to be suddenly interested in the meat that was now becoming temptingly browned. He laid his few meagre dishes upon the rough table, while Grey washed his face and hands in a tin basin near the door. The latter noted the old man's silence, and feared that he had offended him by his jocular remark. It was only after they had sat down to their breakfast that Dan awoke from his reverie. He looked across the table and fixed his faded eyes upon Grey's face.

"Ye hit me to the quick by that question of yours, pardner," he began. "Ye didn't mean no harm, an' I take yer words kindly. But, young man, ye little realised how that thrust stung."

"I'm sorry," Grey faltered, for the man's impressive manner was affecting him more than ordinary.

"That's all right, pardner. Don't ye worry one mite. Ye axed a fair question. But, my God! how kin I answer? Would I like to have a wife? Would I be happier? Am I happy now, d'ye think? Am I happy wanderin' out on the hills all by meself, an' comin' back to this lonely cabin, with never a face to greet me, an' never a word of welcome? Then, when I'm under the weather, an' somewhat petered out, to lie all day long in this shack with never a gentle voice to ax how I am, no one to do fer me, an' no one to care whether I live or die—d'ye think that is happiness? Young man, git a home, an' git it as soon as possible. Buckskin Dan's been over the trail afore ye, an' he knows a thing or two."

"I'm afraid it's too late," Grey sadly replied.

Dan looked keenly at his companion as if trying to read the purport of his words.

"D'ye mean to tell me," he asked, "that you too have lost?"

"That's about it."

"Dead?"

"No, and yes."

"Ah, livin' yit, then?"

"In a way."

"But she's alive, young man. Remember that's somethin'. Ye've got hope yit; it ain't altogether crushed. Look at me, pardner. Didn't I love the sweetest, fairest lass that ever trod God's earth? But she left me!"

The trapper paused, and an expression of agony came into his face. Grey could find no words; he knew not what to say.

"Yes, she left me," the old man continued, "left me in the bright summer time, forty years ago come next July. She faded like the flowers of the garden. The roses fled her cheeks, the roundness left her face, an' the strength desarted her body. But she loved me to the last, an' her partin' word was to me."

"But surely forty years have healed the wound," Grey responded. "It's been long since then, and many a man would have forgotten."

"Never, young man, never! I kin see her as plain to-day as of old. Out on the hills, an' along the trail, my Nan, my lost Nanette, is always with me."

"And have you lived in the wilderness ever since?" Grey queried.

"Most of the time."

"Don't you often long, though, for civilisation?"

"I uster have a hankerin' that way. But when I saw the young fellers with their sweethearts it made me feel so lonely that I could hardly stand it. I like it better out on the hills with my Nanette. But of late I've been somewhat drawn back to this camp more'n usual. Thar's a lassie over yon at that house which minds me much of my Nan. I caught a glimpse of her one day which made me stan' very still. An' since then I have sot on the edge of the woods an' watched her as she walked along the trail a leadin' to the river. She's jist like her in form—but my Nan was never like her."

"Do you mean the young woman at Old Meg's?" Grey demanded.

"Yes; it's her I mean."

"And what do you know about her?"

"Nothin' fer sartin. It's only suspicion. But why should sich a purty lass be out in a hole like this with a cratur' like Old Meg unless thar was somethin' wrong? Tell me that."

"But haven't you heard anything? What do the men in camp say? Don't they go there?"

Grey had now risen to his feet and was standing near the table looking straight at his companion. His heart was beating fast. He expected to hear the truth from this old man. Did he know? Could he tell him anything?

"Yes, the men go thar," Dan replied, noting Grey's excitement. "But I've never axed 'em. When I see her I see my Nanette, an' I want to think it's my Nan livin' over thar an' not—"

"Don't say any more!" cried Grey fiercely, bringing his fist down upon the table with a resounding blow. "You say that you have suffered; that you lost your Nanette long ago. But she left you, and you know she was pure and good when she died. But listen to me. What would be the sufferings of a man who loved a woman whom he believed to be as noble as your Nanette? Loved her with all the true passion of a man's heart. Then lost her, and after years of seeking to find her there, living such a life as that? Could your suffering be compared to his? Far better, don't you think, that your Nanette should be dead than living such a life as that?"

"My God! yes," cried the trapper, as the meaning of the constable's words dawned upon his mind. "But are ye sure she's thar? Mebbe ye've been mistaken."

"Oh, no, there is no mistake. Wouldn't I recognise my Madeline anywhere?"

"Sure, that's only nat'ral. An' so ye tell me she was once like my Nanette? How d'ye account then fer her bein' away up here?"

"I can't. It's a sore puzzle. She was reared in a home of luxury and loving care. Her mother died when she was quite young. She was her father's only comfort, and he planned that at his death the whole of his property, which was large, should go to her. They had relatives in the United States, and Madeline in charge of a trusted friend left England to pay them a visit. On that voyage the steamer was wrecked. Several lives were reported lost, Madeline and her travelling companion among the number. Something always told me that the report was not true, and that Madeline had not been drowned. I could not rid my mind of the idea. It forced itself upon me day and night. That was six years ago, and since then I have travelled far and wide in the hope of obtaining some trace of her. And now to find her there! Oh, God, it is too hard!"

Grey sank upon the bench, and buried his face in his hands. Buckskin Dan watched him compassionately for a while, and thoughtfully stroked his long beard.

"Seems to me thar's somethin' wrong," he at length remarked. "It ain't nat'ral fer sich a lassie, brought up as ye say she was, to be in a place like this. Mebbe if ye had a talk with her she would explain matters."

"I've thought of it," was the slow reply, "but somehow I can't. The first time I saw her enter the house I wanted to rush to her at once. And then last night when she lay unconscious in my arms as I carried her into the cabin the yearning was stronger than ever."

"Young man, what are ye talkin' about?" Dan demanded. "Did ye say she was unconscious? What d'ye mean? What are ye sayin'?"

"I know you must be surprised at my words," Grey responded; then he briefly told the incident of the past night.

Dan said not a word during this recital, but sat bolt upright on his bench. His clinched hands kept moving to and fro by his side, while a deep scowl formed upon his brow.

"The d— skunk!" he ejaculated when Grey ceased. "Oh, if I only had me hands on his measly carcass! An' so he insulted the lassie did he?"

"I should like to know how she is getting along," Grey continued. "But how can I go? If I could feel she is my Madeline as of old, then no power in Hishu could keep me from her side. But I can't go unless I know she wants me. I would like to hear, too, about the boy."

The trapper sat thoughtfully smoking for some time in deep silence. Then he reached out a large hand across the table.

"Put it thar, young man," he said. "Yer tale of sorrow has brought ye very close to me old heart. We're pardners now fer sure. Buckskin Dan don't make friends easy, but when he does it's with links of steel, an' don't ye fergit that. But, come, we've sot here long enough. I jist want to run across to the store fer a little baccy an' ammunition. It'll take only a few minutes. Thar's important bizness ahead of us, an' we ain't got no time to lose."

CHAPTER XIII THE TRAILING SERPENT

Buckskin Dan walked slowly along the trail toward the store. The day was young, and the sun was just swinging clear of the far eastern horizon. It was a cool morning, and the mists of night still hung thick over river and valley. Dan's chest expanded as he drank into his lungs great draughts of the fresh, keen air. "It's the only tonic I need," he had often remarked. "Pills an' tablets an' patent trash may suit some, but give me the medicine the good Lord sends fresh from the hills an' mountains. Thar's no p'isin in that, an' it doesn't twist yer stummick into a groanin' hell wuss than some preachers tell us about."

He found Siwash Bill within the store, looking carefully over his supply of rifles and shot-guns.

"Mornin', Dan," was the curt salutation.

"Mornin'," came the brief reply. "Any baccy?"

"Plenty," and the squaw man crossed the room and handed out a big black plug. "What else?"

"Some ca'tridges. I'm 'bout cleaned out."

"Goin' out on the hills to-day, Dan?" queried the storekeeper.

"Guess likely. Saw some big sheep thar t'other day, an' I need them bad, fer my stock of meat's gittin' low."

"Is the stranger goin' with ye?"

"Mebbe so. 'Cordin' how he feels. Wall, so long, I must be off."

Dan did not notice the interested look in Siwash Bill's face when he learned that the trapper was bound for the hills. Neither did he see the squaw man and Windy Pete engaged in an eager conversation in the back room a few minutes later. He strode forward little realising that his few words were acting like fire to tow in two cunning minds within the store.

He reached Old Meg's house, and rapped upon the door. The owner herself appeared, and stood looking curiously out upon the trapper.

"How's the lassie?" Dan blurted forth. He did not like the expression in the woman's face, and longed to get through with his errand as soon as possible.

"What business is it of yours how she is?" was the quick retort.

"Now don't git cranky, woman," Dan replied; "it doesn't work with me."

"Indeed," and Meg gave a sarcastic laugh. "Don't try any of your bluff game here. It doesn't work with me, either."

"I'm not, woman, an' ye'll soon find it out if ye try any foolin'. If anythin' happens to the lassie wot lives with ye, beware. Buckskin Dan isn't in the habit of talkin' simply to hear his own eloquence. I want to know how the gal is feelin' this mornin'. Will ye tell me? Is it yes or no?"

The defiant look on Old Meg's face changed to one of concern. She was becoming uneasy before those steady eyes which seemed to be reading her inmost soul.

"What does the man know?" she mentally asked herself. "What does he mean by such words?" She knew of Buckskin Dan, and for him to visit her on such business was sufficient cause for anxiety. She shifted uneasily from one foot to the other, and tried to evade his look.

"Is it yes or no? I won't ax ag'in."

"Oh, well, if you must know," she flung forth, "she's all right. It takes a deal to upset her."

"Ah, is that so? An' the kid, how is he gittin' along?"

"Better. Out in a day or two. Now, are you satisfied?"

With that the woman slammed the door, leaving Dan to his own thoughts. And those same thoughts were of no light nature which beat through his brain as he wended his way back to his own house. As he had told Grey the evening before, he had been trained in the wilderness to use his eyes and ears, and he might have included his brain, too, for that matter. He used it now right royally as he moved along the trail. His head was bent forward, and his long beard swept his breast. Every movement of his body bespoke a man of action, while his giant stature denoted strength of no ordinary nature. He was a patriarchal giant of the wild, where endurance and lustihood mean so much.

A slight sigh of relief at length escaped his lips as if some problem had been suddenly and unexpectedly solved. He entered his cabin, and a smile illumined his face as he beheld Grey busily engaged in putting the room in order.

"What!" he cried. "My mornin's work all done, an' the dishes washed, too! Ye've left nuthin' fer me, pardner."

"Didn't you say," Grey laughingly replied, "that we have important business on hand, and that there's no time to lose? I'm still in the dark as to your meaning, but thought it best to straighten things up here a bit so as to be ready."

"Ye're right, young man, thar is important bizness on hand. But mebbe ye won't agree to my plan."

"You lead on, Dan," Grey replied. "You're the Commanding Officer to-day, and I'll follow you to the death."

"Good!" ejaculated the trapper, as he brought forth the plug of tobacco from his pocket, and began to whittle off several thin slices. "I've been thinkin' much since hearin' yer story, an' thar's only one course I see open."

"And what's that?"

"Git out to the hills after the Hishu bunch of miners. If I kin round 'em up afore they come back and git soaked with Bill's and Meg's p'isined whiskey mebbe I kin do somethin'. Will ye go with me? We might run across some game on the way. We'll take a blanket along an' some grub, fer we'll have to spend the night most likely in the open."

"But will it be well to leave Hishu?" Grey queried. "Something might happen to the boy in the meantime, and then how should I feel?"

"Not likely, not likely, young man. The boy's all right, an' the lassie, too, fer I've jist been to inquire."

"What! You were over to the house?"

"Yes; strolled over a little while ago."

"And you say Madeline is all right?"

"Yes, chipper as a young bird."

"Thank God!" fervently broke from Grey's lips. "It's a great relief for me to know that."

"Yes, she'll do fer a while, an' so will the kid. Nuthin' will happen as fer as I kin see until he gits stronger, an' we'll be back fer sure by t'-morrow night at the latest."

"I'll go, then, Dan. But you'll have to loan me a rifle. I left mine over by the rapids."

"Oh, I'll fix ye up all right. Here's a nice light one. She'll spit fire like a wildcat if the right man's behind her."

Half an hour later they emerged from the house, closed the door, and struck a trail, leading in a northeasterly direction away from the river. Dan bore the blanket slung over his shoulder, while Grey carried their scanty supply of food. Little did they think that their every movement was observed from a small window in the store, and that soon after they had headed for the hills the figure of a man stepped lightly across the open and glided along after them. Could they have seen the slinking form keeping so warily out of sight and have read the writing upon the secret chamber of his heart they would not have felt so secure as they moved steadily onward.

It was a beautiful fall morning. The air was clear and bracing. Not a breath of wind stirred the tree tops. Around them stood the mountains, vested to the girdling timber line with snowy robes of dazzling whiteness. Nature was limning her annual masterpiece. A few delicate touches here and there were the only signs of the picture to be completed a few weeks later, with storms raging over the land, streams stricken dumb, and the rasping frost-laden air biting like the whitest of hot iron.

Steadily the two wayfarers sped forward with long, swinging strides. Occasionally a timid rabbit scurried across the trail, and at times the whirr of a startled grouse could be heard a short distance away. For these they paused not. They were forth on a larger quest, for nobler game.

At noon they rested by a small stream, ate their frugal meal, drank of the cold sparkling water, and once more hastened onward. For hours they did not slacken their pace. The sun dipped westward, and the numerous trees were throwing out dark trailing shadows. But darker and more sombre still was that silent figure ever shadowing them from behind. Had they looked back at the right moment they might have caught a fleeting glimpse of his presence as he dodged from tree to tree, from rock to rock, or skirted the edge of some wild meadow which they had just crossed.

Dan and Grey talked but little throughout the day, for the trail was hard and not conducive to much conversation.

"How much farther?" panted Grey, as they toiled painfully up a steep incline.

"Not fer now," was the reply. "Gittin' tired?"

"Somewhat. My feet are rather sore from the snags and stones."

"They'll soon heal, pardner, that's one comfort. Now the snags an' stones ye strike out in civilisation hurt fer a long time. But hello! What's this?"

Grey looked quickly up at this exclamation of surprise, and beheld a man coming slowly toward them. He was bent forward, and limped painfully. A small pack was strapped across his shoulders, and in his right hand he carried a rifle.

"It's 'Crusty' Ike, I do believe!" Dan exclaimed. "He's one of the crankiest cusses in the hull region. What in the name of goodness is he doin' here in sich a condition!"

"Hello, Iky," he shouted as they drew near. "What's wrong with ye? Are ye lost, or bughouse?"

The man addressed lifted his eyes and fixed them upon the trapper's face in a mute appeal, but made no reply.

"What's wrong with ye? Why don't ye speak?" insisted Dan.

"Sprained ankle—left behind," came the curt rejoinder.

"Is that so? Too bad, old chap. But yer headin' the wrong way. Ye'd better face about an' hike it into camp."

"No, no!" cried the other most vehemently. "I can't go back! The gold's over there! Jim Stebbins found it. He brought us word. This confounded sprain kept me back. But I'll get there. By God! I'll stake my claim yet! The boys won't get it all."

"But, man alive," replied Dan, "ye're not fit to travel. Ye'll fall on the trail. Ye'll starve. How fer are the others ahead? When did ye start?"

"This morning, and the boys are hiking like the devil."

The trapper stroked his long beard meditatively. He knew what a stampede meant, and the wild excitement which always ensued. No doubt the stampeders would return in a few days, find "Crusty" and take him back with them. He must let this man do the work he intended to do himself.

"Iky, set down a bit," he demanded. "'Twill do ye good. Thar's somethin' I want to tell ye. I won't keep ye long."

Somewhat reluctantly the lame man seated himself by the side of the trail, unslung his pack, and laid his rifle by his side.

"Fire away, then," he grunted, "and don't be long about it, either."

"Now look here, Iky," Dan began. "I'm mighty glad ye've been knocked out to-day."

"The devil! Well, that's cool."

"Jist keep yer mouth shet fer a minute an' I'll explain what I mean. I've known ye fer years, Iky, as a square man, even though ye are cranky at times. Ye're true to the core, which is more'n I kin say of some I've run ag'inst. If ye knew of a mean ugly game bein' put up ag'inst some poor little kid ye would jist explode like a barrel of dynamite, wouldn't ye?"

"My God! yes. You bet your life I would."

"Wall, then, thar's a poor wee lad at Hishu that's been stole away from its home by a set of measly skunks."

"Who are they?" demanded Ike, half rising to his feet, while his eyes blazed with anger. "Tell me the names of the villains, and I'll bring the boys down to Hishu like greased lightning. D'ye know who they are?"

"Yes, Siwash Bill an' his gang: that's who they are."

"Good Lord! An' did they do that? Let me go. Oh, it's Bill, is it? Steal a baby from his mother's arms! I had a little lad of my own once, but he left me long ago. He's always with me in this hell of a land. I can see his sweet face yet, hear his happy laugh, and feel his small soft hand in mine. Oh, why was he taken from me when I wanted him so much? If I had him now I wouldn't be here. I'd be a better man. But for his sake I'd do anything for someone else's child. Let me go. I'll round up the boys."

He jumped to his feet, forgetting for the instant his sprained ankle. A cry escaped his lips and his body writhed with pain.

"I won't go back!" he cried, straightening himself up with an effort. "Don't delay me any longer."

They watched him as he limped slowly along the trail.

"Poor devil!" exclaimed Dan. "His brain's half turned by that lust of gold, an' now wot I've told him has made him completely daft. But it can't be helped. Guess we'd better turn down into that next valley. Thar's a small stream yonder among some heavy timber, whar we kin spend the night. In the mornin' we'll go to the high hills fer some sheep, an' then hike back to Hishu. I've had quite uneasy thoughts all day about the lassie an' the poor little lad. Let's git on, pardner."

CHAPTER XIV IN THE DEEP OF THE NIGHT

Grey sat before the genial fire with his back propped against a large spruce tree. He watched in a dreamy manner the curling flames sending up countless sparks into the night. Buckskin Dan sat a few feet away, puffing slowly at his black, short-stemmed pipe.

The place they had chosen for their camp was near a small stream in the midst of a sturdy growth of soft-wood trees. The moon was rising in the distance, but its bright beams had not as yet flooded the landscape.

"This is comfort," murmured Grey, as he watched the fire seizing with avidity upon the dry pine sticks. "After the weariness of the trail what can be more delightful than a spot such as this? It makes up for much, does it not, Dan?"

"Ay, ay," was the response. "I've often thought the same thing meself as I sat alone by me little watch-fire in the gloom."

"But didn't you find it lonely at times? Did you ever have a creepy feeling that some danger was surrounding you?"

"Can't say that I ever did. But why d'ye ax, pardner?"

"Oh, I don't exactly know. But as I look into the blackness around us an uncanny feeling comes into my heart. Those great sombre trees fill me with strange forebodings. There seems to be danger lurking within their dark depths. I know it is all nonsense, but somehow it depresses me much to-night."

"Yer tired, young man; that's what's the matter with ye. Ye've had very little sleep fer several nights now, an' ye've been over hard trails of late. It's no wonder yer down in the dumps. A good rest will do ye a world of good. So curl up in yon blanket, an' ye'll soon fergit sich things."

"But you must share the blanket with me, Dan. I won't touch it, otherwise."

"Now don't ye bother about that. Sartinly I'll have a piece of it. Thar's enough fer both of us. We'll need it, too, afore mornin', fer the night is chilly."

Nothing loath, Grey stretched himself upon the ground near the fire, and drew the blanket over his body. He listened for a while to the crackling of the fire, and watched the sparks circling and shooting up into the air. He even tried to count them ere they tumbled and disappeared forever. Presently they faded, and in their stead he saw a face—it was Madeline's—

just where those sparks should be. She was looking at him with fear in her large eyes. An expression of terror was depicted upon her face. She was trying to come to him, but something seemed to be holding her back. He tried to go to her, but felt himself bound by some invisible power. He made an attempt to call to her, but words would not come. The perspiration stood in beads upon his forehead. He must go, he would break those bonds. He made one mighty effort, and felt the cords loosen. Then the vision faded, and he awoke with a start. He looked around. A few embers were still smouldering near by. Dan was lying at his side asleep, and breathing heavily. The moon was now riding high in the heavens, but the camping ground was shrouded by the shadows of the tall trees.

Grey tried to banish the dream which was still so vivid to his mind. He lay there looking up into the sky through the delicate tracery of countless branches. He blamed himself for his childish apprehension. "What a fool I am," he thought, "to be unnerved by a mere dream! But I really wonder if anything is wrong with Madeline. There was much meaning in dreams long ago, and why should it not be the same to-day? Anyway I shall get back to Hishu to-morrow as quickly as possible. I shall find out then how things are going. I was wrong to leave on this wild-goose chase. It was all nonsense."

He closed his eyes, and turned over on his left side. As he did so a slight noise among the trees arrested his attention. He lifted his head slightly from the bunch of fir boughs which formed his pillow, and listened intently. Hearing nothing, he resumed his former posture. "It's only a rabbit or a fox," he said to himself. "Strange that such a thing should startle me." Nevertheless, he moved his head and laid it upon the cool smooth barrel of the rifle lying by his side. The touch was comforting, and he was thankful that he had placed it there.

He now found it impossible to sleep. His eyes would not close, and he kept straining his ears for the faintest sound. His gaze wandered out into the woods among the trees. His eyes were becoming accustomed to the dimness, and he could see fairly distinctly several yards away. Upon one object there he riveted his eyes. He thought he saw it move. Perhaps it was only imagination. It was a stump, no doubt, but it had the appearance of a human being. Presently it moved, he was sure of that, and came a step closer. Then another, and then another. No longer now did Grey doubt that some person was there with malign intent. It was a living object, and that he could face. Whoever it was he was stealing up gradually, and but for that pair of keen, watchful eyes could hardly be detected among the dark tree trunks. Nearer and nearer the form approached, bending somewhat in a wary attitude. In one place a narrow shaft of light shot through the trees. It touched for an instant the slinking figure, and a sudden gleam from polished steel flashed forth. The effect was as an electric shock to Grey's tense nerves. He seized the rifle and sprang to his knees. This sudden action startled the intruder. He paused in his tracks, and then wheeling dashed back among the trees. Quickly Grey brought the rifle to his shoulder and sent a leaden missive after the retreating form. Then all was still. Grey was now thoroughly aroused. A burning rage filled his heart at the thought of the coward who had attempted such a dastardly trick. Quickly reloading his rifle he sprang into the forest in an effort to overtake the assailant. After he had gone some distance he realised the folly of his action. Among the shadows of the trees it would be quite easy for the intruder to hide and shoot him down. Reluctantly he returned to the camping ground, where he found Buckskin Dan standing erect with his rifle in his hand.

"What's the matter, pardner?" he demanded. "What were ye shootin' at? Was it a b'ar?"

"A bear be fiddlesticks!" Grey replied. "Do you think I'd lose a good night's sleep for a bear?"

"What was it then? Ye seem mighty excited."

"It was a sneak, a devil with the form of a man, creeping stealthily upon us with a gleaming knife in his hand. That's what it was."

"Good Lord!" ejaculated the trapper. "A man, d'ye say, with a knife, a creepin' upon us! Are ye sure ye saw aright? Mebbe it was only a shadder."

"A pretty lively shadow, then. I never saw a shadow take to its heels in such a hurry before. A shadow doesn't generally carry a sharp, glittering knife, does it?"

"Wall, no. But things are most deceivin' in the night. I don't like to doubt yer word, young man. But it's so mysterious. I can't savvey it nohow."

"Are there any Indians in this locality, Dan?" Grey inquired.

"Yes, a few scatterin' ones here an' thar, though most of 'em are off in another direction. But it wasn't an Injun, pardner, ye may set yer mind to rest on that score."

"What makes you so sure of that?"

"Bah, the Injuns in these diggin's wouldn't stoop to sich things. When they're on the warpath it's different. But Buckskin Dan 'ud be the last man they'd injure. He's been too good a friend to 'em, an' they wouldn't tech 'im."

"It must be a white man, then," Grey replied, "and if ever I get my hands on his measly skull he'll need to go on the stocks for repairs. God! How I'd like to have him here now!"

The trapper looked with admiration upon the sturdy form before him. He had little doubt of the outcome should Grey meet with the assailant.

"Come, pardner," he commanded, "you lay down now an' git a few winks of sleep. I've had enough fer an old man, so I'll jist stir up the fire a bit an' keep watch."

"But should I not stay awake, too? That snake may come back."

"Let 'im come. I'd like to set me eyes on 'im jist fer an instant. Old Spit-death here knows a thing or two," and Dan fondly stroked the barrel of his rifle. "Many a foamin', frothin' grizzly she's lulled to sleep. Oh, no, don't ye worry. Jist curl up thar, an' fergit everythin'."

Grey found it easy to "curl up," but hard to sleep. He was too much excited, and though at times he did doze off he always awoke with a start, thinking that gliding form was upon him.

Buckskin Dan sat silently near the fire, his rifle lying by his side. He was thinking deeply, and occasionally a deep scowl passed over his face. He was keenly on the alert, nevertheless, and often he peered intently among the trees. It was only when daylight was breaking over the land that he rose from his position, and brought forth some food from a small bag hanging on the limb of a tree.

"Guess we must be movin', young man," he remarked. "Day's dawnin', an' a long trail lies ahead. Better have a snack afore we start."

"I'm going to have a wash first," Grey replied; "it will freshen me up a bit."

Seizing his rifle he hurried down to the stream several yards away, leaving Dan slowly munching his breakfast. Grey had been gone but a short time when he returned, carrying in his hand an old slouch hat.

"What do you think of that?" he inquired. "Do you think now that my trouble was only a nightmare?"

"What is it, pardner?" and Dan paused in his eating.

"Don't you see? A hat with a hole through the crown of it. My bullet didn't go far astray. I just strolled over to where I aimed last night, thinking I might discover something, and here's the result."

"Ye don't say so! Wall, I declare!" exclaimed Dan, taking the hat in his hand and examining it carefully. "Gee whiz, that was a close shave! I bet that skunk's head stung whar the bullet lifted the hat. Hope to goodness it took a slice of his scalp. Now, let me think whar I've seen this headgear afore. Seems quite familiar. Yes, no, ah, I have it. I have it!" and Dan sprang to his feet in the excitement of his discovery. "It's Windy Pete's, that's whose it is! Haven't I seen him with that old thing fer years now. Guess he's worn it ever sence he came North. Stupid of me not to recognise it at fust sight."

"But what would he be doing here?" questioned Grey. "Did we not leave him at Hishu yesterday morning? Was he not there when we started?"

"He was thar, that's true, young man. But ye don't know them divils. They are here to-day an' miles away to-morrer."

"But what object would Pete have in coming here, and stealing upon us as he did last night? And further, how did he know where we were going when we left Hishu?"

The trapper looked intently into Grey's face, although he saw him not. His mind had gone back to his visit to the store the previous morning, and to the information he had imparted to Siwash Bill. He remembered how interested the latter had been in his movements. It all came to him now like a flash, throwing light upon several things which hitherto had been shrouded in darkness.

"Pardner," and his words were slow and impressive, "the hull thing's as clear to me as a rabbit's eye. It's you they're after an' not me. Yer the game, that's sartin."

"After me!" exclaimed Grey. "Why would Pete track me all the way to this place when he could have fixed me in Hishu? You must be mistaken."

"Ye don't know 'em, young man, as well as I do. They were shrewd enough not to meddle with ye down thar. Oh, no, they wouldn't do that. They would git us out in the hills together, creep up when ye was asleep, run ye through, an' skerdaddle. Then it would appear as if we'd had a set-to an' I stabbed ye."

"My God!" cried Grey, "do you think that was their object? Are they such devils as that, to commit such a crime, and cast the blame upon an innocent man?"

"Are they sich divils? Ye don't know 'em yit. Why, man, they'd do anythin'. Thank God, their hellish plans have missed fire this time. But we must be very keerful, pardner. We've had a warnin' which we can't afford to neglect. So let's git out of this uncanny hole, and hit the trail fer Hishu."

CHAPTER XV A CRY ACROSS THE WATER

"If we kin, we must reach Hishu afore Windy Pete gits thar."

It was Buckskin Dan who spoke as he and the constable swung on their way the morning after the night of alarms. They were returning by a different trail, which would bring them to the river a few miles below Hishu. Along this route was a high range of hills where mountain sheep were plentiful. Here they expected to bag a tender lamb to take back with them to the village.

"Yes," continued Dan, "we must git that fust, an' then find out fer sartin if Pete was that skunk wot distarbed us last night."

"We'll have to do some hustling, then," Grey replied. "If we stop for game it will make us late."

"Can't be helped, pardner. Grub's mighty low with me jist now, an' if we don't git it to-day, it'll mean another trip to-morrer, an' I don't like to leave Hishu too often jist at present."

Thus for hours they continued on their way, stopping only once by a small brook to eat their last morsel of food. The afternoon was well advanced as the long terrace-like range loomed up before them on their right.

"Should find some sheep over thar," remarked the trapper. "Guess we'd better leave the trail, and circle yon knoll. Thar's good feedin' ground on t'other side."

Slowly and cautiously they wound their way over broken and twisted rocks, keeping a sharp look-out the while. Creeping guardedly about the side of a hill, with a deep gulch below, they beheld a small flock of sheep feeding calmly several hundred yards away. To Grey it seemed cruel to disturb that peaceful scene. He thought of the assailant stealing upon him in the dead of night, and here he was doing the same to these harmless creatures. But Buckskin Dan evidently had no such qualms of conscience. He needed meat, and the sheep were there for man's use, so that was sufficient. Speedily he advanced, gliding from rock to rock with such agility that Grey, nimble though he was, found it difficult to follow. At length they were forced to creep upon all fours, and when at last they were as close as prudence allowed the trapper took careful aim at a small-sized sheep and fired. The animal gave one great leap into the air, and then dropped to the ground. Its companions, terror stricken, gazed for an instant in the direction from whence the report had come, and then fled wildly across the open space and disappeared like magic among the rocks.

"I've snipped that critter fer sure," Dan remarked, "so I'll jist dodge over an' bring it back."

But this was easier said than done, for they found after they had gone a short distance that the rocks sloped down to the very edge of the precipice like one side of the roof of a house, about fifteen feet in width. Leaving his rifle behind, Dan slowly made his way along the narrow ledge, holding on carefully to the wall towering above. A sharp point jutting out partly barred his progress and as he attempted to go around this his foot lost its hold, and he found himself slipping down the sloping rock, which had been worn smooth by wind and rain. With a cry of terror he clutched frantically for something upon which to fasten his fingers. But not an object could be found. Down and down he moved, and when it seemed as if in another instant he must be hurled to immediate death his hand touched a jagged fissure in the surface. How his tense fingers did dig into the friendly crevice as he hung over that awful place. Below yawned the gulf; above stretched the merciless rock.

So quickly had all this taken place that Grey had hardly time to think, much less to act. A numbing horror overspread his whole body as he watched his companion moving down to apparent destruction. But when he saw him gripping so desperately to the rent in the rock he quickly roused to action. He looked about for something to stretch out to his helpless partner. But not a branch or sapling could he behold—nothing that would serve his purpose. He looked far down into the valley; he might get something there. But it would take considerable time to go and return, and in the meantime what would happen to Dan!

"How long can you hold on?" he called.

"'Bout a minute," came the weak reply. "Me fingers are 'most broke. Fer God's sake do somethin', an' do it quick!"

Then Grey acted. He tore off the buckskin jacket he was wearing, which Dan had loaned him, and gave it a most vigorous pull to test its endurance. Next he unbuckled the cartridge belt which encircled his waist. Tying one end of this to a sleeve of the jacket he fastened the other end securely about his ankle. Finding a suitable stone lying near, with some difficulty he made it fast to the second sleeve of the jacket. This accomplished he stretched himself carefully down the rocky incline, and holding on firmly with one hand to the point of a jagged flinty rift, with the other he let out his improvised rope of salvation. The weight of the stone bore it steadily toward the clinging trapper. Would it reach? And if so would it be strong enough? Dan saw it coming, and a gleam of hope came into his faded eyes. But alas! it was still too far away.

"Let her out some more," he shouted. "I can't tech it yit."

Then Grey stretched himself out full length, and with both hands gripped the rock above. It was all that was needed. Dan's tired fingers closed eagerly upon the sleeve of the jacket. He tested its strength ere letting go of his old precarious support. Finding that it held firm he committed himself to its keeping, and slowly and painfully made his way foot by foot up from that dizzy, frowning ledge. Neither Grey nor Dan spoke. The silence was intense. Would the connecting link hold? Would it bear the strain to the end? Grey could feel the weight attached to his leg, but could not see how his comrade was progressing. He half expected at any instant to hear the jacket or belt give way. The perspiration stood in great beads upon his forehead, and he almost held his breath in the intenseness of the moment. But when he felt Dan's hand laid with a mighty grip upon his other leg, and knew that the old man was scrambling quickly up by the side of his body to a place of safety, a great sigh of relief escaped his lips. It did not take him long to draw himself up from his own perilous position after the weight had been removed.

"God bless ye, pardner!" Dan cried, reaching out a large horny hand. "How kin I ever thank ye fer wot ye've done fer me to-day?"

Grey silently grasped the extended member. Words would not come. His heart was too full for utterance.

The trapper stooped down, and slowly unfastened the buckskin jacket from the leathern belt. He next held it up in both hands, and examined it carefully.

"It stood the test well, that's wot it did," he remarked. "Never thought when I made it that it 'ud be the means of savin' me life."

"And did you make this yourself?" Grey inquired with surprise.

"Sartin, every stitch of it. It's not made with yer measly fancy thread, either, but with good stout raw hide. But even that wouldn't have borne the strain if it hadn't been fer somethin' else which made it strong."

"What was that, Dan?"

"'Twas the good Lord, that's who it was. As I kneeled thar in that awful place, with only that slender thing to keep me from death, I thought how I uster kneel at me mother's knees when a little child. It's been sich a long time sence I said a prayer that I didn't know what to say. But I remembered the prayer she taught me then, an' as I struggled up that rock with me hands clingin' to this jacket I said over in me mind,

Now I lay me down to sleep,

I pray the Lord me soul to keep.

It wasn't altogether suitable, I own, but it was wonderful comfortin', an' I think the Lord knew wot I meant jist as well as if it had been a long one an' fixed up with fine words. But, thar, I've talked 'bout enough. We must git away from here, an' hike it home as fast as we kin. It's gittin' late, an' I'm afeered we can't reach Hishu afore dark."

"But what about the sheep?" Grey questioned. "Are we to leave it behind?"

"Sartin. Not another step do I take after the critter. It nearly cost me me life, an' I don't venture over yon place ag'in. It's too long a way round, an' not worth the trouble. So come, let's git."

The sun had disappeared behind a tall mountain peak as they descended the slope leading to the river. Here they struck upon a well-beaten trail leading to the village. Along this they sped through the steadily deepening twilight.

Suddenly across the water came a piercing cry which stayed their steps and held them spellbound. Again and again it came, and then all was still. It was a cry for help. There was no doubt about that. Grey's heart beat tumultuously, and an horrible dread overwhelmed him. It was a woman's voice, and it sounded like Madeline's! Springing quickly up the bank at the side of the trail he peered over the tops of the trees, and there out in the stream he caught one fleeting glimpse of a canoe ere it swung around a bend in the river and disappeared from view.

"It's the lassie! It's the lassie!" cried Dan, who had sprung to his side. "Thar's somethin' wrong."

"My God, yes!" Grey replied. "What can we do, oh, what can we do? There's some villainy in this! Do you think they've taken the boy, too?"

"Can't tell. But we must git into Hishu as fast as our legs'll take us, an' find out fer sartin."

Grey waited to hear no more. He leaped down the bank and hurried along the trail. That wild pathetic cry for help still rang in his ears. Madeline was in trouble, in danger! That was enough. Forgotten now were his old doubts and fears. He thought of her only as of old. His steps quickened to a trot as he neared the village, then to a run. Down the trail he sped like a greyhound, with Dan following pantingly some distance behind. He flew by the trapper's cabin, the store and the cluster of deserted shacks. He dashed across the open, reached Old Meg's house, beat upon the door, pushed it open, and sprang into the room.

"Where is she?" he cried. "What has happened? For God's sake tell me, quick!"

Little wonder that Meg started back with surprise, mingled with fear, at this sudden intrusion and the towering form standing before her. Grey's unshaven face was drawn and haggard, while his eyes glowed with a light of wild intensity.

"Where is she?" he demanded. "Why don't you speak?"

"W-what do you mean?" the woman replied. She felt there must be some reason for Grey's excited manner. It disconcerted her, leaving her much confused.

"I want to know what has become of Miss Normsell, who has been staying with you, and also the boy? Where are they? Do you know?"

"They went for a stroll to the river some time ago, and should be back by now. It's getting late."

"To the river? My God!" cried Grey. "Then it was Madeline! She's gone, and the boy, too! There's some foul plot."

Grey asked no more questions. He stared for an instant at Old Meg, then turned and left the building, leaving the woman gazing wonderingly after him.

CHAPTER XVI THE SIGNAL FIRE

Grey walked rapidly toward Dan's cabin. His mind was wildly agitated, for his brief interview with Old Meg had given him no satisfaction. In passing the store he was tempted to enter and seek an explanation from Siwash Bill. He banished this thought instantly, however. No, he would see Dan first, and find out what he had learned.

A lighted candle was burning in the cabin, showing that the trapper had been there, although he was nowhere to be seen. Grey entered, and seating himself upon a bench tried to collect his thoughts. What was he to do? Madeline and the boy had been stolen away. What would the Major say when he heard about it? To think that he, Norman Grey, should so neglect his duty as to allow that boy to slip from his grasp! And then there was Madeline. Duty and love were the two forces which stirred his inmost being. He rose to his feet and paced restlessly up and down the small room. Why did not Dan return? Why was he away so long? Without the trapper he felt helpless. A few days before he would have laughed at anyone who even suggested that he could not manage his own affairs. But since coming to Hishu and meeting with this old man, he found how important it was to lean upon him for assistance. Dan knew the people of the place and the whole surrounding country, of which he himself was ignorant.

Thus the moments sped by, and the trapper did not appear. Something must have happened to him. Perhaps he had run across Windy Pete or Siwash Bill, and had got into trouble. At this thought Grey started for the door. He would go to the store and make inquiries. But ere he had time to lay a hand upon the latch the door swung slowly open, and the Indian, Hishu Sam, glided swiftly and noiselessly into the room.

Grey's face brightened perceptibly as he beheld the native who had done so much on behalf of the little child but a short time before. Then he had appeared at the moment when most needed, and now when the darkness was so deep he had suddenly come from the unknown. Grey at once reached out his hand to the native.

"Welcome," he said. "I'm glad to see you again. You're a good friend to the white man."

"Ah, ah," was the reply. "Hishu Sam savvey moche. Bah-bee all sam' lost, eh?"

"Yes, yes, lost," Grey exclaimed in surprise. "How did you know?"

"Hishu Sam see 'um. Beeg canoe go down reever all sam' wild goose."

"And were you along the river? You see canoe? Was the little boy along, too?"

"Ah, ah. Me see bah-bee head. Me see white squaw. Me come to Hishu quick."

"Were they Indians who stole them away?"

"Ah, ah."

"Who?"

"Beeg Lake Injuns."

"What! The Indians who are on the warpath with the Hishus?"

"Ah, ah."

"Look here, Sam; we must get that boy and woman. We must save them quick. What can we do?"

The Indian looked intently into Grey's face for a few seconds.

"Hishu Sam white man's friend," he at length remarked. "Come."

With that he turned toward the door, opened it and passed out into the night. There was nothing left for Grey but to follow. The native took it for granted that he would do so, and did not even once look back.

A short distance from the cabin the Indian turned sharply to the left, and entered upon a rough trail. In the deepening gloom it was hard for Norman to pick his steps, and often he stumbled, and several times fell flat upon the ground. But Hishu Sam walked as easily as in a carpeted room, and evidently knew every inch of the way. Up and up they moved, and after a long hard climb reached the top of a large hill. Here the guide paused and looked slowly around. Then he stretched out a long arm and pointed away to the right.

"Hishu over dere," he began. "Hishu busy. Bime by Hishu all come back."

Grey understood not the meaning of the words until he saw his companion go to a large pile of sticks and underbrush and touch a match to a small piece of bark. Instantly the tiny flame leaped to the inflammable material above, and soon the whole pile was converted into a wild, roaring, seething mass. So intense was the heat that Grey and the Indian were forced to retreat some distance, where the former silently viewed the magnificent spectacle. The hilltop for rods around was illumined by the bright flames, which would make it quite easy to see such a light for miles away.

While Grey stood gazing upon the fire the Indian crouched some distance off, intently peering forth through the darkness. At length Grey took up his position by his side, wondering much what it all meant. Once he questioned the Indian, but receiving no satisfactory reply he was forced to wait. The interest caused by the fire soon waned, and the old longing to be up and doing gripped him hard. He would ere this have hurried down the hillside and have left the Indian alone, but that he believed there was some definite purpose in the Indian's action. The native's silence was to him more eloquent than many words.

Silently they crouched together there on the hilltop. Presently the Indian gave a grunt of satisfaction, and pointed away to the right. At first Grey could see nothing. But as he looked a small light like the faintest star caught his eye. It became brighter. It glowed into a leaping flame, sending blazing cinders high into the air. It was the reply of fire to fire—the natives' crude method of signalling to one another when any great danger was afoot. Presently to the left another light streaked the night from a far-off hilltop, while a little later and to the right another appeared.

Grey understood now the meaning of it all. He recalled, too, the remarkable stories he had heard about the early explorers and their encounters with the natives. Fiery signals from hill to hill had heralded their approach, and brought about them bands of threatening Indians wherever they advanced. So now these fires were being used for a noble purpose. The Hishus would come in a body to his assistance. How long would it take them to return, and in the meantime what would happen to Madeline? He turned to his companion, who was watching the distant fires with much satisfaction.

"Sam," he said, "how long will it take for the Indians to reach Hishu? Will they come at once?"

"Ah, ah. Sun heem come up dere, sun heem go down dere. Hishu come."

"But are you sure they will come?"

"Ugh," grunted the native. "Injun no white man. Injun savvey moche."

"But will they know what the fire means? What will they think?"

"Injun come. Injun savvey fire. Injun savvey Hishu Sam. See?"

"Oh, they think the Big Lakes are coming. Is that it?"

"Ah, ah."

"And you stayed behind to keep watch, eh?"

"Ah, ah."

"Did you ever do this before? Did you ever call the Hishus in this way?"

The native looked thoughtfully before him for a few seconds ere replying.

"Ten winters ago," he at length answered, "bad Injun come up reever. Hishu Sam make beeg fire on hill. Hishu come. Bad Injun run, all sam' dog. Hishu make beeg potlatch. Moche glad."

The fire was smouldering low as Grey rose to his feet. The old impatience was upon him. He longed to be doing. To wait all day for the arrival of the Hishus was more than he could stand. He could do almost anything but wait. How could he tarry at the village while Madeline was being carried farther and farther into the wilderness? No, he must find Buckskin Dan, and discuss matters with him.

Leaving the Indian he hurried down the hill as fast as the roughness of the trail would permit. He reached the cabin, and entered. It was the same as he had left it, but the trapper was nowhere to be seen. A piece of paper lying on the table by the candle arrested his attention. He picked it up, and read the few words scrawled with a lead pencil:

"You'll find me at the store. Dan."

At once Grey left the cabin, and crossed over to the fur-trader's. Entering the building he found the place in darkness, although a faint glimmer of light came from the door at the rear of the room. Groping his way slowly toward this he gave it a push, but found it was securely fastened on the other side.

"Dan," he called, "are you there?"

Receiving no answer he stood for a space, undecided what to do. "Strange," he thought, "that the place should be so still, and the store in darkness. I wonder what has happened to Dan, and why he left that note."

Suddenly a feeling seized him that something was wrong. He became suspicious. Was it a scheme to lure him to the store for some evil purpose? He peered through the darkness in an effort to see what was there. The silence was ominous. He must get away as quickly as possible. Acting upon this impulse he started for the door. He had taken but a few steps forward when a heavy weight suddenly struck him and sent him staggering to the floor. Instantly a rush of feet was heard, and strong hands were laid upon him. Recovering himself as speedily as possible Grey threw out one arm with all the force he could command. It struck what he believed to be a human face, for immediately a groan was heard as something fell heavily to the floor. Then like a tiger he closed with the assailant whose hands were gripping him hard. It was no novice, he at once realised, who had attacked him, but a man of skill, and great muscular strength. But Grey himself was not to be despised when once thoroughly aroused. The blood beat wildly through his veins, and a deep rage filled his heart at the despicable attack which had been made upon a defenceless man, and in the dark at that. But he would show his assailant a thing or two. He caught him with a grip of iron, and hurled him back several steps. Then the two joined in a terrible embrace. Backwards and forwards they surged, and strained at each other. Time and time again Grey felt his opponent's hands reaching out for his throat. They seemed like the slippery, clammy tentacles of a hideous octopus. No word was spoken. Each was reserving his strength for the contest. At length Grey's fingers touched his adversary's throat. It was all that was needed, and almost like the spring of a trap they closed upon the coarse, tense flesh. It was his turn now, and he made the most of it. From his opponent's lips came a hoarse gurgling sound, while he frantically endeavoured to tear away those death-dealing fingers. Grey was madly triumphant now. The sense of victory possessed his soul as he felt his antagonist sink upon the floor. No bulldog held firmer than did he. But even in the midst of his triumph something touched him which brought a chill to his heart. Something was passed swiftly and deftly about his ankles, and then drawn tight. He loosened his grip upon the throat, and tried to regain his feet. But in vain, for his legs were fast bound, as if in a vise. Then in the twinkling of an eye his arms were seized and he was hurled to the floor face downwards, while his arms were fastened behind his back. He had forgotten his second assailant, who had returned to the attack with such marked success. Frantically he struggled to tear away his hands, and to throw off the weight pressing upon his body. But his efforts were all to no purpose, and at last he was forced to give up from sheer exhaustion. He could not see, but he could easily guess the identity of his captors. Two they were, that was evident, and what two except Siwash Bill and Windy Pete would make such a mean, savage attack?

"Lie there, ye young spyin' cur," one of them said, which the constable recognised as Bill's voice. "'Tain't sich fun is it comin' to Hishu? Not a holiday trip, eh? Ye'll think it less so before we git through with ye."

"The more you do with me," Grey replied, "the worse for yourselves. If you want to feel the noose, drive ahead."

"Ha, ha," laughed Pete. "We fear not the noose. All the d— Yellow-legs in the country haven't enough wit to stretch our necks. But come, Bill, lend a hand, and let's git out of this. Have ye the knife?"

"Sure."

Grey began to realise the seriousness of his position as the men lifted him bodily and carried him out into the night toward Buckskin Dan's cabin. This they entered, and laid him in the lower bunk. By the candle light he could see their faces, and they seemed to him like two diabolical fiends standing there in the middle of the room. They began to whisper to each other, while Siwash Bill drew a glittering hunting knife from its sheath at his side. Then the meaning of their action stabbed Grey's mind. They would murder him there in cold blood, in Dan's cabin, and let the blame rest upon the innocent old trapper! He recalled that scene out in the hills, and saw again Pete's form slinking through the night with the bared knife in his hand. The thought almost maddened him. Wildly he tore at his bonds, but they held firm. He sat up in the bunk, and then rolled out upon the floor, and on his knees faced his captors.

"You imps of hell!" he cried. "Would you murder a man in cold blood? Have you no hearts in your bodies? Free my hands and feet and let us fight it out. There are two of you, but I'll fight you both. I dare you to do it, you cowardly dogs."

"Hold yer jaw," cried Pete. "Come, Bill, douse that candle. There's too much light here fer this job."

Grey now felt that his last moment on earth had arrived. He saw a big hand reach out toward the table, and then all was dark. He made one mighty effort to rise, but failing in this he fell forward upon the floor, while from his lips leaped the wild piercing cry of "Dan, Dan! For God's sake, help!"

CHAPTER XVII IN PURSUIT

Instead of going with the constable to Old Meg's house, upon his return from the hill, Buckskin Dan went into his own cabin. Here he lighted a candle, and examined carefully his stock of provisions. Finding it much lower than he had expected he slowly scratched his head in a puzzled manner.

"Wall, I'll be blowed!" he muttered. "I thought thar was more meat left, but that last moose j'int is almost gone, an' what's left is about all bone an' gristle. Guess I'll have to go to the store, though I hate to do so. Mebbe Bill has some on hand."

He was about to blow out the candle, when he suddenly paused.

"No, guess I'd better leave it fer the lad. He'll be back soon. Let me see: he'll wonder whar I am. Ah, that's the idee. I'll jist leave a note to tell 'im I'm at the store. I may be longer than I expect."

Finding a piece of brown paper, and unearthing a stub of a pencil from a few simple treasures kept in an old box, he painfully scrawled the brief sentence: "You'll find me at the store. Dan."

Little dreaming that this simple act would bring his partner into such serious difficulty the worthy trapper closed the cabin door, and walked rapidly toward the store.

He found Siwash Bill alone in the building, smoking an old blackened pipe. The squaw man could hardly conceal his pleasure at seeing Dan alone. He feigned surprise, however, at his early return, and questioned him as to his luck on the hills.

"Brought nuthin' back," Dan replied. "Not even a sheep. Say have ye any meat?"

"No," replied the trader. "I'm clean skinned out. Not a scrap left. I've some in the cache, though, about three miles up-stream."

"Three miles! Good Lord!" groaned the trapper, "an' I want it now."

"Why not wait till the mornin', Dan? Surely yer not so hard up as that?"

"No, I want it to-night. So I'm goin' after it at once. An' look ye, if me pardner comes here tell 'im I'll be back as soon as I kin. I've left a note in the cabin to tell 'im I came to the store. I'll settle with ye fer the meat later."

Dan left the building and walked with a swinging stride along the trail upstream. It was well for his peace of mind that he did not see the form of Windy Pete glide into the store a few minutes later, nor hear the animated conversation which took place between him and the squaw man. Had he seen them, and could he have read their thoughts, he would have bounded back to the cabin with the great leaps of a greyhound.

Well accustomed to the trail he had no difficulty in picking his way through the darkness. He knew where the cache was located, as he had passed it time and time again. In less than an hour the place was reached, and a generous portion of meat obtained. This accomplished, he set his face homeward. Lifting up his eyes, a bright light on the hill above the settlement arrested his steps. He paused for a few minutes, and gazed intently upon the flames which were slowly dying down.

"It's an Injun signal, by jingo!" he exclaimed. "It must be fer the Hishus. I wonder who it kin be. I must git back to camp an' find out. Surely the Big Lakes are not upon us. God help us, if they are!"

Reaching the store he found the place silent and in darkness.

"Queer," he muttered. "What's happened to Bill? Mebbe he's heard about the Big Lakes, an' has taken to the hills. Guess I'll git back to me own shack and see to me ammunition. Hope to goodness me pardner's thar."

Reaching his cabin he paused for a moment, and watched the fire upon the hilltop, half expecting at any instant to hear the sound of approaching Indians. But a cry from a most unexpected quarter fell upon his ears. It was the wild call for help within the cabin, and at once he recognised the voice. Puzzled beyond description as to the meaning of it all he leaped toward the door, gave it a mighty push, and dashed into the room.

The place was in darkness, so he could see nothing. He heard only the scuttling of feet and felt some moving object touch his shoulder. He reached out quickly, but clutched nothing save the yielding air. Soon all was still.

"Laddie, laddie," he called. "What's wrong?"

"I'm here, Dan," came the reply. "But for God's sake get a light."

With trembling hands the old man fumbled in the pocket of his buckskin jacket, brought forth his rude match case made of two cartridge shells, found a match and struck it. He lighted the candle upon the table, and then glanced anxiously about the room. Seeing Grey huddled upon the floor, he sprang to his side with a peculiar cry, half rage and half sympathy.

"Are ye hurt, pardner?" he demanded. "Have the wretches knifed ye?"

"No, Dan," came the reply. "I'm all right now, but unloosen these cords, quick."

With two swift strokes of his hunting knife Dan severed the bonds. Instantly Grey sprang to his feet, and looked around the cabin. He reached out his hand, and clutched a rifle leaning against the wall.

"Give me your revolver, Dan, and some cartridges. You stay here; I don't want you to run any risk."

The trapper, however, maintained his position. He noted the flushed face of his companion and the wild gleam in his eyes.

"Whar are ye goin'?" he asked. "An' what d'ye want with the guns?"

"Going? I'm going after those devils, who trapped, bound and led me here to die. But for your timely arrival I would now be a corpse on this very floor."

Across Dan's face spread an angry cloud. His rough, hard fingers clinched with a sudden grip.

"Was it Bill an' Pete?" he hoarsely whispered. "Was it them varmints?"

"Yes, that's who it was. But come, I want your revolver. I'll take that grinning look from their faces quicker than hell."

"Now look here, pardner," Dan remonstrated, "jist cool down a bit. Yer a little excited, an' don't realise yer persition. Wot's the use of goin' after them divils now? We've more important work on hand, an' I'm thinkin' ye've fergotten the lassie. Guess we'd better go after her fust, an' we kin settle with them skunks later. I admire yer spunk, young man, but we mustn't run any risk at present. Bill an' Pete are mighty handy with the gun, an' mebbe thar wouldn't be anyone left to go after the lassie."

Grey looked hard at Dan for a few minutes without replying. He realised the force of the words he had just heard. But the red rage of battle was hot within him, and he found it difficult to wait.

"Besides," coolly continued the trapper, reading truly the struggle his companion was undergoing, "it's yer duty to keep calm. Ye belong to a great Force, an' I've never yit heard of a member doin' anything that was rash, or that would upset his plans. Caution's the word now, pardner."

"You're right, Dan," and as Grey reached out his hand and gripped that of the trapper, a sigh escaped his lips. "I'm afraid it would bungle matters if I went after those villains. I agree to wait."

"Wall said, pardner. I know how ye feel, an' I jist long meself to git after them snakes. But, come, we must hike away from here. The canoe's in the stream an' the meat's outside, so we kin slip away through the darkness. We've wasted too much time already, an' have given them redskins a big start."

A few minutes later a small trim canoe dropped silently away from the shore a short distance above the cabin. She darted out into midstream where the swift current caught her in its irresistible sweep. Neither Dan nor Norman spoke much as hour after hour they bent to their paddles.

The grey dawn was breaking when at length they ran the canoe ashore, and prepared their breakfast, principally of moose meat. Then it was up and on again. Being on the river, protected by the banks and trees, they escaped the furious storm which was sweeping over the lake miles below. In the afternoon when they did burst into that fine sheet of water, the gale had spent its fury, and only the foamy surf upon the shore, where the long ground swells throbbed and beat, remained to tell of the tempest that had raged but a few hours before.

Grey, although well accustomed to the scenery of the North, felt his heart thrill anew at the superb spectacle which now met his gaze. To the left and right rose massive flinty walls, terrace above terrace, culminating in numerous grand and fantastic peaks hundreds of feet above the surface of the lake. Huge gaping crevices scarred their weather-beaten sides, which every spring belched torrents of icy waters. The afternoon sun touched the snowy peaks with a dazzling halo, forming a sharp contrast to the bluest of skies overhead.

"My, what a sight!" Grey ejaculated, as he rested his paddle across his knees. "I've never seen anything to equal this. Oh, for an artist's skill to catch such a scene!"

"Ay, ay, it's fine, pardner," Dan replied. "But ye should see it when thar's a storm on, an' then ye'd witness somethin'. I saw it once to me sorrow, an' only by a miracle I live to tell the tale. But, laddie, thar's been a storm here to-day. I see signs of it on yonder shore, an' I'm thinkin' the lassie's had a hard time of it. I hope to goodness them redskins made fer shore in time."

Grey looked anxiously into the speaker's face. A new fear seized his heart. Suppose Madeline and the boy had gone down! How could he endure it, and would he dare to go back to Big Glen? What would the Major say, and the Force?

"Look here, Dan," and Grey spoke most impressively, "if we find that an accident has happened, and Madeline and the boy have gone down, do you know what I shall do?"

"No; couldn't guess."

"I shall go back to Hishu, and have it out with those devils there. They may punch me full of holes if they wish, but I don't think they'll ever do it upon anybody else. It'll be the only thing left for me to do in the world, and I think it will be a mighty fine service after all."

A grim smile crossed the trapper's rugged face.

"I guess ye won't have to do that yit awhile, pardner," he remarked. "Them red divils are too cunnin' to take any risk. They know the lake better than they do their prayers. They were sheltered somewhar ye may be sure, an' are now hikin' on like blazes; so we must git after 'em. Thar's a stream some distance ahead which mebbe they reached afore the storm struck. That's their route, an' we must hustle along."

After two more hours of hard paddling an opening appeared upon their right, which proved to be the mouth of a small stream, called by the Indians "Wahsek."

"We'll find the current purty strong," said Dan, as they headed the canoe for the opening. "Thar's a nasty rapids several miles up, an' I'd like to reach the foot of it afore we stop. D'ye think ye can stan' it?"

"Stand it, man! Why I could paddle all night. Of what stuff do you think I am made?"

"Mighty good stuff, if I'm any jedge. Ye've been through enough of late to knock out a dozen men, an' yit yer as chipper as a whisky-jack. But say, pardner, this current's too strong fer the paddles, guess we'll have to pole. I brought two sticks along, fer ye kin never tell what minute ye may have to use 'em, on these tarnel northern streams. I do want to reach the rapids afore landin'. Guess then we'll have to pack the canoe round that rough piece of water."

It was necessary now to keep close to the shore, and with the long poles they slowly and steadily forced the craft against the current, which increased in velocity as they advanced.

The sun had disappeared above the tree tops, and night was settling over the land ere the sound of rushing, swirling waters fell upon their ears.

"It's the rapids, pardner," Dan remarked, as he gave the canoe a vigorous shove which sent her quivering like a thing of life against her rushing adversary. "A little ferther, an' we'll be thar."

When at length they ran into an eddy close to shore and disembarked they could discern through the gloom the white, turbulent waters but a short distance above. Grey was tired, very tired, and after supper was ended he threw himself upon the ground by the small camp fire they had lighted.

"I could sleep for a week," he remarked. "My, this place feels good!"

"No wonder, pardner," was the reply. "Ye haven't had much sleep fer several nights. So fall to now, fer we must make an early start in the mornin'."

CHAPTER XVIII THE CRUEL TRAIL

Standing upon the bank Madeline clutched Donnie in her arms, and gazed at the surf beating and chafing against the shore. She was bewildered and her brain whirled. The wind raved about her, tossing her hair in wild confusion. Her clothes were wet, and she shivered with the cold. She looked at the lad lying in her arms. He was very still. It was the silence of fear, and he gazed up wonderingly into Madeline's eyes. His lips quivered as he noticed her drawn, tense features. He was about to cry, when Madeline suddenly bent her head, and rained a shower of passionate kisses upon the little white face. Tears came to her eyes and fell upon the boy's soft cheeks.

"What's the matter, Malin?" he asked. "What are 'ou crying for? Why don't 'ou take me home to my mamma?"

"I can't, Donnie," was the sobbing reply. "I would if I could. We are alone here with these people, and we must cling together. I want you to be a man, Donnie, and help me to be brave."

For a few brief heart-beats the little lad looked intently into Madeline's face, his bright eyes filled with a questioning, wondering light. Then something seemed to dawn across his mind, and placing one small hand into hers he straightened himself up, and stood proudly by her side.

"I'll take care of 'ou, Malin," he cried. "I'll fight for 'ou. I'll—"

His words were cut short by a gruff voice near at hand. They both started and looked quickly around. The Indian woman was standing near, ordering them to make haste as the men were about to move forward.

Then Madeline noticed that the canoe had been drawn ashore and hidden in a secret place among the trees. The men were making ready to depart, with their few belongings thrown over their shoulders. What did it all mean? She wondered. Why were they leaving the lake, and where were they going? The water, rough and tumultuous though it was, seemed like a friend, and to leave it was to abandon hope. She looked away to the left and beheld a long valley opening up between the shoulders of two mountain ranges. Through this they were to travel. It seemed to her like the gate of death, dark and horrible.

Taking Donnie's hand in her own she followed the natives. The trail, though worn by many feet, was rough. There were rocks, and snags which had not been removed, and over these the boy at times stumbled. He tried bravely to keep up with his companion, but his little legs wearied, and his breath came hard and fast. Madeline looking down saw the effort he was making to be a man. Compunction smote her heart, so, stooping, she lifted the lad in her arms and struggled forward. At times the Indians turned and scowled darkly when she lagged too far behind. But no one offered to assist her with her burden. When her arms ached she would place the boy upon the ground for a brief respite, but only to lift him up again after a few minutes. Thus all through that long day she battled onward. How her strength endured she could not tell. Often she was at the point of sinking upon the trail and giving up in despair. But that little clinging form depending upon her always nerved her to action. For his sake she would be brave and keep up. She longed to lie down and rest, for she was very tired. The strain of the night before and the lack of sleep were telling plainly upon her now. She thought she knew what it was to be weary, but never anything like this. Her whole body ached, her eyes were tired, and her long dark lashes would continually droop. Her head throbbed, and her face was hot and feverish.

"Oh, God!" she mentally prayed. "Why this chastening? Why is the rod so heavy?"

And still she pressed on. She walked mechanically now—a mere machine, a human shuttle crawling through the silent web of trees, streams and hills. And her feet, how they ached! Her shoes were but scant protection against the cruel snags and stones. She was unaccustomed to long marches. At times she almost screamed at the pain she endured, but always with firmly compressed lips she crushed back the cry.

At one terrible moment her foot suddenly struck upon a sharp root, which caused her to stumble and fall forward full length upon the trail. Donnie, fortunately, was walking by her side, and he tried to assist her to her feet. She rose, and gazed about her in a bewildered manner. Should she go on? The Indians were some distance ahead, and were becoming impatient at her slowness. Accustomed to the trail they could not understand such weakness, and in their hearts they despised the white woman.

Standing there a scene appeared to her, clear and bright as the sun in the heavens. It was a picture which hung upon the wall of her old home, showing a weary, thorn-crowned man bearing a heavy cross and sinking beneath its burden. She saw His sorrowful eyes, and they seemed to be looking full upon her. So intense was the vision that she gave a distinct start, caught Donnie once more by the hand and hurried onward. But now a new courage was hers, and though the trail was no less hard, nor did her weariness abate in the least degree, some indefinable power possessed her heart, which wrenched away some of the terrible weight of despair. An unseen presence seemed to be very near, upholding and supporting her, for what purpose she could not guess.

It was late in the afternoon when, after climbing a steep hill, the Indians halted by the side of a swiftly flowing stream, and prepared to camp for the night. Mechanically she watched them as they moved about. She could only taste the poorly cooked food thrust before her. She wished to lie down and rest, no matter where. A small fire had been built, but this was soon allowed to go out, and when night came upon them the desolation of the scene almost overpowered her. A thin blanket was thrown at her feet by one of the Indians. Almost mechanically she picked it up, and began to prepare for the night. One blanket for two! She shuddered at the thought. But there was nothing else to do. So wrapping it carefully about the child where he lay upon the hard ground, and taking her place by his side, she drew one edge over her own body.

Donnie had been wonderfully brave throughout the day, but the long journey had made him very weary. Only a few minutes elapsed after he had taken his place upon his earthen bed ere he was fast asleep.

But not so Madeline. Her eyes would not close. They kept staring up at the great vault above. How far away seemed the stars, and how cold and cruel they looked as they twinkled from their lofty positions. A loneliness which was overwhelming swept upon her. She felt like crying out in anguish of soul. Was there a God beyond those stars and did He care? Why did He allow such misery to exist upon His earth which He had made so beautiful? But as she mused that vision she had seen during the day came once more to her mind. She saw His thorn-crowned head, and the sad face and weary eyes. "He knows, He knows," she whispered to herself. "It was He who said, 'Come unto Me, all ye that labour and are heavy laden, and I will give you rest!'"

Donnie moved in his sleep, and called "Mamma, mamma. Why don't 'ou tum to me?" He started up in afright, looked about, and began to cry.

"Hush, dear," Madeline replied. "You are safe with me."

Then she placed her arms about the lad, and drew him closer to her breast. Her heart was filled with a passionate yearning for the poor child, who had been so cruelly torn away from his home. They were comrades in distress. His curly head was against hers, and she felt the pressure of his soft cheek. Ere long he was fully reassured, so lying down again he was soon in slumber deep.

Slowly the time crept by, but no sleep came to her eyes. Though her body was weary her brain was active. She found herself wondering as to the meaning of it all. Why was she being thus borne off into the wilderness? Was it for the sake of the child? She felt there was some other motive, and that the Indian woman had some sinister purpose in view. Her lowering face and cruel eyes stood out clear and distinct as she lay there. She thought, too, of Norman. Where was he, and would he know what had happened to her? Had he cast her aside as unworthy of his affection?

The night was still and cool. No sound of life broke the intense silence except the deep breathing of the child close by her side. She longed for something to break the quietness which reigned, which was almost maddening her. Presently a slight noise arrested her attention. It was a light step as of someone approaching. Her heart beat fast, and she strained her eyes in an effort to pierce the gloom. Soon a shadowy form became visible. It drew nearer, and then stopped. Slowly it advanced until it was close by her side, when she recognised the form of Nadu, the Indian woman. Madeline lay perfectly still now, although her heart was thumping so loud that she thought it must be heard yards away. The visitor stood for a few seconds like a statue. Then she stooped down and peered intently into Madeline's face. The latter closed her eyes and pretended to be asleep. She almost felt Nadu's warm breath, and pictured those eyes glaring like fiery balls. When it seemed that she could stand the strain no longer she heard the woman move away, and when Madeline opened her eyes the intruder was nowhere to be seen. The darkness had swallowed her up, and Madeline almost imagined she had seen a vision. She lay awake for some time after this incident, staring up vacantly at the stars. At length, however, the tired brain ceased to work, and she drifted away for a time from care and fear into the beneficent land of sleep.

And thus they lay, beneath the twinkling lights of heaven, the child and the woman, two fresh fair flowers, rudely snatched from their natural abode, to be tossed to and fro by the wild winds of passion and greed far out into the frontier of a cold, cruel land.

CHAPTER XIX THE VENOM OF HATRED

The banks of the Takan River, at the head of the Kaska Rapids, were lined with tall fir trees and jack pines. It was a sombre place, this, and the regular camping ground where from time immemorial natives had disembarked to portage overland to the big lake below.

Near one of the large trees stood Nadu, the Indian woman, dark, straight and motionless as the numerous boles around her. But, though very still, a new light shone in her eyes—the light of indecision. For weeks past only grim determination had been expressed in those restless orbs. At Hishu, and all the way down the river, no change or softening gleam could be detected. There was nothing but that savage glitter of a beast of the forest ready to spring upon its victim.

But now something was disturbing that fevered brain, some counter attraction was at work, causing those ever-varying expressions. As dark billowy clouds roll and surge threateningly athwart the sky, while occasionally a brief glimpse of the clear blue is seen, so it was across Nadu's face. Now the storm of passion was seen, and again a sudden rift telling of the violence raging within.

Her form was straight and unbending. A shawl covered her head and swept her comely shoulders. Night was symbolised there—black, desolate Night. Occasionally her eyes turned to the spot where Madeline and Donnie were lying. Then the clouds grew dark, and the staring eyes gleamed cruelly fierce. But anon they shifted to the left, and roamed among the silent arches of the shadowy forest. Then the fire died down to a softer glow, suggesting warmth rather than destruction.

For some time she remained in this position. At length, drawing the loose ends of the shawl closely together about her head, she moved swiftly forward. Down among the trees she sped, following what seemed to be a narrow trail. No mortal eye could see this rough crooked path. But Nadu needed not the light of day for guidance. She was on familiar ground, and intuitively kept the way. Ere long the trees became somewhat sparse, and soon a large clearing appeared in view.

Silently Nadu sped from the midst of the shadows and started across the open. Presently she paused and looked keenly ahead. A light suddenly shone through the darkness. For some time it held her special attention. It fascinated and then drew her steadily on. Brighter and brighter it shone. By this time she was quite near, close enough to see the outline of a rude log house, with the light streaming from the one window on the northern side.

Her form was not straight now, but much bent as she crept warily onward, fearful lest she should be observed. But so silent were her movements that a watchful dog could hardly detect her approach.

She came close to the window, and standing somewhat to one side peered in through the small dust-laden panes. The scene she beheld caused Nadu's bosom to heave, and the hardness of her face to change entirely to an expression of love. Eagerly her eyes dwelt upon various things within that building. The rough deal table, the few stools and benches, and the one lighted candle. But a thin white hand, steadily writing, moved her most, and lifting her eyes they rested upon a bent head covered with hair of snowy whiteness, while a long beard swept the writer's breast.

All unconscious of the eager eyes peering in upon him, the lonely worker continued his task through the silent watches of the night.

For some time Nadu stood by the window, her eyes riveted upon that grey-haired man. After a while she turned aside, glided around the house until she came to the door. Here she paused and looked carefully about. But no sign of life was to be seen. The far-off eastern horizon was now reddening above the tree tops. The light of the rising moon was slowly stealing over the land, bringing into relief the dim outlines of various log houses and tent frames not far away.

Nadu dropped upon the wooden doorstep and leaned her head against her right hand. Occasionally her form trembled, and a half-smothered sob escaped her lips. Some strong emotion was stirring in this Indian woman's heart like a deep lake disturbed by a subtle, unseen volcano. At length she arose and moved slowly away from the building. At times she paused, and looked yearningly back upon the house she had just left. But when once again among the trees her step quickened, and as she neared the river the old hard look returned to her face. She stayed her steps where the woman and the child were lying. Then she crept softly forward, and peered down intently upon the silent pair. What were the thoughts which racked her brain as she saw Madeline's face strained and white lying there amidst the shadows? When she had gazed to her satisfaction she once more glided away, and moving to the bank of the river crouched down upon the ground. A canoe lying in a little eddy near the shore chafed and tugged at its moosehide painter. The cold dark river surged sullenly by, to leap with a roar and a swirl through the dreaded Kaska Rapids several hundred yards down-stream.

Nadu did not sleep, for when the brain becomes the battlefield of strong contending emotions the ministering angel of slumber can find no abiding place. At length she roused to action. Having awakened the men she went to the white woman's side, and looked for a few minutes upon that slight form. Madeline's left arm was thrown about Donnie's body in a protecting embrace. Her right hand pillowed her tired head, while across cheek and brow swept a few loosened tresses of dark brown hair. About the corners of her mouth a faint semblance of a smile was to be detected. Was she dreaming of happy bygone days in her old home far away? If so what a terrible change to awake to her real situation!

Was it the crackling of the fire which one of the Indians had made or the presence of that dark face staring down upon her which caused Madeline to move restlessly, then open her eyes, and start up with a little cry of fright? A malicious gleam of joy shone in Nadu's eyes as she turned away and left the woman and the child together.

Donnie was much refreshed by his sleep. He was standing the ordeal far better than Madeline. He chatted incessantly while she washed his face, and smoothed out his tousled curly locks with her fingers.

Madeline could barely taste the food, and she stood silently by watching Donnie enjoying the few morsels which were given to him. She leaned against a large tree to support her tired and overtaxed form. Every bone in her body ached, for she was so sore and stiff after her long walk of the day before.

Although very early in the morning the moon made the whole land almost as bright as day. The hastily prepared breakfast was soon eaten, the small fire extinguished, and preparations made for a speedy departure.

Madeline and Donnie were standing on the bank near where the canoe was floating. The Indian woman stood by the bow with her hand upon the moosehide thong, while the men conversed together for a few minutes several yards away. Presently they came close to the canoe and began to talk with the woman. What they said Madeline could not tell, but they seemed to be disputing over some question. Ere long one beckoned to the white woman, and pointed to the canoe. With her hand firmly grasping the child's Madeline slipped down the bank and stood close to the craft.

"Git in," commanded Nadu, as she hesitated a moment, "me hand in bah-bee."

Had she at that moment glanced at the Indian woman's malignant, triumphant face she would have shrunk back in terror. But her eyes were upon the rocking canoe, and carefully she stepped over the side, and was about to turn around to receive Donnie, when she felt the craft shoot swiftly out from the shore. The sudden motion caused her to sink upon her knees with a cry of fright. Quickly she turned her eyes to the shore, and there standing close to the water was Donnie with his little arms stretched out appealingly toward her, while his pathetic cry urging her to return smote upon her ears. Nadu was close by his side, one hand fiercely clutching the child's arm, with her eyes full fixed upon the departing canoe. The men were wildly gesticulating, and talking rapidly to her in their own tongue. She heeded them not, but stood like a statue staring out over the swiftly flowing water.

Then the truth flashed across Madeline's mind with a horrible stabbing intensity. It was the Indian woman's devilish plot to get rid of her, to send her to a speedy death into the swirling rapids below. Already their roar sounded in her ears like the knell of doom. Swifter flowed the stream, and the canoe trembled convulsively in its onward rush. Madeline glanced about for a paddle. She would make a struggle for life; she would die fighting. But alas, even that final hope vanished, for the paddles had been carefully removed, by whose hand she could easily guess. But what avail would be a pair of frail arms against that sinuous overmastering current? It was a monster, cruel and relentless, sweeping her onward into the very jaws of death. What earthly hand could break its grip, or what human voice could bid it hold back, and it would obey? Only one Hand could reach out, but there was no sign; only one Voice could give the all-powerful command, and It was silent.

Nearer now were those white foaming waters. Their angry snarl as they dashed and broke over some hidden rock sounded louder and louder. Madeline crouched in the bottom of the canoe, her eyes fascinated by that gleaming, grinning line ahead. She felt the craft quiver, dip, and then with a bound it plunged into that flume of destruction. Instantly Hell opened its horrid jaws to engulf her. She heard the jeering, maddening roar of demons. She felt the white froth spuming her body, and beheld ghostly, merciless claws reaching out to grip and drag her down to their horrid abode. Trees, rocks and sky were blotted out as the craft tore and staggered through that cloud of foam. The canoe was rapidly filling now, and the water was pouring over Madeline's body. It was blinding and deafening her. She rose to her knees; she staggered to her feet; she tried to stand. Her brain reeled. She felt she was going mad. Suddenly the mist cleared. She saw the blue sky above, and lifting up her hands she gave one wild, imploring cry for help. And even as she cried the canoe rushed with a sickening crash upon the edge of a concealed, jagged boulder, hurling Madeline like a rocket, out into the midst of that hissing, seething death.

CHAPTER XX OUT OF THE DEPTHS

When Norman Grey flung himself upon the ground at the foot of the rapids he believed that he would be asleep in a few minutes. In this, however, he was mistaken. His body was tired enough, but his brain was too active. The events of the past night were too vivid to allow him the rest he needed. And ever before his mind rose the vision of Madeline. Where was she, and what was happening to her? Was she calling for him? he wondered, or had she given him up, banished him from her mind? While she was near him at Hishu he was content to wait, to find out the truth gradually. But now it was different. She was alone in the wilderness, needing his assistance. Thinking thus he at length passed into a restless slumber. How long it lasted he could not tell, but he awoke with a start, and looked wildly around. Buckskin Dan was sleeping calmly by his side. Grey laid a heavy hand upon his shoulder, and shook him with impatience.

"Wake up! Wake up!" he cried. "For God's sake, wake up!"

With a roar of surprise and apprehension Dan leaped to his feet, and seized the rifle lying close at hand. He looked about as if expecting to see a bloodthirsty enemy almost on top of them. Then his eyes rested upon his comrade's tossed hair and excited face.

"What's wrong, pardner?" he demanded. "What's up this time? Did ye see that sarpint crawlin' among the trees ag'in? P'int me out the spot, an' I'll riddle the place with bullets. Mebbe one will ketch 'im on the fly, an' if it does he'll git to hell quicker than he imagined."

"No, no, not that beast this time," Grey replied. "But I saw her, yes, her, my Madeline, stretching out her hands, and calling to me for help! There she is, look!" and he clutched Dan by the arm and pointed excitedly among the trees. "There she is! Let me go to her! My God! I never saw her look so beautiful, but she's in the midst of serpents, and they're dragging her down to death. Look! look!"

Dan's eyes followed the direction of the finger, and he carefully scanned the forest for some distance around. Then he turned toward his comrade, while an anxious expression crossed his bronzed face.

"What's wrong with ye, laddie?" he questioned. "Are ye goin' daft? I see nuthin' over thar."

Grey placed his hand to his forehead, while a deep sigh escaped his lips.

"Neither do I, now," he responded. "But I did a minute ago. Oh, it was so clear, and terrible. Perhaps my brain is turning. Lack of sleep, and the events of the two past weeks have been enough to unsettle anyone."

"Indeed yer right thar, pardner," responded the trapper. "Few could have stood it. They'd have buckled under long since this."

"But I can't get that dream and vision out of my mind, Dan. I fear there's something wrong with Madeline."

"Mebbe yer right, pardner, an' I guess we'd better git a move on. It's purty light now, an' the moon makes the land almost as bright as day. If ye'll jist bring some water from the river I'll start a fire. We'll have a hot drink an' a snack of food afore we hike outer this."

Seizing the small tin pail in his hand Grey moved toward the river. He had taken but a few steps when he paused in amazement, for a wild cry for help winged through the crisp morning air and fell upon his ears. His eyes sought the rapids, from which the sound came, and as he looked a never-to-be-forgotten sight met his gaze. For an instant he thought it must be another vision, and would vanish like the one he had recently seen. But how real it was—the leaping billows, the dashing spray, and that fair form with uplifted arms gliding through that channel of death. Surely it must be a spirit, or else he was losing his reason, and it was all the strange fancy of a mad man.

When, however, the shock came, and he saw the woman hurled forward he knew it was no dream, but a terrible reality. With Grey to think was to act. With a shout to Dan he dashed forward, leaped down the bank, and laid his hands upon the canoe. As he did so the trapper was at his heels. He, too, had heard that cry, and had seen the wreck in the rapids, and had bounded forward on the instant. Into the canoe they sprang, and without a word sent it reeling from its moorings. It was caught by the swirling current, and carried a few yards down river. But strong arms held the paddles, and forced its stubborn and rebellious prow against the pressing stream.

A nameless fear clutched at Grey's heart as he drove the paddle through the water with great sweeps until the slender blade bent like a reed beneath a tempest. Could it be Madeline? Who else could be in that staring wilderness with such a form as the one he had just beheld? His eyes noted everything ahead. Would she rise, or had she been carried down to the bottom by some swirling eddy, to reappear bruised and lifeless farther down-stream? Only a brief space of time had elapsed since that cry had fallen upon his ears. Yet in that infinitesimal tick of eternity he had endured the life of the damned. For one who has passed through such an experience it would be easy to realise how much is summed up in "the twinkling of an eye" of the Great Judgment Day.

The canoe was now close to the foaming breakers, where progress was almost imperceptible. Grey's eyes were searching the waters to the right, when a cry from Dan caused him to glance quickly around. As he did so he caught sight of a dark object on the left. Then a hand—oh, so white and small—rose above the surface. With a half-smothered cry Grey dropped his paddle, flung himself into that racing stream, and in an instant sank from view. With titanic strokes he threaded the icy chambers of that watery world. He caught a glimpse of a whirling form a few feet ahead. He reached out one gripping hand; it closed; it held firm, and with his precious burden he rose to the surface with the speed of a nimble bubble.

With a vigorous shake of the head Grey tossed some of the water from his eyes, and endeavoured to look around. A gladsome shout from the left told him that Dan was not far away. Ere long the canoe was a few yards off, then a few feet, and soon the swimmer was able to reach out and seize the trapper's big strong hand. And none too soon, for Grey was almost exhausted, and the helpless form he was supporting was like a great leaden weight.

"Wall done, pardner," was Dan's cheery greeting. "Ye'd better not try to git on board, fer ye'll be likely to capsize the canoe. Jist hold on here to the stern. Thar, that's good. I'll run her ashore now like greased lightnin'!"

Thus Grey clung to the craft with his right hand, while with his left arm he upheld Madeline's limp form. It took Dan several minutes to make land, and by the time the shore was reached they had drifted some distance down-stream.

Grey felt his feet touch bottom, and almost as soon as the trapper had pulled the canoe upon the beach he staggered out of the water with Madeline held tenderly in his arms. At once Dan relieved him of his burden, and carried her up the bank, and laid her upon the ground.

Weak though he was Grey knelt by her side and peered into that drawn, pallid face. No sign of life, however, showed in that drenched form. He called her by name, he pleaded with her to speak, but no response came to his passionate appeal.

"My God! is she dead?" he cried, looking with pitiful eyes into Dan's face.

"Dead? No," was the reassuring reply. "It 'ud take more'n that duckin' to knock out the likes of her. Let me down thar. Mebbe I kin do more good than you."

Dan spoke more cheerfully than he felt in order to encourage his comrade's sinking spirits. His years of practical experience in the wilderness served him in good stead now. He performed the simple method of resuscitation, which he had used on several occasions in the past, and ere long had the satisfaction of seeing signs of returning life, and a faint colour tinge the patient's cheeks.

At length Madeline slowly opened her eyes, and fixed them for an instant upon the trapper's face. Closing them again with a deep sigh, she drifted off into that silent land, whether of sleep or unconsciousness the anxious watchers could not divine.

"We must git her outer this, pardner," Dan remarked. "In her wet condition, and weak as she is, she can't stand much more."

"But what are we to do?" cried Grey, as the helplessness of their position dawned upon him.

The joy of knowing that Madeline still breathed was now replaced by despair. What were they to do with this helpless woman there in the wilderness, with wet clothes clinging to her body? She must be chilled through already, and to remain there much longer would mean certain death.

"Shall I build a fire, Dan?" he asked. "We can lay her close to that, and perhaps her clothes will dry. What else can we do?"

"No, pardner," was the reply. "That won't do; it would take too long to dry clothes as wet as hers. She needs gentle care sich as we can't give her."

"But what—?"

"Jist a moment, pardner," interrupted Dan. "We ain't got no time to waste in words. We've got to act. The last time I was in this region thar was an Injun encampment over thar to the right, on that old cut-off trail, an' mebbe—But hark, what's that?"

"It sounds like the bark of a dog," Grey replied, now standing erect, and listening intently.

"Ay, ay. Didn't I tell ye right? Whar thar's a dog ye may be sure some human critter's not fer away. Come, let's take the lassie an' strike through that openin' over yon. I guess we'll find somethin'."

Stooping, the constable lifted Madeline tenderly in his arms. Dan, however, interposed.

"Ye mustn't do that, laddie. Ye're too weak after yer tryin' experience. Let me carry the lassie."

"No, no, Dan," Grey replied, as he started to leave the place. "Let me carry her for a while. You may take your turn later."

A thrill such as he had not known for years came into Norman's heart, as he bore forward his precious burden. Her face was close to his. Oh, if she would only wake, look into his eyes, and speak to him he would forget and forgive everything, no matter what she had been in the past.

The dog still continued to bark, and by the sound they were able to direct their steps. After a while Grey found it necessary to relinquish his burden to Dan, for he was weaker than he had imagined. This gave him an opportunity to speed on ahead, and in a few minutes the trees became thin, and a clearing burst into view. Looking to the left he saw several log houses, with one in the midst much larger than the others, with smoke issuing from a stovepipe stuck out through the roof. Toward this he hastened, glancing back at times to see whether Dan was following.

Having reached the building, he rapped loudly upon the door, expecting to see it opened by an uncouth native. He heard someone moving within; then a hand was laid upon the wooden latch, and great was his surprise to see standing before him a grey-bearded white man, tall and commanding in appearance. Kindly eyes looked full into his, and a voice musical and soft bade him welcome, followed by an invitation to enter.

Briefly Grey related his story, after which the tall man hurried back into the room. By this time Dan had arrived, entered the building, and laid his burden upon a low cot placed against the wall. Just then the long-bearded man reappeared through a door to the left.

"Bring her in here," he commanded. "It will be more comfortable."

Lifting Madeline in his arms, Norman did as he was bidden, and entered a little room, meant evidently for a study. The floor was bare. A rough deal table stood by the window littered with papers. A few magazine pictures adorned the walls, while in one corner were several shelves filled with books.

"Lay her there," and the owner of the house pointed to a cosy cot covered with the soft glossy skins of a bear, wolf and lynx. "I shall be back in a few minutes."

Saying this, he disappeared, and Grey found himself alone with Madeline, for the trapper had remained in the outer room, where he was filling his pipe preparatory to his usual morning smoke.

Norman looked long and lovingly upon that white face embedded among the furs. Within him raged a fierce contest. He desired to stay by her side, to know how she would fare after her terrible experience. The love in his heart told him to remain. She was all he had in the world. In her was his life and hope. But, on the other hand, he was in duty bound to go forward as quickly as possible after that stolen child. There was his duty. And yet, why should he go? Did not love, the care of this helpless woman, have the first consideration? Suddenly be remembered that this was the day of his discharge from the Force. Was he not a free man, no longer bound by exacting, and at times galling, rules? On the other hand, was he free? That could not be until he returned, and received his discharge from his Commanding Officer. But, then, what was duty, when love stood in the way? One voice whispered, "Stay with her whom you love. This is your first duty." But another voice, clear and distinct, could not be silenced. "You are in honour bound to carry out your Commander's orders. He has intrusted you with a sacred commission, and will you relinquish the quest, bring disgrace upon yourself, and dishonour upon the Force? Hitherto no man has ever turned back when given such a command as yours until his object had been attained, and will you be the first? How can you return to Big Glen, face your Superior Officer, and your comrades? You, Norman Grey, have never shirked your duty before, and will you do it now?" "But what about Madeline?" again insisted the first voice.

Grey glanced through the small window facing the south, and his eyes rested upon the tall man hurrying from one of the cabins with an Indian woman by his side. There was the answer to the question. Madeline would be carefully looked after, and what good would his presence be anyway? He would fulfil his commission, and then come back to her—perhaps she would want him then.

He heard the outer door open, and knew that his attention would not be needed. Swiftly he stooped over that quiet form, and his lips touched her lips in one fond, passionate kiss. When the man and the Indian woman entered the room they beheld the constable standing silently by the cot. They knew nothing of the battle which had taken place within his heart, nor of the victory won.

"You will do your best for her?" and Grey turned his eyes full upon the face of the bearded man as he spoke.

He longed to ask him his name, and what he was doing there alone so far in the wilderness. He regretted that he had not examined the numerous papers on the table to see what they contained. Now it was too late. But as he looked at the quiet man, and the clean, matronly Indian woman he felt that he was leaving Madeline in safe hands.

"You need not fear," came the reply to his question. "I am somewhat of a doctor, and Nancy du Nord here is most trustworthy."

"Thank you, oh, thank you," Grey responded, and with one swift glance at Madeline, he passed into the next room where Buckskin Dan was thoughtfully smoking.

CHAPTER XXI STRATEGY

It did not take Grey long to change his wet clothes for the ones which had been brought for him by the owner of the house. This accomplished, and his cast-off garments hung by the kitchen stove to dry, he started with Dan back to the foot of the rapids, where they had left their outfit and scanty supply of provisions. Little was said until the river was reached, for each was lost in his own thoughts. It was Dan who broke the silence, as they at length stood on the bank of the stream.

"By the fur of a martin!" he ejaculated, "it's clear to me now."

"What's clear?" questioned Grey, as he stooped to roll up their one blanket.

"The place whar them varmints are hikin' to. I wasn't altogether sartin at fust, an' not quite sure that they'd headed up this way. But when that lassie come tumblin' down yon rapids it made everything plain."

"But how do you think she got into that boat alone?" questioned Grey. "That's what I've been trying to solve ever since we left the house over there."

The trapper scratched his head, dove his hand deep into his pocket, and brought forth a plug of tobacco, turned it carefully over and bit off a corner.

"It's one of three things," he began, "an' I've thought 'em all over. In some places it might be an accident, but not among the Big Lake Injuns. Sich a thing 'ud not happen among 'em. Then, the gal might have tried to escape. But as the kid wasn't with her that proposition's outer the question."

"But maybe the boy is dead," Grey suggested. "He has come through much lately, and perhaps the trip has knocked him out."

"No, pardner, I don't think it likely. The lassie 'ud look after 'im. She's the kind that 'ud care fer the little chap fust."

"Well, then, what is your idea, Dan?"

"That woman was sent inter them foamin' white caps to die. That's what it was."

"Dan, Dan!" Grey cried in amazement. "What do you mean? What reason would the Indians have for doing such a deed, and especially to her?"

"Can't tell ye that, laddie. Ye kin never trust them varmints, perticularly when there's an Injun woman along. But come, if we stop here talkin' all day they'll git too fer ahead of us. We're on the right trail, an' if we're goin' to do anythin' let's git on."

At once Grey bent, seized the blanket, threw the strap over his shoulder, and strode rapidly along by Dan's side. His weariness was now gone, and the blood surged madly through his veins. Added to his desire to recover the child was the longing to punish the ones who had sent Madeline through the rapids. Oh, for a dozen or more of his comrades at Big Glen, mounted on their hardy steeds, and he would show the Indians a thing or two! But then, that was not the way of the Force. It never trusted to numbers. As in far-off Hebrew days it believed that "One thousand shall flee at the rebuke of one," and that "One hundred shall put ten thousand to flight."

Having reached the head of the rapids they carefully examined the remains of the recent camp fire. From the few ashes lying on the ground they could tell how pitifully small it had been—typical of Indian ways. Grey looked down thoughtfully upon that thin black layer and the several charred sticks scattered around. He pictured Madeline sitting at that very spot, enfolding, perhaps, in her arms the tired, homeless child. What were her thoughts as she sat there? Did she think of him? He glanced toward the river flowing sullenly by. If it would only speak what a tale it could unfold. Dan saw the look and divined the meaning.

"Yes, laddie," he remarked, "it was hard—it was devilish. But never mind, yon trail will reveal somethin' afore night shets down or else I'm much mistaken."

For several miles above the rapids stretched as wild and rugged a portion of land as ever met the eye of man. A long range of hills sloped toward the river in a terrace-like formation, terminating in an abrupt, jagged wall of rock from ten to thirty feet in height. The narrow strip of ground between this and the river was strewn with thousands of small and large boulders, which had been hurled from the flinty summit of the range, so the Indians believed, by the Great Spirit in a terrible battle with the monsters of the mountains.

Among these boulders twisted the slender trail, winding at times close to the overshadowing wall of rock. At one of these places Grey paused, and looked about with wonder, mingled with awe. Above him towered two gigantic flinty columns of rock. The chisels of ages had cut strange figures upon their hard surfaces, and rounded into rugged symmetry their stately forms. Silent hoodoo sentinels were they frowning down upon the trail at their feet. To the Indians they were objects of fear and reverence, and their steps always quickened as with furtive eyes they glided speedily by.

"Talk about the monuments of civilisation," said Grey, placing his hand upon the nearer column. "But where will you find such shafts as these cut by the hand of man? Why, the wonderful Cleopatra's needle is a pigmy to these."

"Ay, ay, laddie, yer right thar. When I was in New York they p'inted out to me a number of stones stuck up in the city, an' they showed me the picters in their Art Galleries. But sez I to 'em, 'Come with me to the grand North land, an' I'll show ye picters jist as the Lord made 'em, with no smell of paint upon 'em either. An' as fer stones, I'll show ye monements which the Lord made, with their heads playin' with the clouds, an' their roots grippin' down inter the bowels of the arth.' That's wot I said to 'em, an' they smiled to their selves, so they did, an' nudged one another. They thought I was a bit daft. But, my! if they could see sich wonders as these, they'd then know it wasn't me who was daft."

During this speech Grey was peering around the colossal shaft, exploring the space beyond. Something was interesting him there, and he took a few paces forward.

"Come, Dan," he cried, "what a fine cave is hidden behind these columns."

They both now stood at the opening, looking into the yawning mouth of the cavern.

"It sartinly is great!" ejaculated the trapper. "Who'd a thought thar was sich a hole as this!"

"I should like to explore it," Grey replied, for his curiosity was by this time thoroughly aroused. "Who can tell what wonderful things lie concealed in there. What strange pranks nature plays in this part of the world."

"Seems to me nater had nuthin' to do with this," and Dan carefully examined the opening as he spoke. "Looks as if some two-legged critters with hands an' brains did the work. Guess them Rooshians, who once was here, dug the place. But, come, that's not our bizness now. We've lost too much precious time by foolin' around here, while them Injuns are hikin' it along the trail. No more sich stoppin', mind ye, to-day, examinin' holes an' rocks. Let's git on. I'm agoin' to set the pace, an' ye kin foller if ye like."

And Dan was true to his word. How he did swing forward with that long steady gait, which seemed never to weary. Grey found it difficult to follow close, but he was determined that he would not be outdone. Across a long stretch of wild meadows they sped, up a steep hill, through a densely wooded region, where the trees stood tall and sombre. Grey lost count of time and distance. He was a mere machine—he was simply a bundle of cogs, fitting into another set of cogs ahead, which some irresistible power was driving. Could he keep it up much longer?

It was late in the afternoon as they climbed a hill steeper than any they had yet encountered. Reaching the summit they involuntarily stayed their steps, and looked down upon a body of water lying like a gem in a setting of dark firs and jack pines. Not a ripple ruffled the surface of this mountain lake, while all around the edge ran a fringe of surpassing beauty, where the trees stood mirrored in its liquid depths.

"It's Lake Klawan," whispered Dan, "an' the Injuns are sure to stop here fer the night. We need to be very keerful now, fer the time has arrived when we must do somethin' that'll count."

The trapper was about to move forward, when he suddenly paused, gripped his companion by the arm, and pointed down through the tops of the trees.

"See, they're campin' thar!" he hoarsely whispered. "The varmints are down yon fer sure gettin' their supper."

As Grey looked he could see a thin line of smoke rising above the firs. He turned to the trapper.

"What next, Dan? What's your move?" he inquired.

The trapper's eyes were searching the forest to the left, while his ears were carefully attentive to a faint sound murmuring up through the trees.

"The river, pardner, is down in the valley, an' we must investigate. We'll have to depend much, I'm thinkin' upon that stream."

Saying thus he plunged at once down the hillside, Grey following close at his heels. After a hard fight through the thick underbrush they gained the river's bank and looked carefully around.

"Ah, that's good!" ejaculated Dan. "Thar's plenty of driftwood here, an' some of a fair size. We must make a small raft, laddie, fer I'm thinkin' we'll have to trust our carcasses to it afore long."

Quickly they set to work, and rolled to the edge of the water a dozen of the largest sticks. With his small axe Dan soon fashioned a number of withes from several trees standing near. With these he skilfully bound the logs together, placed several more across the top, and ere long the raft was finished.

"Fine job that," and Dan stepped back a few paces to view his work. "She'll run like a greyhound down the stream. We'll make her fast an' snug in the eddy, fer we can't tell how soon we may need her."

"What's your plan now?" questioned Grey.

"We must git that kid."

"In what way?"

"Wall, I'm jist thinkin' about it. We might creep down upon 'em, an' pick 'em off. But I don't want to do that. It 'ud stir up the hull tribe if we knocked out them two bucks. Then, we might wait till it gits dark, steal upon 'em, an' pinch the lad. But mebbe they intend to git on over the lake, an' we'd be out of it fer sure then. They ginerally keep a canoe handy. No, them plans won't work. But I've another. We must git the men away. It's fer me to do that, an' it's up to you to look after the boy. See?"

"Partly. But how?"

"You leave that to me. I'm goin' up around the lake to the right, an' you jist creep up close like, whar them varmints are squattin'. Be very cautious or ye might spile the hull thing. But when ye see the men leave the kid with the woman, then you drop in like a whirlwind an' do the rest. When ye git the kid hike back to this place, an' wait fer me. But if the bucks git here fust, cast off, an' I'll meet ye down-stream. If it comes to a fight, yer a match fer the hull consarn. I'm off now."

Left to himself Grey stood for a few minutes looking down upon the water. He was realising how dependent he was upon this rugged frontier trapper. He had imagined that his own strength of mind, nerve and body was sufficient to overcome almost any difficulty. In the vicinity of Big Glen it had sufficed. But here where the vast wilderness was the stage, with rushing rivers, foaming rapids, wind-swept lakes, sweeping plains and towering mountains, the setting, and dare-devil white men and roving Indians the chief actors, it was altogether different.

At length he turned, and walked along the bank of the river up toward the lake. There was no footpath here, and he found travelling most difficult. But he considered it safer than on the trail higher up. Slowly and warily he picked his way, taking care not to make the slightest noise to warn the natives of his approach. At times he paused and listened, but hearing nothing he advanced. Ere long, after pushing his way through a tangled thicket of underbrush, the lake burst suddenly into view. One glance was sufficient, and Grey dropped quickly to his knees, and crouched behind a low scrubby bush. There on the shore, only a few rods away, were the Indians, squatting about their camp fire. He counted them—two men, one woman, and something lying on the ground, which no doubt was the stolen child.

Grey's right hand pressed firmly his smooth rifle barrel as he peered down upon that group. How he longed to pick off those two dusky braves. Two quick reports and the deed would be done. He could deal with the woman;

he had no doubt of that. But another voice soon silenced this blood-thirsty desire. "Coward," it whispered, "would you shoot them down without giving them a chance? You call yourself a man. You a member of a famous Force, and would you stain its honourable annals with such a contemptible deed?"

At that instant a sound broke upon the still evening air. It came from the right, around the curve in the lake. It was the hoarse cry of a moose calling to its mate. Again it came, clearer than before.

The effect of that call acted like magic upon the two Indian bucks. Seizing their rifles they glided to a canoe lying upon the shore, shoved it off, and leaped in. With noiseless paddle dips they sped swiftly over the still waters, keeping well within the dark fringe-like shadow, which was growing larger and larger as the evening waned.

"How strange," Grey murmured to himself, "that such a thing should happen at the right moment."

Then he thought of Dan, and as light dawned upon his mind he almost gave a shout of delight. He restrained himself, however, in time, and turned his attention to the camp fire. Only the woman to contend with now.

He was about to slip from his hiding place, rush down and seize the child, when he happened to glance out over the lake to the left. As he did so he stared with amazement, for coming swiftly onward was a flotilla of canoes, driven by strong, determined arms. Spectres they seemed, bearing down suddenly from the unknown. Grey rubbed his eyes to make sure that he beheld aright. But there was no mistake. It was a stern reality.

By this time the Indian woman had seen them, too, and had hurried to the shore, and was wildly waving her arms. It was his opportunity, and he must not delay.

But now there fell upon his ears another sound. It was the voice of a child crying out in its loneliness.

"Mamma, mamma," it called. "I wants 'ou, mamma."

Grey hesitated no longer. He sprang forward, bounded like a tiger down the slope, seized the lad in his arms, and speeded back to cover. Scarcely had he reached the shelter of the forest ere the wild shrieks of the Indian woman made the evening hideous. Well did Grey know its meaning, and he smiled grimly, as, pressing the child to his breast, he once again threaded the tangled maze of underbrush, and reached the place where the raft was floating. Here he placed his burden upon the ground, and listened attentively.

"My! this is getting hot!" he panted. "We'll have the whole tribe after us now. I hope to goodness Dan will show up soon."

CHAPTER XXII AT BAY

So intent was Grey upon listening for any sound from the Indians that he did not notice Donnie rise to his feet and toddle toward him. But when a small hand touched him, he started and looked quickly down upon the forlorn little figure standing near.

"Hello, laddie," he said, placing one hand upon the boy's shoulder. "What's wrong now?"

But the child did not reply. He only stood there looking intently upward. Then Grey noticed how drawn and pinched was his face, while his large eyes gazed straight into his with the pathetic expression of a dumb animal. Stooping, he lifted the waif in his strong arms, and pressed him close to his heart.

"Poor laddie! poor laddie!" he murmured. "Your lot is certainly a hard one. But never mind, I'll defend you to the last."

"I wants my mamma. Oh, take me to my mamma," moaned the child, as he laid his head trustingly on his rescuer's arm.

"I shall take you to your mamma, little one," Grey replied. "All the Indians and white men in the North will not take you from me now."

"Dood man," whispered Donnie sleepily. "I love 'ou, dood man. I'll pray to Dod for 'ou, dood man."

In a few minutes the weary, tired eyes closed, and then Grey laid him upon the ground, and taking off his own jacket he wrapped it carefully about the child. This done he paced slowly up and down listening anxiously for any sound from the silent forest around. Once he thought he heard the Indians coming, and he was about to place Donnie upon the raft, and hurry down-stream. But hearing nothing more he decided to wait a while longer. Night had by this time deepened, and the whole forest was brooding in a sombre shade. Upon the alert ear must he now depend. What was keeping Dan? he wondered. Why this delay? Had something befallen the trapper?

While Grey thought on these things a slight noise to the right aroused him. Grasping his rifle he tried to peer into those gloomy reaches. A twig snapped, and then silence. He was sure that someone was approaching. Presently a peculiar low call of a bird sounded upon the air, and Grey's heart lightened, for he recognised the signal which Dan had taught him some time before to be used in time of need. At once Grey responded with the same call, and a moment later the trapper appeared before him.

"Gee whiz!" he panted. "I got mixed up somehow, an' lost me bearin's, an' have been flounderin' around fer some time. I nearly ran full ag'inst a bunch of Injuns on the shore up yon, an' jist had time to creep back under cover. They're gittin' ready to come down-stream after us in their canoes to head us off, so we must git outer this like lightnin'. But say whar's the kid; did ye git 'im?"

"Yes, he's right here," and Grey stooped and lifted the sleeping child in his arms. "But can we run the stream through the darkness? Would it not be better to let the Indians pass, and try to evade them on land?"

"An' starve in the meantime wanderin' about with this kid? Not on yer life. If the Injuns once git ahead of us we might as well give up fust as last. But we're not goin' to give up. We're goin' down this river, dark as it is. Then, if they do overtake us we'll give 'em the hottest reception they ever got. Is yer gun all right?"

"Yes, the magazine's full."

"How many ca'tridges?"

"Belt full, except for the ones in the rifle."

"Good. Mine's jist the same. Aha, we'll show 'em a thing or two if they're not keerful. They're not foolin' with jack rabbits this time."

In a few minutes they had loosened the raft from its moorings, and were bearing steadily down-stream. Provided with two long slender sticks Grey and Dan managed to steer their frail craft without much difficulty. The current was strong, which held the raft in deep water, and swung it safely around the numerous sand-bars which lined the river. Donnie slept soundly on his hard rough bed, covered with Grey's jacket, with his head pillowed upon Dan's buckskin coat. Little did the bereaved and heart-broken mother at Big Glen know where her darling boy was sleeping this night, nor the efforts of two brave and great-hearted men on his behalf.

No sound broke the stillness as steadily the raft surged forward at the rate of three miles an hour. Slowly the moon rose and swung clear of the horizon. The river for the most part lay wrapped in shadow from the closely crowding forest. But here and there where the trees were low and thin, bright shafts of light shot downward, which falling athwart the rippling water caused it to glitter like polished steel.

Dan, who was standing well astern, kept his eyes fixed upon those gleaming places. In fact ever since embarking his eyes and ears had been strained to their utmost in an effort to detect some sign of their pursuers. At length he started, and reached instinctively for his rifle lying close at hand.

"They're comin'!" he hoarsely whispered to his companion. "The divils are after us!"

Grey looked back, and was able to see dark specks in the distance where the moon shone bright. Fleeting spectres they were, appearing and disappearing, yet drawing steadily nearer.

"What are we to do?" he replied. "We can't fight here, and they'll be upon us in a few minutes."

"Make fer the shore, quick," Dan commanded, and suiting the action to the word he gave the raft a vigorous shove which sent her reeling toward the bank.

With some difficulty they were able to make a landing, and while Dan held the raft Grey carried Donnie quickly ashore. There was now no time to lose, for the Indians were almost abreast of the place. Then a wild blood-curdling yell of derision fell upon their ears. The pursuers had expected to overtake the raft in midstream. They feared the deadly rifles of the pale faces, and followed silently and cautiously. But when they saw them make for land, and disappear among the trees they gave full vent to their savage delight. What could two men and a little child do against such overwhelming odds?

And as Grey and Dan sped forward, carrying Donnie by turns, they felt how almost hopeless was their position. But they determined to fight to the last, and looked anxiously as they ran for some place where they could make a firm stand. Ere long several large boulders were seen, and the sight brought a new hope into Dan's heart.

"We're somewhar near that cave," he panted, "an' if we once git in thar I'll riddle some of them d—d redskins like a sieve."

Presently they reached the open trail, and to the left appeared the dim forms of the two giant shafts of stone.

"Run fer it!" breathed the trapper to Grey, who was now carrying the child. "I'll foller a little behind to cut off them varmints if they come too near. Give me yer gun."

With Donnie enfolded in his arms, and head bent, Grey ran as he had never run before. So much depended upon that last lap—the honour of the Force, the safety of a little child, the happiness of a home far away, and their own lives. And he could run as well as fight, this hound of the North. He was not running because he was afraid, but that he might fight the better later on. How interminably far away seemed those huge columns. Would he ever reach them? He felt his strength growing weaker, for his burden was heavy. Suddenly a report split the air, and a bullet whistled past his head. The effect was magical. Forgotten was his weariness. It nerved him to greater effort, and his feet fairly spurned the ground. How he maintained his footing on that rough and crooked trail he could not tell. But not once did he fall, and at last to his relief he beheld the cave but a few rods away. He glanced back, and saw Dan nimbly speeding after. He was near to shelter now, and as he hurried by the nearer column a bullet spat against the hard stone, telling plainly that the Indians were not far behind, although somewhat astray in their aim.

Having deposited Donnie within the mouth of the cave, he leaped back, seized his rifle from the trapper, and took up his position on the opposite side of the column. Peering cautiously forth he was able to discern several forms lurking in the distance, which he knew to be the baffled Indians.

"What do you say if we pick a few of them off, Dan?" he remarked. "It might teach the others a lesson, and send them back wiser than they came."

"Don't do it, pardner," was the reply. "Ye don't know them Big Lakes. We mustn't shoot unless they come at us fust."

"But, man, we can't stay here very long. We haven't a scrap of grub left, and what about that poor child? Listen to him now crying there in the cave as if his heart would break. What are we to do?"

"I don't really know, pardner," and Dan ran the fingers of his right hand through his long hair. "Seems to me we're in a trap."

"Can't we make peace with the Indians?" Grey questioned. "What have they against us? We never harmed them."

"We pinched the kid, though. Give 'im up, an' mebbe, then, they'd leave us alone."

"Not otherwise?"

"Ye bet yer life, no."

"But they won't have him," cried Grey fiercely. "At least not as long as there's any life in my body."

Dan looked grimly around, and his eyes rapidly scanned the beetling wall of rock towering high above them.

"In a place like this," he slowly drawled, "with grub, water an' ammunition, two of us could stand off a bunch of redskins without any trouble. They can't come down atop of us, an' if they begin pokin' their noses around the front door we'll hand 'em somethin' purty hot. But seems to me they won't come very close. They don't like this place, as I told ye afore, so I guess they'll keep at a distance an' try to starve us out."

"I'd rather face the whole bunch of them, and die fighting like a man, than starve to death here."

Gloomily Grey uttered these words. He was weary after his long tramp and want of sleep. Little food had he eaten since the night before, and there was now no prospect of any for the coming day. He thought of Donnie, who would certainly cry for something to eat. He and Dan could stand starvation and hardships, but to listen to an innocent child pleading for a mere morsel of bread which could not be supplied, would be maddening.

The trapper surmised the thoughts which were throbbing through his companion's mind. He glanced at the tall, erect figure standing before him, and noted the expression of determination upon his strong, tense face. He realised how hard it was to keep such a spirit as his within bounds. He had often secretly marvelled why this sturdy limb of the law should follow him, an old trapper, so implicitly, and yield so readily to his will. But Dan did not know that Grey had been trained to obey as well as to command, and that the former is at times the wiser course to pursue.

The sobbing of the child at the mouth of the cave still continued. It was a pleading, pathetic cry, and sounded strangely unnatural from those dark depths.

"Ye'd better go to the laddie, pardner," Dan remarked. "Ye might be able to comfort the poor chap a little. I'll keep watch, an' call ye if necessary."

Grey found Donnie standing just within the deep shadow of the high wall of rock. The blackness of the cave had frightened him, and he had moved toward the light outside. His little form was quivering with deep sobs, and he gave a cry of joy as Grey drew near, and dropped upon the ground by his side. Placing his arms tenderly about the boy, he drew him to his heart, and tried to soothe his fears.

"I wants my mamma," Donnie moaned. "Take me to my mamma."

"Yes, dear, just as soon as I can," comforted Grey. "You will trust me, will you not?"

"Ya. But I wants my mamma. Why doesn't she tum to her 'ittle boy-boy?"

"She can't come just now, but she will after a while."

"Then I wants Malin. Oh, where is Malin?" and he started suddenly up. "Me saw her go away, and she would not tum back to Donnie."

"You love her, do you not?" Grey queried.

"Ya, me love Malin. Do 'ou?"

"Yes, yes, little one, I love her, too."

"Den me love 'ou," and Donnie threw his arms about Grey's neck. "But I wants Malin, too. Oh, please take me to Malin."

"She is not far away, dearie, and is waiting for you."

Grey spoke bravely for the child's sake. There was no need to alarm the lad now. But his heart was heavy. He thought of the Indians prowling around outside. Then his mind turned to Madeline. What was her condition? he wondered, after her terrible experience in the river. Suppose she— He crushed back the thought. No, it could not be possible. He could not imagine Madeline, his Madeline, lying in that house cold in death. All his old doubts and fears were swept away like chaff before the wind. His love for her filled, his heart with an overwhelming intensity. Let her be what she might, he loved her still, and would love her to the end. She had been sinned against, cruelly and wilfully, he felt sure of that. He saw her as in days gone by; the trim lines of her form, her dark-brown hair, and large affectionate eyes, looking up so trustingly into his. His hands clinched, and his teeth ground hard together.

"Some villain has done this," he muttered. "There has been dark work in connection with this matter. Surely there is a God in Israel who will avenge that innocent woman and this poor child."

Listening attentively he found that Donnie was fast asleep, with his curly head leaning against his breast. Grey's arms closed slightly in a loving embrace. The feeling of affection which had stolen into his heart when he had rescued him from the icy waters below Klikhausia Rapids burned now like a flame. He realised that this child was unconsciously playing an important part in his life. The boy had suffered much, and been cruelly wronged, but for all that he had been the guiding star which had led him to his long-lost loved one.

And while Grey crouched upon the ground with the child in his arms, the trapper stood outside with rifle in hand, and eyes keenly alert. The sun rose slowly above the tree tops, and at its appearing the slinking Indians crouched back among the trees, like tigers lying in wait for their prey.

CHAPTER XXIII THE HAVEN

Slowly Madeline opened her eyes, and looked wearily around. The swirl of raging water still sounded in her ears. Dimly she saw two forms standing by the bed, and then oblivion. When she again awoke the morning was well advanced. Her sleep had been deep, and she felt much refreshed. But how pleasant it was to be there in that quiet room! Her mind went back with a rush to the terrible experience in the rapids. She remembered standing for an instant in the reeling canoe, calling for help, ere she had taken that mad plunge into the icy water. How had she been rescued? Who had dared to snatch her from that horrible place, and what was she doing here in this room? Where was Donnie? She recalled his pathetic figure standing upon the shore, holding out to her his little pleading hands. What had become of the boy? And the Indian woman, Nadu, where was she? A sense of fear smote her heart as she saw again that sinister dusky face, and those cruel, glaring eyes. She was her bitter enemy, she realised that now. In what way had she offended the Indian woman? Why had she tried to destroy her? And she had been saved from the rapids! Who had done it? She must know. She must find out. Perhaps the Indians did it. But why was she lying in this quiet room? Her bed was a small cot placed against the wall. The coverings were only dark blankets, but they seemed perfectly clean.

The room was simply furnished; a large bear skin on the rough floor, a rude table close to the window, littered with papers, and a small bench near by. Her eyes rested upon a few books on a shelf upon the wall. The owner of the place, she thought, must do some reading. Several pictures tacked to the roughly hewn logs attracted her attention. Some were evidently taken from magazines, while others were crayon drawings, and a few were done in water colours by no mean hand. One of the latter aroused her interest. It was that of a young Indian woman, with bright eyes, with a gentle smile upon her lips, and her black hair, parted in the middle, was combed smoothly back. The expression upon her face exhibited confidence and sweet peace. As Madeline studied this picture something told her that she had seen that face before, and she started as Nadu flashed into her mind. Why had she thought of her? she wondered. What connection had such a creature with that fair vision before her? In those clear, trusting eyes there was no resemblance to the fiery orbs of jealousy upon which she had recently gazed, and those slightly parted lips had no suggestion of the cruel smile of hatred. No, it could not be. The two faces were so different. It must be her own fancy which was deceiving her. And yet, why did she think of Nadu when looking at the picture?

Her musing was interrupted by a light step on the right. Turning her head she saw a middle-aged Indian entering, and in her hands a small wooden tray upon which were several dishes. This she placed upon the table, and then came to the bedside. Her lips parted in a pleased smile as she gazed down upon the white face enwreathed with loose tresses of dark-brown hair. To Madeline it was pleasant to look into those kindly eyes, and to feel that she was among friends. With this clean and neatly dressed native near she knew that she had no cause to fear.

"I am so glad to see you," she faintly murmured. "Will you tell me how I came here?"

But the Indian woman only smiled, and crossing the room brought over the tray and placed it upon the edge of the bed.

"Soup," she said. "Eat. Good."

Rising on her elbow Madeline dipped the spoon into the dish and tasted the broth. It was certainly pleasant after the horrible stuff which had been tossed before her on that dreadful journey. Seeing that her patient was doing justice to the food she had brought, the Indian woman again smiled and left the room.

A few minutes later the long-bearded, white-haired man entered. His tall commanding figure was drawn to its full height, and to Madeline he seemed like a veritable giant. Sad grey eyes, somewhat faded, gazed into hers from beneath beetling brows. Little did Madeline know that those same eyes had for forty years faced death unflinchingly many a time in the far Northland. Swiftly the visitor crossed the room and stood by her side.

"I am so glad you are better."

It was a soft, low voice which spoke, accompanied by a slight accent of embarrassment. The speaker did not appear to be perfectly at ease, and this Madeline noted.

"I am feeling stronger now," she replied, holding out to him a firm white hand. "This soup has done me much good. Won't you sit by my side, for I wish to ask you some questions? There, that's better," she continued, as he quietly obeyed.

"Do you feel strong enough to talk?" questioned the man. "You are very weak."

"But I must talk," Madeline pleaded. "Oh, please tell me how I came here, and what has happened to Donnie. Is he safe?"

"I can tell you but little. You were brought here early this morning by two men, but I saw nothing of any boy."

"Oh, where is he—the poor darling!" cried Madeline as she half started from the bed. "I last saw him standing on the shore, stretching out his little hands to me as the canoe swept me down toward that horrible place."

"Do not excite yourself," remonstrated the man. "You must reserve your strength."

"I know it. I know it. But I have been through so much to-day."

Then she briefly told the story of the capture, the journey overland, and the base act of the Indian woman. "When I shot from the canoe," she concluded, "I gave up all hope. I cannot understand how I was saved."

"Those men must have been near."

"Do you know who they were?"

"No. I asked no questions. They left so quickly that I really had no opportunity."

"But you saw them, though. What did they look like?"

"One was an old man of powerful build, with a long beard and white hair. He wore, I think, a buckskin jacket."

"And the other?" Madeline's heart beat fast, for an idea had suddenly seized her mind.

"He was a young man, tall, and straight as an arrow."

"And did he have dark-brown eyes?" she questioned.

"I believe he did. As a rule I am not good at remembering such things. I noticed his, however, for they were so full of trouble, and looked as if they had not closed in sleep for several nights."

"And his hair, was it dark and wavy?"

"It was dark, but soaked with water, as were his clothes."

"And you did not ask him his name," she mused. "That was strange. Were you not curious to know?"

"As I said before, there was little time for that. Besides," and here he hesitated, "we learn in the North not to ask too many questions."

Madeline noted his hesitation, and glanced quickly up. What did he mean? she mentally asked herself. What did his words signify? There was something about this tall, reserved man which filled her with confidence. He was so different from many she had met. He seemed to belong to another world from the one which had been hers for years. It brought back memories of other days. A mistiness filled her eyes, and despite her efforts tears flowed down her cheeks. She tried to repress her emotion, but in vain. Burying her face in her hands, she sobbed like a child, while the man looked at her in wonderment. At length she brushed away the tears, and tried to smile.

"Forgive me," she simply remarked. "But you know not what I have suffered. You believe me to be one of those creatures you sometimes see in the North. But I am not! Before God, I say I am not! Listen! I had a home, surrounded by loved ones. I left on a visit to America. The ship was wrecked. I was rescued by a woman, who has held me in bondage for years. I have tried time and again to escape, but without avail. We came North, and at last to Hishu. I had given up all hope when suddenly one day, over a week ago, a man came to the place, bringing in a child he had rescued from death. He was a Mounted Policeman, and I knew him to be Norman Grey, a friend of mine in the dear old happy days. He saw me, and believed me to be a fallen woman. I believe it was he who saved me from death this morning."

"And who was the other?" came the question.

"It must be Buckskin Dan, a fine old trapper living at Hishu."

"You are a long way from Hishu," the man quietly remarked. "Were the Indians Hishus who stole you away?"

"The woman belongs there," Madeline replied. "She is the wife of Siwash Bill, and her name is Nadu. I cannot imagine what she has against me. I saw her only occasionally at Hishu."

It was now the man's turn to start, while a pained expression crossed his face. He was about to reply, but instead he moved a little and looked long and silently at the picture of the young Indian maiden hanging on the wall near the table.

"And you say it was Nadu?" he at length asked, while a deep sigh escaped his lips. "Are you sure?"

"Certain. I have good reason to know, have I not?"

"Yes, yes. Indeed, you have. But, oh, this is a blow to me. Could you believe that was once Nadu?" and he pointed toward the picture.

"I did think of her," Madeline replied, "when I saw it first, but thought I must be mistaken."

"No, you were not. Would to God that you were. That was Nadu when she was a sweet, innocent child, the flower of the Northland. Her father, a chief, was killed in a fierce battle. We loved her—my dear wife and I—and it almost broke our hearts when we gave her to that white man. They were joined in holy wedlock, but we feared, yes, we feared, for her. And oh, how changed must she be! My poor Nadu! My darling child!"

"Is that your wife who brought me this delicious broth?" Then seeing the astonished look upon the old man's face she hastily added, "Forgive me. I fear I have made a mistake. But as trappers are sometimes married to Indian women in the North, I took it for granted it was so in your case."

"But with me it was not so," and the old man placed his hand to his forehead in an abstracted manner as he replied. "I had a wife, good and true. We came to the North together forty years ago. It's five years now since she left me, and she lies over yonder in the Indian Cemetery. It was she who made those drawings, and painted that picture. She was ever skilful with the pencil and brush. She loved Nadu dearly, and never could become reconciled to the girl marrying that fur-trader. I believe it had much to do with her death."

"Have you really lived as a trapper and hunter for forty years in the North!" exclaimed Madeline in astonishment. "And to think of your wife being here for most of that time! How lonely she must have been when you were away from home."

A slight expression of amusement shone in the old man's eyes as he listened.

"I have been a hunter for forty years," he replied, "but I have trapped very little. I have followed the chase, but have had meagre success."

"Is game scarce? I should think it would be plentiful here."

"Miss—" Here the old man paused. It was the first time that he had even hinted as to her name.

"Normsell—Madeline Normsell," she added.

"Well, Miss Normsell, there is an abundance of game, but the hunters are few, and scattered. I think it was expressed much better many years ago by One when He said, 'The field is already white unto the harvest, but the labourers are few.'"

Madeline had been looking straight before her during the greater part of this conversation. But now she glanced quickly up, while a new light of understanding overspread her face. These last words set her thinking.

"Have I made a stupid blunder?" she asked. "I mistook you for a trapper."

"It was quite natural, Miss Normsell."

"And you are really a missionary."

"Yes. That is why I am here."

"Oh, now I see. Now I comprehend."

"Are you a bishop? You look like one."

"No; merely Charles Nordis—who is trying to do some work for the Master among these Northern natives."

"And you have been here for forty years?"

"Not on this side of the mountain. Thirty years were passed on the great Mackenzie River—and only the last ten here."

"And all that time among the Indians! How they must love you."

"If they do they seldom show it. This want of response has so often discouraged the missionaries. They look for some gratitude for what they have done. I have learned not to expect it, and so am never disappointed. I think the Indians beyond the mountains loved me in their own way, and were sorry when I left. But the natives here are hard and cruel. I cannot seem to make any impression upon them at all. They are held in thrall by the crafty Medicine Men, and are fond of tribal wars."

"But you have one faithful Indian in that woman who brought me the soup," Madeline remarked.

"Ah, Nancy du Nord, you mean. Yes, she is a good soul. But she is from the Mackenzie River. She and her husband followed me across the mountains, and have been here ever since. My dear wife did much for her."

"Are the Indians away now?" Madeline asked.

"Yes, although they may return at any moment. There are nasty reports abroad, and I fear there will be trouble with the Hishus. They have been trespassing, so it seems, upon the Big Lakes' ancestral hunting-grounds. From time immemorial this has been the cause of strife. The Hishus are ugly people when once aroused. Oh, for a missionary to work among them!"

"There is one of the Hishus," Madeline replied, "who appears to be rather a superior Indian. That is, Hishu Sam. He has been very good to me."

"Hishu Sam, did you say?" and the missionary leaned forward. "I remember the name. When did I meet him? Ah, yes, now I recollect. It was several years ago. I was up the river in the direction of Hishu. I camped near him one night. He had a very sick child, a little girl, and I was able to give her some medicine so that she recovered. You see here in the North one has to be a doctor as well as a missionary. I had forgotten the incident until you mentioned the name."

"Was that all you did?" Madeline queried.

"Yes; I can't think of anything else."

"Did you talk any with the Indian? Did you teach him anything?"

"Why, yes, to be sure. I stayed with him and his wife for several days, and during that time I told them the old, old story, to which they listened most attentively. But I fear it was of little use."

"Indeed it was, Mr. Nordis," Madeline replied. "I have often wondered about that Indian; he is so different from the other Hishus. Several times when he came to our house he asked me questions in broken English about Christ, and was so anxious to learn. Now I understand. It was the little seed you sowed in his heart which did so much for him."

The missionary did not reply to these words, but sat very still with head bent forward, as if in deep thought. Madeline lay there, and watched him with much interest. She felt tired after this conversation, and wished to think over what she had heard. Her mind turned to Norman, for she firmly believed it was he who had rescued her. Had he gone after Donnie, she wondered, and would he come back to her?

Presently she was aroused from her reverie by the sudden entrance of Nancy du Nord. Upon her face was a look of fear, and her agitated manner plainly showed that something was wrong. She spoke rapidly in the Indian tongue, and all that Madeline could understand was the one word "Hishu."

The effect upon the missionary was magical. Deep concern gave place to the meditative expression as he started to his feet and hurried from the room.

CHAPTER XXIV THE MEDIATOR

As Charles Nordis passed out of the house into the open he met an old Indian with a look of intense fear stamped upon his face. He was trembling violently, and his staring eyes were directed toward the river. As the missionary appeared he turned and began to speak rapidly in the native tongue.

"The Hishus!" he cried, while a shiver shook his form. "They come up the river. They carry their canoes around the rapids. They are cruel men, and will kill us."

"Hush, hush, du Nord," commanded the missionary. "If all the Big Lakes are like you there will be little done to oppose the Hishus. You cower and fear like a cur."

"I am old, Master," replied the native. "How can I fight? If the Big Lakes were only here!"

Charles Nordis looked intently at the poor creature standing before him, and his face softened. He remembered how faithful the man had been to him through long years. He, too, had been brave. But now in his old age it was only natural that he should fear a scene which years before had been all too common in his life.

"Poor du Nord," said the missionary to himself. "Who am I that I should feel contempt for him?"

Then he began to pace up and down before the house. His steps were long and rapid, a sure sign of his agitated thoughts.

"And is this the end of it all?" he murmured. "After years of patient toil and prayer, has it come to this—a deadly battle between these two tribes? What fond hopes were mine ten years ago. How I trusted that these Indians would lay aside their strife forever. But now they are at it again. And Nadu—poor child—of whom we hoped so much. Little did I think she would fall so low. Have all the teaching, prayers and patient care amounted to nothing? What have I to show for all these years of work?"

The report of a rifle in the distance startled him. Then another, and still another.

"I feared it! I feared it!" the missionary hoarsely breathed. "The battle has begun, and oh, what horrible things will happen! God in Heaven," he cried, falling upon his knees on the hard ground, "stop this fight! Let not these people engage in deadly conflict. Show Thine arm, put forth Thy strength, and let them have a glimpse of Thy glory, that they may turn to nobler, higher things."

Presently his lips ceased to move, and across his face spread a wonderful transforming light. His eyes gleamed with a new lustre, and he gazed before him into space. His surroundings were forgotten, neither did he see old du Nord standing awe-stricken a few yards away. Another series of shots ripped through the air like messengers of woe. The missionary sprang to his feet. He listened intently. Again came those ominous reports. With not a look behind Charles Nordis sprang forward, crossed the open, and disappeared among the trees.

Meanwhile over at the mouth of the cave, behind the giant pillars, the two weary men maintained their long watch. Dan continued on guard until the dawn had ripened into day. Donnie still slept, while Grey remained by his side. He, too, had fallen asleep, but it was only a fitful slumber, and he awoke with a start thinking the Indians were upon them. At length he went to the trapper's side, where he stood leaning upon his rifle.

"The Indians are quiet, Dan," he began.

"Quiet now," was the reply. "Guess they kin afford to be quiet, fer it seems they intend to starve us out."

"Do you really think so?"

"Feel quite sartin about it. If not they'd've rushed us long afore this."

"But it was almost as bright as day, Dan. Perhaps they'll wait until to-night and come upon us ere the moon rises. It will be dark then."

"I was thinkin' of that, pardner. It's one thing or t'other, mark my word."

"But what shall we do in the meantime?"

"God only knows. But we might make a rush fer it when night shets down. That's our only hope, an' what will that poor child do in the meantime without grub? We kin stand it; but a child is different. He wants to eat about all the time."

"Look here, Dan," and Grey picked up his rifle lying on the ground. "It's my turn now. You go and lie down awhile, for I intend to watch."

"An' ye'll be sure to wake me if the Injuns come?"

Grey almost laughed outright at such a request, and even a smile flitted across the trapper's face as he slowly wended his way to the dark entrance of the cave.

"An' so he thinks I'll sleep, does he?" he mumbled. "Wall, I'll see about that."

Thrusting his hand into a pocket in his jacket he brought forth a small candle. This he deliberately lighted with a match produced from his match case of two cartridge shells fitted neatly together. Glancing first at the constable and then at the sleeping child, he moved forward within the cave. The flickering light of the candle showed up dimly the rugged wall about him. Here and there large wooden logs, much decayed, were seen sticking forth where the earth had tumbled in.

"Ha, ha! I thought so," he muttered. "This has been a mine as sure as sunrise. Hello! what's this?"

Stooping, he picked up a piece of iron against which his foot had struck.

"A pick, by jimminy, an' a queer old one at that. None of yer new-fangled ones. My! the man wot swung that must have been a monster. He was a Rooshian, that's who he was. Now it's sartin that they dug this place."

Holding the candle high he slowly advanced, the passage becoming narrower all the time, owing to the falling earth.

"Guess I've gone fer enough from the entrance," he muttered, "an' had better go back."

He was about to turn when a glitter on the right wall caught his eye. Stepping quickly forward, he thrust the candle close to the spot, and with an exclamation of surprise reached out and grasped a big handful of gravel.

"Good Lord!" he gasped. "It's gold! Nuggets of 'em!"

The prospector's fever now possessed him, and holding the candle in his left hand he clawed into the bank, and exposed to view the precious gravel. And rich it was, he could tell at a glance, and it seemed to be the beginning of a rich vein which had been unearthed. Forgotten for a few brief moments were the Indians as he stood there with staring eyes looking upon his discovery.

"I wasn't fer wrong in my surmise," he mused. "Jist think how much them Rooshians must have scooped outer this place. But they left some behind, an' it took Buckskin Dan to find it, ha, ha!"

Suddenly he thought of the Indians, and the light of discovery faded from his face.

"Yes, I've got the gold, but the Injuns have got me, an' the lads out yon. This is sartinly a purty fix fer an old trapper to git into, ain't it now?" and he scratched his head in perplexity. "With all this gold mebbe I could make some dicker with them redskins, an' buy 'em off. But no, darn it! I won't give 'em the satisfaction, nor Siwash Bill either. He's at the bottom of this hull hellish bizness, an' we've got to git more'n even with 'im. I'm goin' back to me pardner now, an' see how things are shapin' out thar."

When he reached the mouth of the mine he found Donnie awake and crying piteously. He glanced toward the constable, and noted that he was not heeding the child, but was keenly intent upon something beyond. Having soothed the lad's cries, he hurried to Grey's side.

"What is it, pardner?" he whispered. "Are the Injuns comin'?"

"Look," and Grey pointed to the left. "I saw several forms moving among the trees. There they are, see, creeping up behind those boulders. They are Indians, it strikes me, but they do not seem to be the Big Lakes, and they are not coming directly toward us either."

Dan looked keenly at the creeping figures, and then an expression of satisfaction crossed his face.

"They're the Hishus, pardner!" he whispered. "An' they mean bizness at that. They're divils when they're on the warpath. Mark my word, somethin's goin' to happen in the twinklin' of an eye. The Big Lakes haven't seen 'em yet. But when they do we'll see sparks a flyin'. Thank God, they've arrived in the nick of time! We'll just wait until they git busy with the Big Lakes, an' we'll hike it outer this."

The Big Lakes had certainly been caught napping. They little expected the arrival of the Hishus, and merely kept a vigilant watch lest the prisoners behind the big columns should escape. They were delighted that they had the fugitives in such a trap. They could afford to wait until hunger drove the pale faces from their hiding place, and that this would not be long they felt sure. So while several kept strict guard the rest lolled around, laughing and chatting about the imprisoned whites.

But when several sharp reports ripped the stillness of the day, and as many bullets sang their menacing danger about their heads, they sprang to their feet in dismay, seized their rifles and dashed for cover. At first they imagined the volley came from the besieged, but when yells of derision followed the shots they knew that the Hishus were upon them.

When the first shock of surprise had passed their coolness and cunning returned. The wild savage nature was aroused. Their old implacable enemy was before them, and now old scores were to be settled. Creeping cautiously from boulder to boulder they watched their opportunity. Whenever a head showed for an instant it became a target for sure marksmen. At first they returned yell for yell, but now they were silent!

Both sides realised how deadly was the game, and like tigers they crouched and watched.

From their rocky fastness Dan and Grey looked out upon the scene of conflict. Owing to their somewhat elevated position they were able to obtain a good view of all that took place. The two tribes were much closer together now, and the shots became more frequent. It seemed to be only a matter of a few minutes ere they would be engaged in a hand-to-hand encounter. The wild hatred of their savage nature would be unleashed, and terrible would be the lot of the vanquished. This Dan and Grey knew. Their fate depended upon which side should win.

"If the Hishus conquer," said the trapper, "we are safe; but if the Big Lakes, God help us! We must be ready to step outer this at the fust opportunity. Ye'd better keep the kid close."

Scarcely had Dan finished speaking ere he leaned forward, while a roar of surprise broke from his lips.

Grey looked, too, and what he saw caused his eyes to open wide with amazement. Speeding across the open, and not far away from where they were hiding, they beheld the old man whom they had met the day before. His arms were lifted in an imploring attitude. He seemed not to mind the unevenness of the ground, nor the danger to which he was exposed. He appeared to lead a charmed life as he sped into the midst of that rain of death. Grey almost held his breath as he watched. What did the man mean? Surely he must be crazy! But still he kept on. Presently he fell, and when he rose he was seen to be limping painfully. With much difficulty he scrambled to the top of a big boulder, and lifting up his arms began to speak in the Indian tongue. What he said neither Grey nor Dan could tell. That his words had little effect was evident, for the shots were as frequent as ever. How he escaped for so long was marvellous.

Grey now realised the old man's purpose. He would stop the fight between these two tribes. He was willing to act as a mediator, to lay down his life that their strife might cease. Surely the man must be crazy, or a fanatic, he thought, to risk his life in such a way for no apparent purpose. But he was no coward, that was certain, and Grey felt a thrill of admiration as he watched him standing erect in the face of that deadly fire. Then an overwhelming pity possessed him. He could not see the old man die without an effort to save his life. He longed to hurry him away, if possible, from such danger. Only a few wild heart-beats had passed since the missionary mounted the boulder, but it was sufficient time for Grey to think, and to make up his mind.

Forgetting his own peril and without one word to Dan he sprang from his hiding place, and bounded across the open. He had almost reached the old man when he saw him reel and then pitch headlong with widely extended arms among the rugged rocks. Grey was by his side in an instant. He seized the man and raised him somewhat from the ground with the hope of carrying him away. But, strong though he was, he had not sufficient strength to bear such a burden. Rising to his feet he lifted up his hands to the natives. Would they not understand—would they not heed such an appeal? Surely their hearts were not altogether turned to stone. There must be some spark of nobleness mingled with their savage nature. In fact the fire did slacken, and it seemed as if the Indians were about to cease their strife for a while. But alas! his hope was in vain. He suddenly felt the ground reel beneath him. A horrible blackness rose before his eyes. He tried to stand. He groped about for an instant. He tottered, and then fell forward unconscious upon the prostrate form at his feet.

CHAPTER XXV THE HEART OF A WOMAN

After Charles Nordis, the missionary, had hurriedly left the room Madeline listened intently for a few minutes. Hearing nothing more she concluded that the matter was of little importance. She knew how easily Indian women were excited and ready at times to believe almost anything, whether an unsubstantial dream or the wild imaginings of an overheated brain. Her mind gradually turned to other things. She thought of the old man and of the lonely life he must have led since his wife's death; of Nadu, and often her eyes would turn toward the picture upon the wall. But she thought mostly of Norman and Donnie. What had happened to them? How she longed to have the child close by her side again. It grieved her to think that he was somewhere out in the wilderness among the Indians, with no one to comfort him or to soothe his cries. But surely Norman would find him—he would if it were possible—she felt sure of that.

During the past six terrible years the hope that Norman would come and save her had buoyed her up. She clung to the idea like a drowning person. He had always been her hero, and often she had pictured him seizing her in his strong arms and carrying her away from her uncongenial surroundings. And he had come, had looked upon her, and believed her to be unworthy of his love. He had saved her from the icy waters, but that was only by chance. He had followed her, but only for the sake of the child whom he was in duty bound to seek. He would return, no doubt, bringing the lad with him. Then he would take the little one to Big Glen, and leave her in the wilderness. Why had he not left her to die in the rapids? It would have been more merciful. But would he speak to her when he returned? she wondered. Would he give her a chance to explain or would words be unnecessary? He had seen her living with Old Meg, and perhaps that would be sufficient to poison his mind against her. But he had touched her in the water. He had enfolded her in his arms as he carried her to the house. Did he look into her face, and loathe the burden that he bore? The thought was almost more than she could endure. She felt so tired, and she closed her eyes in an effort to shut out the many scenes which were moving like horrible spectres before her mind.

A pretty picture she presented as she lay there. Her loose dark-brown hair was tossed over cheek and pillow. Her face was white and worn, for the experiences of the last few days had left their mark. She had struggled hard, and had endured without a murmur. Her prayers during the whole of this ordeal of years had been a pitiful, intense pleading to the Great Father for help. And what was the answer? Nothing but silence! Thrown among savages, and cast off by the very one upon whom she had most relied, what was left to her now? Hope gone, to return no more forever!

She lay very still for a time, and was only aroused by Nancy du Nord entering the room. Fear was still depicted upon the Indian woman's face, and she cast furtive glances around as if expecting pursuit.

"What is it, Nancy?" Madeline questioned, surprised at her agitated manner.

"Hishus! Hishus!" she cried. "Dey come! Dey kill! Oh! Oh! Oh!"

Madeline, who had no fear of the Hishus, for they had always been friendly to her, could not understand the poor creature's fright.

"They will not harm us, Nancy," she soothed. "They have been good to me. Why are you afraid?"

"Hishu bad; all same black bear. Ugh!"

Then she started violently, and laid a sudden hand upon Madeline's arm.

"Hark!" she gasped. "Dey meet Big Lakes! Dey shoot! Dey fight!"

Listening, Madeline could hear faint rifle reports away in the distance. That there was trouble she had no doubt. But what did it matter to her? It made little difference which side won. She might as well live with the Big Lakes as among the Hishus. If they killed her the sooner would her troubles end. But this terrified woman appealed to her. She felt sorry for her, and longed to do something to calm her distress. And, besides, it might do herself good to move around a little, for she felt stronger now.

"Nancy," she said. "I want to get up. Are my clothes dry?"

"Clothes no dry," the native replied, slowly shaking her head.

"But did you hang them by the fire?"

"Ah, ah, me hang 'um."

"Right after you put me here?"

"Ah, ah."

"Surely, Nancy, they must be dry by this time. Has there been a good fire on ever since?"

"Ah, ah, good fire."

"Well, then, Nancy, I'm going to see for myself," and Madeline started to rise.

"No! no!" cried the old woman. "No get up!"

"But why?" insisted Madeline. "Why do you not want me to get up?"

"Heem say she stay in bed. She no get up."

"Who told you that?"

"De meesion man."

"Oh, I see. So you thought you would make me stay here by saying my clothes were not dry?"

"Ah, ah."

Madeline's heart was touched by this woman's faithfulness to her master's orders.

"Well, look here, Nancy," she at length remarked. "I am going to get up anyway. You have done your best to make me stay in bed, so your master cannot blame you, see?"

"Ah, ah, me see."

"Bring my clothes, then, Nancy, or I shall go for them myself."

After a brief hesitation the old woman shuffled across the room, and a few minutes later returned with the dried garments.

"Thank you, Nancy. You are very kind," said Madeline. "Will you help me now, for I do not feel very strong yet."

After Madeline was dressed she walked for a few minutes slowly around the room, examining the pictures more closely, but especially Nadu's. Her eyes rested on the papers lying upon the table. A Bible lay open where the missionary had left it. The papers contained writing which she could not understand, but which she surmised to be a translation of the English into the Indian dialect. The portion upon which the old man had been working when Nadu had watched him through the window the night before was the latter half of the tenth chapter of St. Matthew's Gospel. It was not finished, and he had ceased with the thirty-ninth verse. He had sat meditating upon the closing words for some time: "And he that loseth his life for My sake shall find it." He had remained for a while lost in thought ere retiring to rest. Madeline next went into the kitchen, and was looking out of one of the small windows at the log buildings beyond, when she saw a man hurrying toward the house bearing something in his arms. She started as she recognised Buckskin Dan, and knew that his burden must be none other than Donnie. Moving to the door she opened it just as the trapper was about to knock. The latter uttered not a word as he placed Donnie upon the floor, and wiped the perspiration from his forehead with his sleeve. Instantly Madeline caught the child in her arms, and pressed him close to her breast.

"Donnie, Donnie!" she cried. "Oh, thank God, you are safe!"

She could say no more. Words would not come as she placed her face against the boy's soft cheek and held him tight. Donnie squirmed a little, freed his arms, threw them about Madeline's neck, and kissed her lips.

"I love 'ou, Malin," he simply said. "Don't leave me again. Don't let the bad men det me. I'm hungry, Malin."

Dan watched the two in silence for a few minutes. He was not accustomed to such a scene, and he hardly knew what to say. He was delighted to see Madeline alive and so well, but he wondered what effect the news he brought would have upon her. He wished to prepare her, but how should he begin? Twice he cleared his throat in an effort to speak, but the words would not come. It was Madeline who at length helped him out of the difficulty.

"You did well," she said, turning to the trapper and placing Donnie upon the floor. "Did you have much trouble? And where is—?"

She hesitated, and her face flushed. It had been the first thought which had flashed into her mind when she saw Dan from the window. She longed to ask him the moment he entered the building, but something held her back. Why should she inquire? Why should she care? She did not intend to speak about him, but the question partly came almost before she was aware of it. Dan noted her hesitation and the flush which suffused her cheek.

"This ain't none of them craturs," he said to himself. "She's as innocent as any babe, I kin tell that at a glance. An' she cares fer 'im, too. Poor lassie, it'll be hard for her when she hears."

When Dan did not answer Madeline's question immediately, the colour fled her cheeks, and taking a step forward she laid her hand lightly upon the trapper's arm.

"Tell me," she began, in a voice scarcely above a whisper, "what has happened."

"Thar was a fight, miss, an' the old man who ran out atween the Injuns went down."

"Oh! Is he dead?"

"Can't tell fer sartin."

"But did no one go to help him?"

"Yes, me pardner leaped out like a wildcat, an'—oh, well."

"He was shot, too," Madeline interrupted, as Dan floundered around in an attempt to find some suitable word. "Don't be afraid to tell me. I saw it in your face."

"Why bless ye, miss, so ye did. I never thought of that. It's wonderful what sharp eyes some people have."

"So you left him there, did you, without trying to find out whether he was dead or alive, and came away?"

Across Dan's face spread a crimson flush. Madeline's words cut deeper than she imagined. Did she think that he was a coward and would leave a partner to die? He had been accused of many things in the past, but never of that! How he loathed even the name. And here was this beautiful woman standing before him with flashing eyes saying as much.

Madeline saw the injured look upon his face, and hastened to explain.

"Forgive me," she said. "I spoke too quickly. I should have waited to hear more."

"Sartin, miss, I fergive ye. But yer words stung hard. If ye'd been a man I know what the answer 'ud have been, but what kin one say to a woman? When I saw me pardner fall I was agoin' after 'im like a whirlwind. But jist then several Injuns jumped forward, with Hishu Sam in the lead. It was lucky fer 'em that the Big Lakes stopped firin'. Whether their ammunition gave out, or whether their hearts took a sudden kink of marcy, I can't tell. Anyway, Sam an' the ones with 'im got me pardner an' the old man out from behint the rocks, an' are bringin' 'em in. I grabbed the kid, and hiked on ahead. I wasn't sure that you was livin', but if I foun' ye was, a bit of warnin' wouldn't be outer the way."

"Thank you, it was good of you," and Madeline placed her hand to her forehead. Suppose Norman were dead! How could she bear to look upon him?

"Malin, I'm hungry."

She stooped and put her arms about the child.

"Poor little lad," she replied, "I forgot all about you. Nancy will give you something, will you not?" and she turned to the Indian woman who was standing by the stove trying to comprehend the meaning of the conversation. Hunger the native could understand, so going to a small pantry she brought forth a piece of cold meat and a slice of bread.

Dan's eyes looked longingly upon the food, and he was about to ask Nancy for some, too, when Madeline gave a cry and rushed to the door. Through the window she had caught a glimpse of several Indians approaching the house, bearing some heavy burden between them. Ere they reached the building she had the door open, and was standing watching them with fast-beating heart. There were four men, and Hishu Sam was one of them. Madeline stood aside to let them enter. Questions were unnecessary, for she saw at a glance Norman's unconscious form in their arms. Quickly and without a word they glided over the threshold, and placed their burden upon the small cot near the wall—the same one upon which Madeline had been laid by Grey the day before.

As the Indians stepped back Madeline moved swiftly forward and looked down searchingly into Grey's face. How he had changed since the evening he had brought Donnie to Old Meg's. His beard was days' old, and his face drawn and haggard. His eyes were closed, and he had all the appearance of a dead man. Madeline stooped and put her ear close to his face, but could detect no sign of life.

"He is dead!" she cried, turning suddenly to the men standing near. "Oh, he is dead!"

At once Dan stepped to the cot and placed his fingers upon Grey's wrist.

"No," he replied, "thar's life in 'im yit, but it's mighty weak. We must examine 'im a bit an' see what's wrong."

Then he paused and looked intently at something.

"See," he said, "thar's the trouble, right on the side of his head. That's whar the bullet grazed 'im an' knocked 'im out. My! it was a close call that. Sixteenth of an inch more an' it 'ud have shattered his skull. As it is, it burnt away some hair, an' has left a nasty, bloody scar. Ye'd better step inter the next room, miss, while we undress the poor chap an' put 'im to bed. I'm somewhat handy at docterin', havin' had to do quite a lot of it to meself an' the Injuns, so if ye'll jist leave me fer a while I shall see what I kin do."

Madeline realised the wisdom of this injunction, although it grieved her to quit Norman's side for even a few minutes. Entering the next room and closing the door she walked slowly up and down, listening anxiously for the faintest sound which came from the kitchen. She was surprised at her own strength, for the weakness she had felt upon rising from the bed seemed to have left her entirely. Her mind was upon Norman. She thought of nothing else. "Was he to die?" she asked herself over and over again. "Would he never look upon her more, nor open his lips to speak to her?"

As she slowly walked, heeding nothing around her, a small soft hand slipped gently into hers. She started, and looked quickly down. It was Donnie, standing there, with a mute, wistful appeal upon his small shrunken face. He appeared like a little old man instead of a mere child. His eyes were unnaturally large, and the fear of a hunted creature lurked in their clear depths. Stooping, Madeline placed her arms about the boy and drew him close to her.

"Poor laddie," she said, "I'm so sorry I forgot you. But I won't do so any more."

"You'll 'tay wif me, Malin?" he whispered, looking up into her face. "You won't leave Donnie any more?"

"No, no, dearie. Nothing shall separate us until you get back to your mother."

"Will 'ou take me to my mamma, Malin? Oh, I'm so glad!"

"Somebody will take you, Donnie. You are sure to go back to her now."

"But 'ou must tum, too, Malin. 'Ou must go wif Donnie. Will 'ou?"

"I should like to go, dearie. But then you will not want me. You will have your mother to take care of you. You will not need Malin any more."

The thought of going back to Big Glen brought to her no gladness. Why should she go? Why should she leave the wilderness? Would it not be better for her to throw in her lot with the Indians? She shuddered at the thought. If Norman got better he, too, would go away, and then what would life contain for her? What would she do in Big Glen? She had no money, and no friends. People would hear in some way about her. They would shake their heads, and shun her. Donnie's parents would thank her, no doubt, but they would not care to have much to do with a woman about whom there were strange stories.

"Malin."

"Yes, dearie."

"Why do 'ou look dat way, Malin? 'Ou make me 'fraid."

"Do I, darling? I'm sorry," and Madeline gave the boy a closer hug.

"An' 'ou won't leave me, Malin? 'Ou won't let the bad men det me?"

"No, no, Donnie. You are safe with me. So don't be afraid."

"Dis is a funny house. I was never here before. Whose house is it, Malin?"

"A good man lives here. He will take care of us."

"Will he tum soon? I want to see 'im. Maybe he'll take me to my mamma an' papa."

Madeline did not answer. She was thinking of what Dan had told her about the missionary. She had not forgotten him. But why had he not been brought back to the house? she wondered. Where had they taken him? Would he ever return? Had he given his life for the sake of the Indians?

And even as these thoughts filled her mind a knock sounded upon the door. Opening it she saw Dan standing there. She looked keenly into his face. But it told her nothing.

"Ye may come now, miss," he said. "I've done me best; the good Lord'll have to do the rest."

CHAPTER XXVI WITHIN THE DEEP SHADOW

Madeline said not a word as she hastened to Norman's side, and looked down anxiously into his face. She had hoped to behold some sign of returning consciousness, to see him look up and recognise her. But she saw no change, nothing but that deep, terrible stupor which seemed so much like death.

Dan had carefully washed the wound and applied bandages which the Indian woman had procured from a small closet where the missionary kept his medical supplies. It was a rough, clumsy bandage, but Madeline felt grateful to the trapper for the trouble he had taken. She little knew how anxiously he had examined the wound, washed it, and applied some soothing oil he found among the neatly arranged bottles on the shelf. His hands had trembled as he wound the bandages around Grey's head, and he wondered why his fingers were so awkward as he tied the ends together. He thought little of the scratch; it was the blow which worried him.

"It's a wonder, miss," he remarked, "that he escaped at all. It sartinly 'ud be a pity to see sich a fine feller knocked out. I haven't seen his like in many a day. He's got real spunk, an' is all man."

"Do you think he will recover?" Madeline asked as she turned toward the trapper. "Isn't there anything that we can do?"

"Wall, I'm hopin' he'll come outer this stupor. But if he doesn't we must try to git 'im back to Big Glen, whar he will have treatment from the doctors. I understan' they have purty skilful ones thar."

"But when can we start? How can we take him all the way over that hard trail?"

"We can't leave jist yet, miss; thar's important work on hand. We must lay that poor old man to rest, an'—"

"Oh! is he dead? Do you mean to tell me that he was shot?"

"Yes, miss; it's only too true. A bullet passed through his body, an' he went down like a log. I'm mighty sorry."

Madeline pressed her left hand to her heart. It did not seem possible that the venerable man who had talked so kindly to her but a short time before should now be lying cold in death. What would happen next!

"Where is he?" she faintly asked. "Why did they not bring him in here?"

"They've taken 'im inter the church, miss. The Injuns thought it would be the best place. I guess I'll have to read the Burial Service to-morrer. My! it was a sight to see 'im stand thar in the midst of that rain of lead, an' try to git them Injuns to stop their fightin'! I've seen some brave deeds in me life, miss, an' things that 'ud make yer blood turn to icicles. But that scene beat 'em all."

"And were you hemmed in by the Indians the whole day?" Madeline questioned.

"Only fer part of the night and mornin'."

"How did you manage to find Donnie and get back to the cave?"

"It was this way, miss," and in a few words Dan related the experience through which they had passed the night before. It was a simple tale, told in his own quaint style, with all embellishment left out. It thrilled Madeline's heart, and she looked fondly into the honest, rugged face. She had known him only as Buckskin Dan, the trapper. Formerly he had figured little in her thoughts. But she saw beneath his rough exterior now and knew him as never before.

"And you did all that for the little child!" she mused when he had finished. "You risked your own life to find him and to bring him back to his mother! You are a noble man."

"Tut, tut, miss; that was nothin'. Anyone 'ud have done that much, an' more. But come, we've been talkin' too long, seems to me. This poor chap needs grub. He hasn't tasted a bite fer some time."

"Nor you, either," interposed Madeline.

"Oh, I kin stand it, miss, although I do feel somewhat holler. Mebbe that Injun woman out thar in the yard will be able to throw some stuff together."

"No, I intend to do it myself," Madeline calmly replied. "You call for Nancy. She can show me where the provisions are kept, and will be able to give me a hand. I shall feel better when doing something. It will keep me from worrying too much."

With the Indian woman's aid Madeline was soon busy at the sheet-iron stove. From the larder, which led off from the kitchen, were brought several pieces of moose meat, and these were soon sizzling in the frying pan. Cold beans were warmed up, and some desiccated potatoes prepared, with a little water and salt added. Tea, too, was found, and a loaf of sour-dough bread. For Norman a piece of meat was placed in a kettle upon the stove, for the preparation of soup.

With admiring eyes Dan sat back and watched Madeline moving about the room. He noted her lithesome figure, the erect poise of her head, and the flush which now animated her face, caused partly by the heat, and partly by the exercise. He saw, too, how occasionally she glanced toward the unconscious form lying upon the cot, and the look of deep concern expressed in her eyes.

"She's a good woman," he said to himself; "thar's nothin' wrong about her. She's been badly treated in some way. That's clear as light. Eyes an' face sich as hers speak fer themselves."

It suited Madeline to be busy. She could not bear to remain quiet and watch Norman lying there so very still with that blank look upon his face. And yet her heart was somewhat fearful. Suppose he should open his eyes, see her, and turn away his head in disgust! When the food was prepared she placed it upon the table, and sat near watching the hungry trapper as he ate.

"My, this is fine!" he ejaculated. "I haven't enjoyed sich grub in a long time. It was sartinly good of ye, miss, to think of an old man like me. I don't desarve it."

"You deserve more than I can ever do for you," Madeline replied. "Just think what you have done for me and that poor child. The Lord will reward you, I am sure of that. I cannot imagine why you have done so much for us. We were such strangers to you."

"Don't say that, miss; please don't. Why shouldn't I do it fer you an' the kid? Didn't I once have a lassie of me own, long years ago it was, an' ye remind me much of her. But she was taken away from me, an' I was left all alone. I did it at fust, miss, fer her sake, an' also to help me pardner out. But now I'd do anything fer yer own sake, 'cause I know yer worthy of it."

"And you thought I was not a true woman?" questioned Madeline. "You imagined I was one of those poor fallen creatures who so often come North?"

"I had me doubts, miss. Sometimes I thought ye was, an' ag'in I thought ye wasn't. But I couldn't tell fer sartin. Appearances was ag'in ye."

"I know it! I know it!" Madeline cried almost fiercely. "Everything has been against me for the last six years. Oh, my life has been terrible!"

"I believe ye, miss. I believe ye. But thar's an end to that now. I'll take ye outer this, an' back to yer own people."

"But what will he think?" and Madeline glanced toward the cot. "Oh, if you only knew! If you only understood!"

"I do understand somethin', miss. I know a thing or two."

"And did be really tell you? Did he explain?"

"He told me a little, an' I guessed the rest."

"And did he think I had fallen; that I was a disgrace to womankind?"

"He didn't know what to believe, miss. Poor feller, I was sorry fer 'im. He took it mighty hard."

Madeline was leaning anxiously forward now, with her eyes fixed full upon Dan's face.

"Did he say that he loathed me, that he had cast me off forever?"

It cost her an effort to ask this question, which for days had been beating through her brain.

"No, miss, he said nuthin' of the kind. His heart was almost broke when he found that ye was livin' with Old Meg. But he thought mebbe ye was thar cause ye wanted to be. He wasn't sartin, however, an' said he was agoin' to find out. If he larned that ye was thar of yer own free will he would jist leave ye alone. But if he discovered that ye was thar ag'inst yer will he said nuthin' on arth 'ud stop 'im from savin' ye."

"Oh!"

Madeline drew a deep breath of relief as she listened to these words. So he did care. He wanted to know the truth.

"Yes, miss," Dan continued, "never ye doubt that young man alyin' thar, an' if ye'll excuse a rough old trapper I'll jist tell ye that his love fer ye is like a blazin' fire. Haven't I watched 'im fer days now, an' heerd him murmur yer name in his sleep? I tell ye he was most wild when he found that the Injuns had stole ye away."

Madeline asked no further questions just then. She wished to think over what Dan had told her. A new hope and joy came into her heart. So Norman really cared for her after all. She repeated the words to herself time and time again.

Dan finished his meal, and pushed back the stool upon which he was sitting.

"I'm agoin' to leave ye fer a while, miss," he said, slowly drawing his pipe from his pocket. "I've been a wonderin' what them Injuns are up to over thar, an' so I'll jist stroll cautiously around an' size things up a bit."

"Do you think the Indians will continue their fighting?" Madeline anxiously asked.

"Can't tell what them varmints 'ill do, miss. They're very unsartin critters. But if they do git at it ag'in an' the Big Lakes win out I'm afeered it'll go purty hard with us. We got outer their clutches by a close shave, an' I'm thinkin' they're rather sore over it. It seems to me it's that Injun woman, Nadu, wot's doin' much of the mischief. She's a vixin, that I kin tell it by her eye."

"Oh, don't speak of her!" and a shudder shook Madeline's body, while her face turned pale. "She is terrible! It was she who sent me adrift in the canoe. She hates me, and I do not know why."

"An' did she do that deed?" Dan cried. "Did she send ye through the rapids?"

"Yes; it's only too true. But please don't speak about it again. I want to forget it."

Madeline rose and examined the meat cooking upon the stove.

"I think we might give our patient a little of this soup now," she said; "it's not very strong, but he should have something nourishing as soon as possible."

"Right ye are, miss," Dan replied, as he sprang to his feet. "I'll jist hold his head up a little while ye feed 'im. Thar, that's good!" he exclaimed, when the task had been accomplished. "That's the fust taste of food he's had since I don't know when. I'll jist hike off now, an' leave ye a while on watch."

When the door had closed, and Dan's footsteps had died away in the distance, Madeline drew a stool up close to the cot. Nancy du Nord had left some time before, so she was alone with Norman. Quietly she sat by his side, and looked down earnestly into his face. How often she had seen it in her day and night dreams through those long, terrible years. It had been an inspiration to her when hope had almost fled. Oh, if he would only open his lips and eyes, speak to her, and look upon her! She longed to tell him everything, to clear the cloud of doubt from his mind. But no sign did he give. He lay there helpless and unconscious. His right hand was lying by his side. Reaching over she held it in her own. A thrill shot through her heart as she did so, and a flush suffused her cheeks. It was the same hand that had pressed hers so fondly one night at the little garden gate so long ago, and it was the same strong, firm hand that had reached out, gripped her, and drew her from the icy waters of death. Suddenly she bent her head, lifted the hand to her lips, and kissed it fervently. Then she quickly dropped it, and looked around, fearful lest someone had seen her.

Thus she sat keeping faithful watch as the hours wore slowly away. Occasionally she arose and gave Norman some of the soup, which by this time was much stronger and contained more nourishment. When at length Dan returned she was still at her post and smiled upon the trapper as he entered the room.

"You've been away a long time," she said. "You must have found much to occupy your attention."

"Indeed I have, miss," Dan replied, glancing toward the constable. "The Injuns are havin' a big pow-wow. They can't decide whether to have peace, or fight it out. Guess they'll keep it up all night by the look of things. I watched 'em fer some time, an' made out the drift of their harangues, which are sartinly mighty long. Hishu Sam had the floor, or I should say, the ground, when I left. He's got a purty level head. Anyway I do hope it will be peace, fer I'm gittin' mighty anxious to be away an' take this poor chap back to Big Glen. I see thar's no change in 'im yit."

"None," Madeline replied. "He's just the same as when you left."

"An' ye've been watchin' 'im ever since? Ye look tired, miss. Don't ye think ye should have a bite to eat, an' take a little rest? But whar's the kid? He must be hungry."

At these words Madeline sprang to her feet in alarm. So intent had she been with thinking of other things that she had forgotten all about the child. It was not natural for him to be so quiet. She had left him playing in the next room, and he had always come to her when he needed anything. Hurrying to the door she looked at the place on the floor where she had left him. He was not there. She glanced about the room until her eyes rested upon the bed, and there among the tossed blankets nestled the little lad fast asleep. Madeline gave a sigh of relief as she stood and watched him.

"Poor, wee chap," she remarked, turning to the trapper. "He was certainly worn out, and crawled into bed himself, and fell asleep."

"Ay, ay, indeed he needs rest," Dan responded. "An' so do you, miss. Jist swaller some of yon grub, an' take yerself off, or else I'll have two patients on me hands. Ye'll need all yer strength fer what lies ahead."

"I know it, I know it. You are kind to think of me," and Madeline gave the old man a bright smile of gratitude as he turned and left the room.

CHAPTER XXVII THE COST

All through the night Dan kept watch by the constable's side. His pipe was seldom out of his mouth as he sat silently on the rough bench with his back against the wall. Twice Grey had moved a little, and once a moan escaped his lips. But otherwise there was no perceptible change. When Madeline appeared in the morning she looked much refreshed after her sleep. An expression of pleasure crossed Dan's face as he saw her standing before him. Her presence revived him after his long vigil, like the inspiring breath of dewy morn over a drowsy world. The room did not seem so close and sombre when she was present. A new spirit pervaded the place, which made it a restful abode.

That morning after breakfast Dan started forth and walked slowly to the little church. He was joined there by three natives who had returned to the village. A few moments later they came out bearing the body of Charles Nordis, the missionary. A single blanket enshrouded that stiffened form, for a coffin was out of the question. Silently they bore their burden down a gentle slope, across a narrow valley, then up a steep hill to the cemetery at the summit, for Indians choose high places in which to bury their dead. Here a grave had been dug the day before, and by its gaping mouth they laid the body down.

Dan stood for a few moments looking at the white face of the old man lying at his feet, and then glanced at the expressionless features of the three natives standing near. Deep, bitter thoughts were surging through the trapper's mind as he stood there. Was this all that the missionary had gained? A lifetime spent in the wilderness for the sake of a wandering people, and was this all—a violent death, a lonely grave in the wild, without one mourner to shed a tear? What was the use of such a life? he mused. The Indians had not responded to his care and teaching; but seemed to be as hard and cruel as ever.

A startled exclamation from one of the Indians aroused him. He lifted his head, and saw the three men looking anxiously away to the left. Dan turned sharply around to ascertain the cause of their excitement. It was certainly a magnificent view which met his eyes. Down below stretched the valley, partly wooded. Beyond, glimpses of the river gleamed like burnished silver beneath the sun, while away in the distance towered the rugged mountains to their tapering coronets of snow. At another time Dan would have drunk in the beauty with a true lover's ardent admiration. But now something else occupied his mind. Shading his eyes with his right hand he soon discerned a long, black, sinuous line trailing out from the forest beyond the Mission

House. It held him spellbound for an instant, and then an exclamation of fear and concern burst from his lips. They were Indians, coming from their recent pow-wow, for what purpose he could not tell. Were they heading for the Mission House to carry away the woman and child? His first impulse was to rush down the hill, hurry to meet them, and guard the defenceless ones. This he at once realised would be folly. He could not get there in time, and what could one man do against so many?

He watched them with almost breathless interest as they drew near the house, and when the foremost ones had passed without turning aside he gave a deep sigh of relief. Through the village they threaded their way, then down the slope straight toward the hill upon which they were standing.

"They're comin' here!" he ejaculated, turning to his now thoroughly frightened companions. "What kin they be up to, anyway?"

His hand slipped to his hip and rested upon the butt of his revolver.

"If they're after mischief an' want me," he muttered, "they'll git a warm reception from my old comrade here. She's never failed me yit, an' I guess she won't now."

Up the hill the Indians swung with their easy, tireless gait, and soon the leaders were but a few hundred yards away. As Dan looked he drew his hand from his revolver, and meditatively stroked his long beard. Although armed the Indians showed no signs of hostility. On they came and without a word reached the top of the hill. Here they paused and waited for the rear to come up. Then from the midst stepped Hishu Sam. He gave one word which sounded like a command, and at once he walked over to where the dead man was lying, gave one quick glance at the cold, white face, and moved on. Others now came forward, stopped, looked, and moved away. It took them some time to do this, and Dan stood silently by wondering at the meaning of this unusual procedure.

The Hishus and Big Lakes were there—some bent and withered by the weight of years, others were young in the full strength and flush of virile manhood. But not a word was uttered, and not a movement of their impassive faces revealed the hearts within.

As the Indians moved away they turned to the right and formed in a circle several lines deep around the grave, where they stood silently leaning upon their rifles. At the end of the procession came Nadu, the Indian woman. She advanced slowly with bent head, over which a scarf had been carelessly thrown. She stopped before the body, gazed for an instant upon the face, and then sinking on her knees upon the ground remained silent for a few minutes. A stillness as deep as death pervaded the onlookers, while Dan stared in amazement. Then from the woman's lips came a low wail which steadily increased in intensity. Once Dan had heard such a sound. He had been in an Indian village where a little child had just died. He had heard the mother's cry ringing out upon the night air from the rude cabin. It had haunted him for days—that low, plaintive wail of a bereaved heart, which swelled to a wild, piercing shriek. Until then Dan had not believed that so much pathos and agony could be expressed in the human voice. And here was this woman kneeling on the ground giving vent to the same heart-rending cry. What did it all mean? Why should she, from Hishu, feel so keenly the death of the old man? What was he to her?

As he listened and wondered the sounds grew fainter and fainter until they ceased altogether, and she knelt as before with bowed head. For a few moments an intense silence reigned on the hilltop.

Dan was about to give orders to lower the body into the grave when Hishu Sam stepped forward and stood close to where Nadu was kneeling. His tall commanding figure was drawn to its full height as he surveyed the silent natives before him. Then he began to speak in the Hishu tongue, which made it quite easy for Dan to understand what he was saying.

"The sun shines in the sky," he began, "the mountains stand as of old, the rivers flow through the land, the fish swim in the water, the moose roam the forest; but the hearts of the Indians are sad. The Hishus and the Big Lakes are all of one family. But they have not lived as brothers. They have been always fighting as did their fathers before them. They lived for war. Their hearts were hard and cruel. They thought only of evil, of killing one another. Ten winters ago a pale face came from the great river beyond the big mountains. With his own hands he built those houses down there. He learned to speak our language. He taught our little ones from a book he brought with him. He made more books, and he gave them to our children to read. He lived with us. When we were sick he healed us, when we were hungry he gave us food, when we were cold he gave us clothes. But our hearts were hard. He worked for us, and loved us, but when he asked us to give up fighting we laughed at him. When he would teach us a better way we would not listen. One night my little child was sick. The pale face came. He made her well. He taught me wonderful things. He told me of the Great Chief who died to save us all. I listened, and my heart, which was like a frozen river, thawed. I became a new man. The pale face came into our land. He did not come to rob us. He did not come to give us fire-water. He did not come to ruin our young women. He came to help us, to save us. And what have we done to him?" Here the speaker paused, and raised his right hand in an impressive manner. "We killed him, and he now lies before us. We were fighting. We wished to kill one another. But the pale face came between us. He tried to stop us, and he died. Now our eyes have been opened. We see what he has done for us, and how he loved us. We have had a great meeting. We have talked much. Our hearts and mouths spoke peace. We have given up fighting with one another. We have promised to be friends as long as the sun rises in the sky and the water flows in the river. We will have a big pot-latch—the tribes will all come to witness our agreement of peace. The pale face has done it. He is dead. We cannot speak to him. But if another teacher comes from beyond the great mountains we will listen."

Hishu Sam paused, and from the assembled Indians came the murmur of assent. Several others stepped forward and spoke. They were natural orators, and with much gesticulation they emphasised the greatness of their race. But they all agreed with the first speaker that they had met with a deep loss in the death of the pale face, and were anxious now for peace.

During these harangues Dan stood silently by. He was accustomed to the ways of the Indians. In his heart he was most thankful at the happy termination of the trouble. When the speakers were through he gave the signal, and the body was lowered into the ground. Seizing a handful of gravel he stepped close to the grave, and bared his head.

"Great God in Heaven," he prayed, "listen to the words of these people. They have killed this old man, but punish 'em not fer the sin they have committed. They are sorry now, O Lord, an' want to do better. This old man has died fer 'em, an' by his death they've been united. I can't make a long prayer, O Lord, nor tell ye all that's in me heart jist now. But I ax ye to bless these Injuns fer the sake of the old man who died fer 'em, an' in their presence I commit his body to the ground, arth to arth, dust to dust, ashes to ashes, sartin that sich a man as this'll rise ag'in to the life etarnal. Hear an old trapper's words, O Lord. Amen."

Dan stood long and silently by the grave and watched the three Indians toss in the earth upon the body. The Big Lakes and the Hishus remained for a few moments, and then filed quickly away. When at last the grave had been filled, the trapper, too, turned and walked slowly back to the Mission House. His heart was deeply touched by what he had heard and seen. Much had been accomplished, but, oh, at what a cost! It was the story of history repeated here on this far-off frontier, that without the shedding of blood there is no advancement, no remission of sins.

CHAPTER XXVIII THE LIFTED VEIL

After Dan had left the Mission House Madeline was kept busy for a while getting breakfast for herself and Donnie. The latter had slept soundly, and awoke much refreshed, with more of the old healthy colour in his cheeks. He opened his eyes, and looked around. Hearing sounds in the kitchen he tumbled out of bed, and standing in the doorway gave a chuckle of delight when he saw that Madeline was really there, and had not left him again. Soon he was enfolded in her arms, and his lips and cheeks showered with fervent kisses of welcome. Then he was carried off bodily to have his face and hands washed, and his tangled hair combed into something approaching order. He was hungry, too, and could hardly wait until Madeline had finished before beginning his breakfast. His little tongue wagged incessantly as he sat at the side of the table opposite Madeline. He asked many questions, especially about the unconscious man lying on the cot.

"What's the matter wif 'im?" he asked. "Why is he so still? Is he asleep?"

"He was hurt, dearie," was the quiet reply.

"Who hurt 'im, Malin?" and Donnie's eyes opened wide.

"The Indians, dear. They shot at him."

"Oh, I'm sorry. He was so dood to me. He said he loved 'ou, Malin, an' would take me to 'ou."

"Did he say that, dearie? Are you sure?" and Madeline leaned eagerly forward.

"Ya, me sure," was the simple response.

Madeline sat silently for a while lost in thought. Then it must he true, she said to herself, while a sweet joy stole into her heart. She had meditated much over what Dan had told her, and wondered if the old trapper had said those things merely to cheer her drooping spirits. But such words from the lips of a little child she could not doubt. Norman must have told him. They were surely true.

After breakfast was over Madeline washed the few dishes, put them carefully away, and then tidied up the room. This done she took her place by Norman's side. She could see no change, nothing but that deep heavy stupor. She felt now in her heart that he had loved her during those terrible days when she thought he had cast her away forever. But if he would only awake and tell her so. What joy to hear the blessed truth from his own lips.

For some time Donnie had remained seated upon the floor, looking over several picture books Madeline had found for him on one of the shelves. These satisfied him for a while, but at length, wearying of this amusement, he rose and came to Madeline's side.

"Tell me a 'tory, Malin, pleath."

"What shall it be, dearie?" was the reply, as Madeline lifted him upon her lap.

"When 'ou was 'ittle, Malin. I like dat."

It was not so hard for Madeline to tell of her old home life now. She remembered how she had first told it to Donnie on that terrible night when he had been torn from her arms. How much had happened since then! Slowly and simply she told again of her happy home across the great water, the big house, the garden with the beautiful flowers, and the many kind people she knew. To all this Donnie listened with wondering ears, his little head leaning against her arm.

"There," Madeline at length said, "I've told you enough now. Are you not satisfied?"

"I like dat 'tory, Malin. 'Ou will tell it again some time, won't 'ou?"

"Yes, dearie."

"An' 'ou will sing to me, Malin, won't 'ou?" he pleaded. "I like to hear 'ou sing. 'Ou sounds just like my mamma."

"What shall I sing, dearie? A hymn? It must be only one, and short, too, for it might hurt him," and she nodded toward the cot.

"Oh, do 'ou fink it would?" and Donnie's eyes opened wide. "But maybe a 'ittle one wouldn't hurt 'im; dat one about de star. 'Ou sang it one night when I was tired, an' I went to sleep."

"So I did, Donnie, and you shall have it now. But you mustn't go to sleep, you know. I want you to watch with me and keep me company."

"All right, Malin. I won't go sleep."

In a low, sweet voice Madeline sang the simple song she had learned years before:

"Lead me, O Thou Star of Heaven,

Guide me through the world's dark night,

Lead me to the restful haven,

Bring me to the morning light.

Star of Heaven, bright and fair,

Keep me ever in Thy care.

Brighten, O Thou Star of Heaven,

Death's dark valley deep and wide,

Lighten up the way before me,

Till I reach the other side.

Star of Heaven, lead me on,

When the light of earth is gone."

Scarcely had Madeline begun to sing ere an invisible veil lifted from the brain of the wounded man by her side. He came forth from the blank world of darkness, and a voice fell upon his ears which made him lie very still. It was so sweet and familiar. He had heard it before, and it led him into gardens of the most beautiful and fragrant flowers. And in the centre—the fairest flower of all—stood Madeline as of old.

Presently the singing ceased, and Grey opened his eyes, and fixed them full upon the bright scene before him.

Madeline turning, saw him, noted the look of intelligence upon his face, and her heart bounded with joy. Grey tried to speak, but words would not come. He gave a weary smile, and stretched out his hand. Madeline seized it, and pressed it gently.

"Hush," she whispered. "Don't try to talk. You are weak, so go to sleep now."

Again he smiled, and gave her such a look of love and gratitude that she trembled with emotion, while a deep blush suffused her cheeks. She longed for Norman to speak, to hear the truth from his own lips. She read it in his eyes, however, and was happy. But she did not wish to excite him in his present condition, and knew that a deep refreshing sleep would be the best thing for him.

"My head!" Grey faintly murmured, as he lifted his hand to the wound.

"Yes, I know," she replied. "Go to sleep, and it will feel better."

With a deep sigh of extreme weariness he closed his eyes in a slumber which Madeline knew was natural and refreshing.

"Thank God! Oh, thank God!" she breathed to herself. "The veil is lifted. He knew me, and did not turn away from me in disgust."

She sat watching him for a few minutes, and then some subtle influence caused her to turn her face toward the door. It was partly open, for the morning was mild, and the room warm. And as she looked out upon the world beyond in a half-abstracted manner, she became aware that someone was approaching the house. Then she started, placed Donnie upon the floor, rose to her feet, and took a few steps forward. Her face, which but a few moments before had flushed with joy, was now as white as death. The person coming toward her was the Indian woman, Nadu. She recognised her in an instant, and her first impulse was to close and securely fasten the door. But something seemed to hold her spellbound. She was unable to move and stood perfectly still, fascinated by that slowly advancing figure.

Nadu walked with her eyes fixed upon the ground, and her head covered with the old scarf. She was moving as in a dream, heeding nothing about her. Was she coming to visit for the last time the house in which she had passed so many happy days, to look upon the scenes so familiar to her? Was she thinking of the missionary and his wife who would never live there again, the two who had been so kind to her, and who had taught her about the nobler things of life? Was there any feeling of remorse in her heart for the woman she had sent so ruthlessly through the swirling rapids? She reached the door, placed a foot upon the threshold, and lifted her head. As she did so a look of wonder, quickly succeeded by a wild fear, leaped into her eyes. She started back and threw out her arms as if to drive away the scene, while from her lips came a piercing shriek of terror. There before her stood the white woman. It could not be, she was drowned in the rapids, and was this her ghost returned to confront her? The teaching she had received at the Mission House and the years she had spent among white people could not altogether eradicate from Nadu's mind the ingrained superstition of her race. The roaring of the wind, the roll of thunder and the rippling of the stream were to her so many voices of the unseen spirits. Only in times of extreme passion were the voices silent. She heeded nothing then, but rushed madly forward like some impetuous torrent. Only when the violent force had been exhausted did the voices return as before. So on this day her passion of jealousy and hatred was subdued by the sight of her old friend and teacher lying cold in death. And then to be confronted by this spirit, as she thought, of the very one she wished to banish from her mind was most startling. Pain, hardship and even death she would have suffered without a complaint. But this vision of the supernatural, this spirit of the woman she had sent to her death, was more than her sturdy stoicism could endure. Sinking to her knees upon the floor, she buried her face in her hands to blot out that strange sight. And as she knelt there Madeline stepped forward and laid her hand gently upon the bowed woman's shoulder. The touch caused Nadu to shrink back with a gurgling, inarticulate cry.

"Don't be afraid," Madeline said, half surmising the cause of the Indian woman's fear. "I won't hurt you. I forgive you."

Lowering her hands and lifting her head Nadu looked slowly up, while her eyes scanned the white woman's face intently for an instant. Then she reached out fearfully a trembling hand and touched Madeline's dress.

"You not dead?" she gasped. "You not speerit?"

"No, no," came the laughing reply. "Do I seem like a dead person? Get up, and take a good look at me."

Realising how she had been mistaken, Nadu quickly regained her feet, while the old expression of hatred leaped back into her eyes.

"Don't look at me that way!" Madeline cried, laying her hand upon the woman's arm. "Why do you hate me? I have not hurt you. Why do you want to kill me?"

"White woman steal Bill's heart, savvey?" came the quick response.

"Steal Bill's heart!" repeated Madeline. "What do you mean?"

"White woman no savvey?" and Nadu gave a sarcastic laugh. "No savvey Siwash Bill at Hishu?"

In an instant the truth flashed upon Madeline's mind. Why had she been so dull of comprehension? she wondered. She recalled now the squaw man's numerous advances, and his protestations of love that night she had fainted at the door of Old Meg's house. So here was the secret of it all. The Indian woman believed it was her fault, which caused the hatred to burn like a wild, consuming fire.

"Look at me, Nadu," she commanded, drawing closer, "and know that I am telling you the truth. I did not try to steal the heart of your husband. It is a lie! He came to me, but I would not listen. He is bad, bad! You see that man lying there?" and she pointed to the constable. "I knew him a long time ago. I never forgot him. See? Why should I want Siwash Bill?"

Nadu's eyes turned toward the cot, and for the first time she saw the sleeping man lying there. She remained silent for a few minutes, and then a new light shone in her eyes as she turned them upon Madeline's face.

"You no love Bill?" she asked. "You no steal his heart?"

"I tell you, no," was the emphatic reply. "You are wrong. You have tried to kill me when I did nothing to you. It is that man, Bill, who is bad; oh, he is terrible!"

Madeline hardly expected to convince this woman that what she said was true. It was, therefore, a great surprise when Nadu suddenly dropped upon the kitchen floor, seized Madeline's right hand in hers, and pressed it to her lips.

"Me sorry. Me sorry," she moaned. "Nadu once happy here. But Bill take Nadu away. Nadu savvey now."

Then she sprang to her feet with a look of wild determination in her face.

"Me hate heem! Me hate heem!" she cried, while her hands clinched hard. "Heem bad, ugh!"

With that she turned and hurried out of the house, leaving Madeline standing gazing wonderingly after her. She felt that Nadu's hatred would now be turned toward Siwash Bill. What course her anger would take she could not tell, but a sigh of relief escaped her lips as she realised that she herself was no longer the object of this strange woman's revengeful moods.

She was still standing there when Buckskin Dan crossed the threshold. He glanced at Madeline, and then toward the cot. His eye brightened as he noted the natural expression upon Norman's face.

"So the change has come fer the better, miss," he said.

"Yes, and he is sleeping quietly now," was the reply. "But you have been away most of the morning. I did not think a funeral, especially here, would take so long."

"Set down, miss, while I tell ye all about it, an' then ye must give me an account of when yon laddie come to."

Grey slept for the remainder of the day, and did not awake again until early the next morning. He started up and looked around. Daylight was streaming into the room, and the objects within were quite discernible. He saw Dan lying on the floor a short distance away, and wondered what he was doing there. Then slowly his mind cleared and the past stood out vividly before him. He remembered the stand they had made behind the columns of stone, and how he had rushed forward to rescue the old man. But where was Madeline? He had a faint idea that she had been close by his side, had held his hand, and spoken to him. But he now believed it was all a dream. He wished to get up, for he felt strong enough for that. He was also hungry, and longed to explore the room to see what it contained in the way of food. But he did not wish to disturb the old trapper, who must be very tired. So he lay quietly on the cot, thinking and wondering about many things.

At length Dan opened his eyes, and with an ejaculation of annoyance sprang to his feet.

"Wall, I'll be blowed," he exclaimed. "I only intended to rest a bit thar on the floor, an' didn't I go fast asleep."

His delight knew no bounds when he saw Grey's improved condition, and he set hastily to work getting breakfast. But occasionally he cast his eyes in the direction of Madeline's room, and when at length he heard her moving across the floor toward the door he slipped quickly and quietly out of the kitchen into the fresh morning air.

"Guess I'm better out here," he chuckled with delight. "They don't want an old humbug hangin' around at sich a critical time like this. I'll jist slip over to whar the Injuns are camped, an' have a few words with 'em. I've been thinkin' things over a bit lately, an' want thar help. They're a queer lot of varmints, but they kin help us to git outer this hole."

When he returned a half hour later the jubilant expression had left his face, and his furrowed brow was troubled. He noted the happy scene in the Mission House, Norman and Madeline sitting close to each other, with Donnie playing near by.

"They're gone!" he exclaimed. "Them Injuns, the mean wretches, have cleared out."

"Well, what does it matter, Dan?" Grey replied. "We don't need them now, do we?"

"Don't need 'em? Don't need 'em, do ye say? It's jist the time we do need 'em. Jist as soon as ye git a little more strength into yer body we've got to hike outer this back to Hishu. I wanted them Injuns to go with us, fer I'm thinkin' thar'll be trouble up yon with Siwash Bill an' his gang. With them Injuns at me back I'd soon settle thar hash. But now they've hiked off to the interior—both Hishus an' Big Lakes—to hold a great pot-latch. Blame their dusky skins. They're jist as troublesome an' unsartin as a hull nest of fleas."

"But we can face them, Dan," Grey insisted. "I feel stronger every minute, and I have good cause for it, too, have I not? Oh, Dan, this is the happiest day of my life. The veil is not only lifted from my mind, but the veil so dark and terrible which separated Madeline and me is lifted, too. Come, banish that gloom from your face, and be happy with us for to-day. We've had enough darkness and hardship together of late, Dan, so let us enjoy the sunshine and joy for a few hours at least. To-morrow we can start back to Hishu. I do not fear those vile serpents now, though, they were ten to one."

"Very wall, pardner," and Dan scratched his head doubtfully. "I don't want to spile yer pleasure to-day. So I'll jist think me thoughts, an' hold me tongue fer a change."

CHAPTER XXIX STRENGTH FROM THE HILLS

The night Siwash Bill and Windy Pete had been foiled in their dastardly work within Buckskin Dan's cabin, they sat late in the store scheming for a speedy revenge. They were tigers in human forms, and by the flickering candle light their faces expressed the rage burning in their hearts. Oaths of the most blood-curdling nature poured in a sulphurous stream from their foul mouths. There was nothing about their appearance to arouse even the slightest feeling of sympathy or approval. Through years of baseness, guile and debauchery, they had extinguished the faintest spark of nobleness within their hearts. Subject to no restraint, free to follow the dictates of their own passions, they found it now unbearable to be checked in their mad career.

They sat for hours, and the candle spluttered low ere they ceased. Neither did they see two forms speeding swiftly and quietly from Dan's cabin to the canoe by the river's bank.

At length Windy Pete yawned, rose and threw himself into a bunk in the adjoining room, leaving Bill alone with the dying candle. The squaw man's eyes often turned toward the door as if expecting it to open at any minute, and that Nadu would enter. But as the night lengthened and she did not appear, a sigh of relief escaped his lips. He was sure that she had fulfilled his command, and had sped with the child down-stream. A sense of elation swept over him as he mused upon the success of his scheme. How easily he had cleared himself of the troublesome, suspicious squaw. He had the field to himself now, and there was no one to interfere with his design upon that woman at Old Meg's. She had repelled him, it was true, but what of that? There were other ways, and he thought with satisfaction upon her daily, lonely walk down the trail to the river. There would be no Nadu prowling around, either. He would have the beautiful woman to himself, and then he would see if she would scorn him again. To-morrow she would be there. He would wait no longer. And so he sat in the darkness, for the light had gone out. That kindly ministrant had slowly flickered down to nothing, and night mercifully blotted out the coarse passion-inflamed features of the wretched squaw man sitting alone in the room.

No sleep came to his eyes, and at the earliest break of day he arose, lighted the fire and prepared breakfast. Windy Pete still slept on, unheeding the noise his companion was making. Occasionally the squaw man went to the door and looked intently toward Buckskin Dan's cabin. The trapper was an unusually early riser, and when an hour or two had passed, and no smoke was seen issuing from the stovepipe stuck through the roof, the squaw man was much surprised. He talked it over with Pete when he awoke, and together the two watched the cabin for some sign of life. They waited and watched for the greater part of the morning, and observing nothing they went over to the building, and looked cautiously through the small window into the room. Seeing no one, they tried the door, and found it fastened.

Then from Bill's lips broke an exclamation of triumph.

"They've hiked, Pete! Ha, ha!" he cried. "We've routed the d— skunks at last. The place was gittin' too hot fer 'em. Oh, this is a good one. Say, old man, let's go over to the store an' have a drink on it. That was the best job we've done in a long time. I didn't think that spyin' Yellow-leg would show sich a chicken liver so soon. How he did squak last night when the light went out. Oh, oh, this is rich."

They retraced their steps, and had almost reached the store when their attention was arrested by the clatter of hoofs some distance away. Looking around they beheld Shifty Nick tearing down the trail, mounted upon his lean and wiry cayuse. He reined up close to where they were standing, with his characteristic brutality and string of oaths.

"Got the dough, Nick?" queried Bill.

"Dough be d—!" was the reply, as the rider leaped to the ground, tore off saddle and bridle, and turned the much-abused animal loose to seek for a meal as best it could. "Come inside, and we'll talk it over. I'm dead beat, an' almost starved."

"They didn't bite," growled Shifty, as he gulped down his food. "How many times have I got to tell ye that?"

"But didn't ye see anybody?" insisted Bill. "Did no one come near the place where we ordered the money to be left?"

"Come? No. But I kept well out of sight, an' saw several d— Yellow-legs in the distance. They were on the lookout, but I kept close. They thought somebody'd be squattin' like a fool by the rock, with folded hands, an' meek eyes, waitin' fer the money. But Shifty knows a thing or two. Good Lord! How my fingers itched and quivered to draw a bead on their numbskulls."

"Oh, well, Nick," Bill replied, "don't feel too bad about it. We've got the kid, an' as that old cuss Si didn't fork out, but set those hounds of hell on us, it'll be some consolation to make 'im squirm. But I'd like to see his face when he gits the news of what has happened to his little tootsy-wootsie boy."

"Where is the kid, anyway?" questioned Nick. "I halted at Old Meg's, an' she told me the news."

"Ha, ha," and Bill laughed outright. "We've got 'im cinched all right. He's gone down to the Big Lakes. They'll keep 'im until called fer."

"An' ye sent the gal along to look after 'im, eh?"

"Sartin. I didn't want her pryin' around. She's been somewhat suspicious of me lately, so I sent her to her own people with the two Injuns who came spyin' upon Hishu."

"Oh, I don't mean your squaw, Bill. But the gal over yon."

"Why, what about her?" and the squaw man's eyes opened wide in wonder.

"She's gone, too. Haven't ye heard?"

"The divil!" and Bill leaped to his feet. "What are ye givin' us? Who's stuffed ye with all this nonsense?"

"Ask Old Meg, then. She'll tell ye, fer she's more'n worked up over it; said that the gal went away with the kid in the canoe. Guess them Big Lakes must have an eye fer beauty, too, Bill, an' one of 'em needed a white squaw. Ha, ha, that's a good one."

Siwash Bill hardly heard these closing words. He stood as in a dream. So she was gone, and his plans were all upset. But why did they take her? What did it all mean?

"How did Old Meg know of this, Nick?" he hoarsely asked. "We didn't hear a word."

"Oh, that d— Yellow-leg told her. He burst into her cabin like a tornado. His eyes were starin' wild, an' his voice was like a roar of thunder, so she said, when he asked her about the gal. Where is the cur now, anyway?"

Siwash Bill was more mystified than ever. He stood looking at Shifty in an abstracted manner, and then an angry snarl of rage broke from his lips.

"We're fools, d— fools!" he cried. "While we've been gloatin' over Buckskin Dan an' that Yellow-leg, callin' 'em cowards an' all kinds of names, they've been hikin' after them Injuns to save the boy an' that gal. Oh, I see it all as plain as day."

The squaw man had been outwitted at his own game. His companions knew when to be silent, and discreetly left him to his own thoughts. They sauntered from the building, and discussed the matter outside. Within the store sat Bill, alone, the very incarnation of baffled rage and hatred. The day wore on, and he prowled around waiting for something to happen. Mingled with his rage was a feeling of insecurity. He had formerly believed that his word was law at Hishu; that his plans could not be overturned, and that his commands would be obeyed. But his eyes were being slowly opened. There was some undercurrent which was working against him. The very air seemed ominous with unforeseen events.

The feeling of dread was deepened when toward evening he saw canoes gliding down the river, filled with natives. He believed they would stop at Hishu, but, instead, they pushed steadily on in deep silence. He ran to the bank of the river, and watched them until they had disappeared around a bend in the distance. He noted that one craft ran close to the shore, and a tall, lithe figure stepped lightly in. He could not tell who this passenger was, but it increased his anxiety. Why had not the Hishus stopped? What did they mean by going by without a word? Had they, too, turned against him? He felt that their action had something to do with the stolen woman and child. But how could they know about it so far off in the wilderness, while he, only a few hundred yards away, had been in entire ignorance?

Anxiously now he discussed the whole question with his companions. Would Dan and the constable return, and the Hishus with them? If so, their position at the village would be unenviable. Or had the Indians gone down to meet the Big Lakes? This latter idea gave them some relief. Anyway, they considered it safer to be prepared, and if the worst came they could fade away into the wilderness. A couple of cayuses, grazing in a wild meadow, several miles from Hishu, were caught and brought to the village to be held in readiness, while packs of food were made up for a speedy departure. In addition to these precautions Shifty Nick each day patrolled the river for miles below Hishu. He lived upon the trail. By day he scanned the river for the slightest object, while at night his alert ears were strained for the faintest paddle dip. It had often been said that Shifty could sleep in the saddle, and could see with his eyes closed.

Days passed and nothing happened. The river gave no sign, and the air breathed no secrets. But late one afternoon Shifty rode madly into Hishu, leaped from the cayuse, and burst into the store.

"They're comin'!" he shouted. "Five miles down river."

Siwash Bill dropped the rifle he was cleaning and stared.

"How many?" he gasped. "Injuns, too?"

"No, only one canoe. Injuns nowhere in sight. All whites but one, an' that's Nadu. Now we've got to act, an' what's yer plan? Are ye goin' to let 'em git through Hishu?"

"How long 'fore they'll git here, Nick?" questioned the squaw man, who was now thinking deeply.

"'Bout two hours. Heavy tide that."

"Two hours. It'll be quite dark then," Bill mused, as he glanced toward the window. "Two hours. Let me see. Thar's Dan; he's a divil, an' the Yellow-leg's 'bout as bad. The rest'll be easy to handle, eh?"

"What's yer plan, Bill?"

"Listen," and the squaw man leaned over and spoke low. "See? Dead men tell no tales. Night. Confusion. Cries of fright. River swift. Good grave, eh? Easy. What? We kin do it. Three to one. It's our only way, Nick. We'll have to do it later, so might as well settle the job now."

"But what about the Yellow-legs at Big Glen?" questioned Shifty.

"What about 'em? I care not fer the hull bunch. They can't prove anything. We're desperate men, anyway, so a few lives more or less won't matter, eh? Now you had better git down-stream early, in case they come faster'n we expect. I'll be along later, fer I've got some things to look after around the store. We'll have a big blowout when we git this affair settled. I'll stand treat to-night, an' a good one it'll be, too. So ye'd better be off at once."

Slowly the darkness deepened as the squaw man moved around the store. He felt confident now that his plans would not miscarry. He could trust his two companions to do the deed from which his cowardly heart shrank. He had really nothing to detain him, and his excuse of work was only a weak sham. But he resolved to be near, watching within the shadows, at the right moment. Occasionally he went to the door to listen, hoping to hear the report of rifles and the sounds of clamour down-stream. At last, thinking it about time the canoe should be near, he seized his cap, and was about to blow out the candle standing on the table, when a peculiar noise fell upon his ears. He paused and listened. It was the steady tramp of numerous feet approaching the building. He started, and his face grew ashy white, for he recognised that sound. The prospectors and miners had returned from the hills! But why were they coming so soon? Formerly their arrival had always filled him with joy, for it had meant big sales, and much drinking. Now, however, it was different. He did not wish them near at this critical time, and, besides, something warned him that they had returned for a special purpose.

He glanced quickly around, with the idea of flight, but at that instant the store door was thrust open with a bang, and a number of men surged into the room. To the squaw man trembling by the counter they seemed like a veritable army of giants. And in fact they were splendid types of men physically. No carpet knights these, but rugged pioneers and pathfinders, who for long years had followed the lure of gold wherever it beckoned with its mystic charm.

They entered without a word, and almost filled the store. Their silence to the shrinking man was most ominous. Why had he remained behind? he asked himself. Why had he not gone with his companions? He would have had their assistance at any rate, and here he was alone to face these men!

"Evenin', men," he at length blurted out. "It's g-good t' see ye. Yer back early from the hills. Have a drink, eh? Free to all. It's my treat t'night."

If he thought in this manner to win the good will of these men he was sadly mistaken. He partly turned toward the black bottles standing on the shelves, when certain sickening clicks caused him to wheel suddenly about, and he found his eyes looking straight down the smooth barrels of a dozen levelled revolvers.

"Fer heaven's sake!" he gasped. "What does this mean? What d'ye want?"

"Throw up your hands," came the stern command. "There, that's better. Now look here, Bill," and the speaker took a step closer. "Where's that kid you pinched from Big Glen?"

"K-kid! What kid?"

"Look, none of that. You can't fool with us. We've come too far to listen to nonsense. So out with it at once."

The squaw man was in a trap, and he knew that to parley was useless.

"He's down river," he muttered. "I don't know whar he is now."

"But ye do know. Ye sent 'im, an' if ye don't cough up at once we'll leave your d— carcass here on the floor in the twinkling of an eye. D'ye hear?"

Siwash Bill heard, and shaking with fear told briefly what he knew.

Muttered oaths and agitated movements greeted this contemptible story. The speaker lifted his hand for silence.

"You mean, cowardly sneak," he cried, turning to the prisoner. "You deserve to be tied to a stake and tortured to death. The men here are just in the right mood for such a job, too. They left their claims, tramped the whole distance to Hishu, and are hungry enough to be mad for action."

"No, no, fer God's sake, don't do that!" gasped Bill.

"No, we won't do it just now. We'll reserve that for a little later. There are two others to be dealt with, and we'll make one job of the whole nasty affair. So you say Shifty and Windy are lying in wait down-stream, eh?"

"Yes. They've been thar fer some time."

"Well, then, boys," ordered the speaker, "some stay here, and guard this cur. The rest of us will step over to the landing. We'd like to have a hand in that racket. I hope to God we're not too late."

At that instant the faint report of a rifle fell upon their ears. Then another, and still another. At once a mad rush was made for the door, while Siwash Bill was left in the safe-keeping of half a dozen able-bodied prospectors.

CHAPTER XXX UPHOLDING THE LAW

All day long the pointed prow of the little canoe had disturbed the surface of the Hishu in its steady progress up-stream. The monotonous swish of the paddle continued hour after hour as Buckskin Dan and Grey bent to their task. The latter was still somewhat weak after the trying experiences through which he had recently passed. But the energy and fire of manhood, now intensified by a new hope within his breast, converted toil into play. Madeline was sitting well astern, with Donnie seated comfortably by her side. Upon her face a new light had dawned. She thought much of the terrible journey she had made down that same river but a few days before. Then she was helpless. But now the two strong forms bending and swinging before her were near to shield her from harm.

Her eyes often roamed to Nadu's muffled figure sitting so quietly in the bow. The Indian woman had suddenly appeared below the Kaska Rapids as they were about to embark, and implored to be taken back to Hishu. After careful consideration Dan and Grey had conceded to her request. Why she wished to go they could not tell. Neither did they ask her, well knowing that questions would be useless.

It was a weary way up that crooked stream, and the shadows of a second night were gathering ere they neared the end of their voyage. They had hoped to arrive at Hishu before dark, but in this they were disappointed. Grey's mind was somewhat troubled as he thought of the reception which probably awaited them there. What had Siwash Bill and his companions been doing during the past week? Would they oppose them, and strive to wrench the child from their grasp? He glanced at his rifle lying near his side, and thought of the revolver at his hip. His teeth closed firmly together as he pictured the gang surrounding them. He would show them a thing or two if they attempted any of their vile tricks. There was also that cabin affair, and their dastardly attempt upon his life to be settled. How he longed to be at them.

He was roused from his reverie by a low cry from Nadu. Glancing quickly up he saw the woman pointing excitedly ahead to the left bank.

"See, see!" she cried. "There, there!"

Following the pointed finger Grey was able to discern in the distance a horseman speeding along the trail close to the river. At times he was lost to view behind a clump of trees, only to reappear farther on. Ere long he was lost to sight amidst the forest and the deepening gloom. Dan ceased paddling, turned and looked into Grey's face.

"It's that skunk, Shifty Nick!" he exclaimed. "He's spotted us, an' is hikin' back to Hishu with the news! He's been waitin' fer us to appear, that's sartin. What mischief are them villains up to now, I wonder?"

"They haven't given us up, then," Grey replied, heading the canoe up-stream. "We're in for it, and there's nothing else for us to do but to drive ahead as fast as we can and have it over with them as soon as possible. I'm tired of this hide-and-seek game. It's getting on my nerves."

Dan did not reply, but bent to his paddle with more determination than ever. How the canoe did thrill along through the water. Nearer and nearer they came to the village, and after a while dim forms of the cabins could be discerned in the distance. Instead of following the left bank of the stream, Dan headed the canoe to the right. Grey wondered at this, but said nothing. He believed the trapper had some purpose in mind which he would soon explain. When almost opposite the village Dan ran the canoe sharply ashore, and when its keel grated gently upon the beach he laid down his paddle and stood up.

"If yez don't mind," he commenced, "I'll jist leave yez here fer awhile an' slip over to Hishu alone an' size things up a bit. We must be cautious."

"And I had better go with you, Dan," Grey replied. "You may need my help."

"No, pardner. You stay here an' guard the lassie an' the kid. It's best not to leave 'em alone. Ye can't tell what might happen."

"Oh, don't go, Norman," pleaded Madeline, leaning forward and laying her hand gently on his arm. "Stay with us. So many things have happened lately that I dread to be alone."

"Well, I'll stay then," Grey assented. "Only I don't like to have Dan go over there by himself. Two are better than one."

All had now left the canoe except Nadu, who made no effort to move.

"Come," commanded Dan, as he was about to shove the canoe back into the water. "Ain't ye goin' to git out, too?"

"No. Me go to Hishu," was the brief reply.

Dan hesitated only for an instant, and then sent the craft reeling into the current. It was nothing to him whether the woman stayed or went. Seizing a paddle he headed the canoe for the opposite shore, intending to land about one hundred yards below the store. The evening was still, and hardly a sound did he make as he paddled swiftly forward.

As he neared the shore a rifle report suddenly broke the silence, followed immediately by a second, while a bullet whistled past his head. A scream of pain and fright came from Nadu, and looking quickly in her direction Dan saw her lift herself to her feet, reel and fall with a sickening splash into the dark water. A feeling of wild rage possessed the trapper. He realised now the cowardly nature of the attack, in which the Indian woman was the victim. He wheeled the canoe around in an effort to see some sign of Nadu. But nothing could he observe, although he drifted some distance down the river in the hope of seeing her body rise to the surface.

Resolved to search no longer he headed the canoe for the place where the others were waiting, when again the rifles spoke. Dan threw himself forward, and the bullet whistled harmlessly overhead.

"Them villains! Them sarpints!" he cried, as he ran the canoe upon the beach and leaped out. "I'll git me hands on 'em afore long, see if I don't," and he shook his fist in the direction of Hishu.

When Madeline heard about Nadu's death she sank upon the ground and buried her face in her hands. Her heart had held no bitterness for the poor distracted Indian woman since that day she had talked with her in the Mission House. And now Nadu was gone! All her earthly troubles over in an instant.

"Oh, it is terrible, terrible!" she cried, springing to her feet. "When will these things end! Can nothing stop those horrible men?"

Ere an answer could be made a noise from the opposite shore arrested their attention. Shouts, yells and oaths fell upon their ears. They listened, and at length the sounds moved up-stream toward the store.

"The miners! The miners!" exclaimed the trapper, now much excited. "They've come from the hills, an' none too soon. Oh, if they'd only arrived a few minutes earlier, that poor creature 'ud not be lyin' out thar in the river. We'll go over now, fer the miners have got things in their own hands, an' Buckskin Dan wants a finger in the mess, too. He's got a few words to say. Hurry up. Let's go, quick."

As they paddled rapidly across the river straight toward the store, a bright light suddenly sprang up right before them. Larger and larger it grew, until huge forked flames were leaping wildly into the air. It was a bonfire which had been built, and the light was illumining the village for some distance around.

"We must keep back in the shadders," Dan remarked as they landed upon the shore, "an' git the lassie an' kid inter my cabin. It's no place fer 'em outside on sich an occasion as this. You take 'em thar, pardner," he said, turning to Grey, who was carrying Donnie. "I can't wait any longer. I want to jine the crowd. Here's the key to me shack."

Heeding not the confusion near the store, Norman turned somewhat to the left, and keeping well within the shadows gradually worked his way around toward Dan's cabin. Madeline followed close behind, and after what seemed to be a long time they came upon the shack on the opposite side from the store. The light from the fire was broken by the building, up to which they were able to creep unnoticed. It took Norman but a minute to place the child upon the ground, unlock the door, and throw it open. When once inside he breathed a sigh of relief.

"Thank God, we are here at last, Madeline," and he turned as he spoke to the woman by his side.

The small window faced the store, and the light shining through illuminated the whole room. It showed Madeline's face, white and tired after the journey and the trying ordeal of the evening. Grey laid Donnie, who had fallen asleep in his arms, gently in the lower bunk, and turned to the woman standing quietly near.

"Madeline," he said, taking her hands in his, and looking into her weary eyes, "you are tired and need food and rest. Sit in this big chair, while I build a fire, and we shall soon have a lunch together."

"I am tired," Madeline replied as she took the seat and watched Norman as he at once applied himself to his task.

The large chair was Buckskin Dan's special pride. He had made it big and luxurious, and had covered it with skins of wild animals. To Madeline it was the essence of comfort to nestle among the soft furs and lean her head against the high back. She watched Norman as he moved about the stove piling in dry wood, pouring water into the kettle, and laying the few dishes upon the table. Neither spoke, for words were unnecessary. To each that humble cabin was more beautiful than a gorgeous palace. Love pervaded the room. It had a language without words, and a music without sound.

But Grey's mind was not at rest. The gathering near the store worried him. He realised what those men might do when carried away in the heat of excitement. He thought of the whisky on the shelves, and what the result would be should the men get hold of it. Once he went to the door and listened. Siwash Bill and his companions were standing with their backs against the store, surrounded by the miners. Dan was speaking, and ever and anon above the crackling of the fire Grey could catch a few words. He was telling in fiery language of the murderous attack made by Windy Pete out in the hills that dark night, and of the cowardly attempt at murder in his own cabin.

As the speaker proceeded the cries of rage became fiercer, and it was quite evident to the listening constable that the whisky had been liberally sampled. When he re-entered the cabin his face was graver than usual. He had depended upon Dan, and now he was stirring these men to passionate action.

"Is anything wrong, Norman?" Madeline asked, noting the expression of concern upon his brow.

"I'm afraid so," was the reply. "We can't tell what the miners will do to-night. They are almost beside themselves now. That cursed whisky has let loose the evil demon within them. It always does."

Yells and cries more vehement than before caused Grey to hurry again outside. He heard several shouting for ropes, and noted that the miners had formed more closely about the three wretched men. He realised that there was no time to lose. Hastening across the opening he reached the circle of men, pushed his way through, and stood for a moment and viewed the situation. Several ropes had been found within the store, and nooses had been quickly formed. Extending for several feet from the eaves of the building were two rough-hewn log plates, upon which the roof rested. These, as is often the case, had not been cut off, and on them the storekeeper had often hung articles for safety from the numerous starving Indian dogs which frequented the place when the natives were at Hishu. Over one of these a rope was now thrown, and the noose in the other end was about to be slipped over the head of the terrified squaw man, when Grey stepped quickly to his side.

"What's the meaning of this?" he cried, facing the miners. "Surely you're not going to string these men up?"

"That's what we're going to do, pardner," shouted several. "They deserve more'n that. They stole the kid, an' tried to kill you, didn't they? Step back, and don't interfere."

"But I will interfere," insisted Grey. "I know they deserve severe punishment, but you must not take the law into your own hands. They'll be dealt with, so don't you stain your hands with their blood."

"Come, come, don't stand there preachin' to us," came the cry as the men surged closer. "We want to see 'em go up now. Our law is quicker, an' there's no chance of their gittin' away."

It was a critical moment, and Grey knew it. Before him stood these men, mad and inflamed by the poisonous trash they had been drinking. They were certainly not in a fit condition to hearken to reason. Yet sometimes such hearts could be stirred by sentiment.

"Listen," he cried, raising his right hand for silence. "In the name of the Queen, I demand protection for these men."

His words had some effect upon several of the miners.

"The Queen; God bless her," they shouted. "Long may she live."

But some had been born under other flags, and this appeal to loyalty moved them not.

"That won't do," they cried. "The Queen's all right, but she'd do the same as us if she was here. So stand back, an' let us to our job."

"Then you'll do it in the barking mouth of this," Grey calmly replied as his hand slipped to his hip, and ripped forth his revolver. "As a member of a Force whose duty it is to uphold the law of our land I shall stand by these men. Lay hands upon them at your peril."

A yell of anger burst from the miners at Grey's words and action. Their rage for the moment was diverted from Bill and his companions to the constable. They were not men to be startled or cowed by the gleam of a revolver. Instantly their hands slipped to their hips, and as many weapons flashed in the firelight.

"We kin play at that game, too, pardner," said one sturdy miner in the front row. "Ye can't bully us, an' it ain't no use tryin'."

"I'm not trying to bully you," Grey responded. "I'm only trying to bring you to your senses. Though you're forty to one, I'll make your number less if you're not careful."

At that moment Buckskin Dan sprang to Grey's side. He had watched the proceedings for a while without interfering. But he knew that his words had done much to cause this disturbance. He longed to see the three rascals strung up. But now that his partner was in danger it was a different matter, and he must help him.

"Have a care, pardners," he roared. "If yez touch this man, yez'll answer to the hull Force, an' the British Empire back of 'em. I'll stand by the laddie here, and yez know what Buckskin Dan's like when he gits his gun to work."

On any other occasion the men would have listened to these words of reason. But they were in no mood for that now. They were mad, clean crazy for something, they hardly knew what, and their passion was like a furiously blazing fire.

"Come out of that, Dan," yelled several. "We don't want to hurt you. Let's git at that d— cur. We're not afraid of the whole British Empire."

"Hear, hear," roared the rest. "Down with them, and let us at our men."

They surged nearer, and in an instant more the rush would take place. Grey's finger was upon the trigger. The revolver was all ready to spit messages of death, when suddenly his hand dropped, and his eyes stared in amazement. There at his side stood Madeline, confronting the men before her. How she had got there he could not tell. Her slight form was drawn to its full height, while her face was as white as death. Had an angel dropped suddenly into their midst the miners could not have been more surprised. They hesitated, lowered their weapons, and surged back a pace or two. For ten heart beats no one spoke, and the roaring fire was the only sound heard. Then Madeline took a step to the right, and placed herself directly in front of the constable, keeping her face to the miners.

"You are men," she began in a trembling voice, "and will respect a woman, for your mothers were women. But if you shoot this man you will do it through my body. He saved my life, and I love him."

"Madeline! Madeline! What are you doing here?" Grey demanded. "This is no place for you. Oh, please go away for my sake."

"For your sake I shall stay," was the reply.

But there was no need for Madeline's fear. She was safe in the presence of those men. Where reason and appeal to loyalty had failed, the presence of this woman had succeeded. Their hearts were stirred by the scene before them, and the true chivalry of their nature conquered.

"Three cheers for the lady," shouted one.

"Three cheers," was the cry, and how they did roar out the three rounds and a "tiger."

"Thank you very much," Madeline responded. "But you will prove that you are in earnest by sparing those men."

"An' let 'em escape the noose?" roared one. "Not a bit of it."

"Wait until the morning, then," Madeline pleaded. "Not to-night. For my sake."

"Come, Jake, don't be stubborn," was the cry. "Let's do as the lady wishes. But we'll take good care they won't git away. Come, boys, let's make 'em fast, an' tie 'em up good an' tight till mornin'."

In the confusion and cries which followed Grey seized Madeline by the arm, and hurried back to the cabin. Neither spoke until they were within the building and the door shut. Then Grey reached out and took Madeline's hands in his.

"God bless you, darling!" he murmured. "You have saved my life to-night."

"Oh, I am so thankful," Madeline replied. "But it was terrible to face those men!"

At that instant Dan entered the room. A smile crossed his rugged face as he saw the two standing before him.

"Wall, that job's over," he exclaimed. "An' mighty glad I am, too."

"Are they securely tied?" questioned Grey.

"Like rats in a trap. They'll be thar in the mornin', never ye fear."

"But will the miners leave them alone?" asked Madeline. "They may change their minds."

"Not a bit of it, miss. They've come to their senses somewhat, so don't worry."

"But I'm not going to run any risk," Grey replied. "Those three men must go back to Big Glen alive, and I'm going to keep guard to-night. You need a good rest, Madeline, so you and Donnie will have the cabin to yourselves. Dan can sleep in the store. So come, I'm off."

Madeline said not a word, but her eyes spoke all that was necessary, causing Grey to go forward to his watch with a spirit of joy and elation.

CHAPTER XXXI OLD TRAILS AND NEW

It was late ere the confusion in Hishu subsided. The miners from the hills remained around the store until after midnight. They wished to be sure that Siwash Bill and his two companions had no possible means of escape. When they saw them fast bound within the building, and guarded not only by several of their own men, but by the constable and Buckskin Dan, they gradually drifted away to their little shacks in the village. Grey breathed a deep sigh of relief when he saw the last depart, and quietness settle down over the place. He could not trust the miners on guard, for he felt quite sure that as the night wore on sleep would overcome them. They were tired men, and he could not blame them if they slept. Dan, he knew, would not fail him, but he must not leave him alone.

In separate corners of the room huddled the three wretched prisoners. By the faint glimmering light of the candle their dim forms could be seen. Their heads, bowed almost to their knees, told their own tale of miserable despair.

At times Grey opened the door and looked at Dan's cabin. All was still there, and he knew that Madeline and Donnie were resting after the fatigue of the day. As morning dawned he stepped out into the open, and paced up and down before the store. The fresh air was invigorating, and his body throbbed with new life. Slowly the night waned, the east brightened, and the sun rose big and red above the tree tops. Then the village stirred to action. Sounds of axes could be heard as the men prepared their firewood, and smoke could be seen curling from a score of stovepipes stuck through the cabin roofs.

Grey wondered what the day would bring forth. He wished to get away from Hishu as speedily as possible. He knew the trapper would go along to assist with the prisoners. But when he considered the distance to Big Glen and the difficulties of the way he realised what a task it would mean. As he was debating with himself whether he should ask several of the miners to accompany them his attention was aroused by the clatter of hoofs on the trail. Looking up, what was his joy to behold two men of the Force mounted on weary horses riding slowly toward him! They greeted him as one from the dead. Blackbird had wandered back to Big Glen, so they told him, and the Major, fearing the worst, had sent them out to find some trace of the lost rider.

Grey told them very little of what had taken place—he would report first to his Commanding Officer. He told the constables to look after the prisoners, and be ready to start back to Big Glen in a few hours.

During the morning Madeline's mind turned often to Old Meg. She felt sorry now for the poor creature alone in her cabin. Should she go away without one word of farewell? There was another reason why she wished to see her. Perhaps at last she might prevail upon her to reveal the mystery of the past six years, and why she had been kept away in the wilderness. Old Meg had never told her. Perhaps she might tell now.

She and Grey were standing at the door waiting for the trapper and a couple of miners to return with the cayuses, which the gang had rounded up for their own retreat if necessary.

"Norman," said Madeline suddenly, "I should like to see Old Meg before leaving Hishu. Will you go with me?"

"Yes, Madeline," was the reply, "if you wish it. But I should think you had seen enough of that woman."

"I have, Norman. But there is a reason. We have time to go, have we not?"

"Certainly. We shall make time, especially for you."

Donnie was delighted with the walk along the trail, and his little tongue kept up an incessant chatter as he trotted by Madeline's side. Reaching Old Meg's cabin Grey knocked upon the door. Receiving no answer, he pushed it open and entered. All was silent within the building, and Madeline wondered what had become of the old woman. She looked first into the kitchen, then into her own room. Next she softly and timidly opened the door of Old Meg's private room. As she did so, a cry of fear fell from her lips, which caused Grey to spring quickly to her side. There, lying upon the bed, they saw her, with eyes staring wildly before her. Her features were contorted with agony, while her hands clutched convulsively the worn grey blankets.

"Meg, Meg!" cried Madeline, rushing to her side. "What is the matter?"

The sufferer rolled her eyes, and fixed them upon the young woman's face.

"You here?" she replied. "Do you come to mock me?"

"No, no. I only came to see you before going away."

"And so you're going?"

"Yes; to-day."

"I thought so. And that man; he would like to take me. But he won't, no, he won't!" and her voice rose to a shriek. "I knew he would come to take me. But I won't go. He'll never take me alive—oh!"

Here the pain again convulsed her body, and silenced her speech.

"Can't I do something for you?" Madeline asked, taking the sufferer's cold, bony hand. "You know I want to help you. I am sorry for you."

Into Old Meg's eyes came a faint expression of softness. She turned them upon the face of the fair woman at her side.

"I'm bad," she replied. "I've wronged you, and do you wish to help me? Are you sorry for me?"

"Yes, indeed I am. And if there is anything I can do to assist you, tell me at once."

"You can't do anything for my body, or to give me peace of mind. But there's something I want you to know before I die. Look. Put your hand under the pillow. You'll find something there."

Madeline did as she was commanded, and brought forth a package of papers tied with a string.

"Open it," Meg ordered. "Yes—no—Ah, that's the one. See the name. That's the man who put me up to this job. He sent me in the ship to spirit you away when we reached America. I thought it would be a hard thing to accomplish, but the storm and the wreck helped me out."

Madeline only dimly realised what the woman was saying, for her eyes were fixed upon the name written upon the paper. It was that of her cousin, living in England.

"What is the meaning of this?" she asked. "What had he to do with my trouble?"

"Can't you guess? Were not you the only one standing between him and your father's vast estate?"

"Yes. I know that, but—"

"You don't see yet? Your cousin needed money—was bankrupt—driven to the verge of despair—a desperate man—and you alone stood in his way. With you gone, everything would be his."

Swiftly now the horrible truth flashed into Madeline's mind. It almost overpowered her.

"And he hired you to kill me?"

"No, no, not that," cried the woman. "But you were young, and many things can happen in a big city. Young girls can disappear—there are places they can enter, and the world will hear of them no more. But that wreck came. There was a girl drowned. Money did the rest. Money will do anything. There were men willing to swear that you had been drowned—that they saw you go down. The story was believed, and your cousin got what he wanted. Wait," she commanded, as Madeline was about to interrupt her. "Don't stop me. I want to tell my story, for I can't last long. Your cousin knew the truth. I told him everything, and he supplied me with money. But I could not ruin you. I am bad, God knows, but I could not put you into those dens of hell. I fled with you from place to place. But I was always fearful lest I should be discovered. Farther and farther North I sped—to Winnipeg—and beyond, ever Northward—always away from the crowded cities—until we came here. People thought I kept you for an evil purpose. I have fought with men. I have threatened to shoot them. But I kept you safe—and—and—you are pure. You may think it strange, but I loved you. I tried not to show it. I struggled to crush back the feeling. I scolded you. I spoke sharply to you, but I loved you. When you were stolen away by the Indians my heart almost broke. Then when I heard that you were going back to Big Glen, and that I should lose you forever, I could stand no more. How could I live here in this lonely cabin—and you gone! The thought is terrible. I don't deserve your pity—your sympathy, for I am a bad woman. But when you say your prayers to-night put in one little word for Old Meg—the outcast. And see, I wrote it all out before I took that stuff. I thought no one would come to me until I was dead. It's all there—my story is on that paper, though I'm glad I've told you with my own lips, for it makes me feel better."

Tears were streaming down Madeline's cheeks as she listened to the poor creature. She now bent forward, and imprinted a kiss upon the sufferer's brow. Old Meg's face brightened, and she seized the young woman's hands in a firm clasp.

"Don't leave me!" she cried. "I'm afraid to be alone. I'm afraid to die. God, have mercy upon my wretched soul!"

There was a struggle, a gasp for breath, and in a twinkling all was over. Old Meg was dead.

* * * * * * *

One week later a little company moved slowly through the principal street of Big Glen. Horses and riders were weary, for the journey had been a hard one. The three shackled prisoners shuffled along on foot, with heads bent forward and downcast eyes. They had fondly cherished hopes of escape on the trail, but they were doomed to a bitter disappointment. Now they knew that their last chance was gone.

Madeline rode her horse with much ease and grace. Although tired, her cheeks were flushed and her eyes were bright. She was again back to the ways of civilisation. No more loneliness in the great wilderness, with all the many longings and heartaches. The stores interested her, and the people on the streets. Men, women and children paused to gaze upon the spectacle. Word passed from lip to lip that Silas Farwell's child had been found, and the kidnappers had been captured. The excitement grew, and the crowd increased. Men left their stores, women their homes, and followed the little cavalcade. Madeline shrank from the curious gaze bestowed upon her, and her face paled. Grey, riding with Donnie before him, noting her embarrassment, reined his horse to her side.

"They are friendly, Madeline," he whispered. "They are overjoyed at seeing us back again."

Turning into a side street they at length reined up before the finest residence in Big Glen. Presently a pale face appeared at one of the windows, then the door was flung open and a tall woman with a cry of joy rushed down the steps, seized Donnie in her arms, and fairly smothered him in a sea of rapturous kisses. For an instant only there was a death-like silence, and then from the watching crowd arose three rousing cheers of joy. The people remained until Mrs. Farwell, Madeline and Donnie had entered the house, the constables had marched the prisoners off to the Guard Room, and Grey and Buckskin Dan had headed their horses for the Barracks Square. Then they dispersed to discuss the news, and to await anxiously the detailed account which they felt sure would be published in the local evening paper.

An hour later Grey sat alone with his Commanding Officer. He presented a more respectable appearance than upon his entrance into Big Glen. He gave the Major a complete account of his experience in the wilderness, embellishing nothing, and speaking of himself as little as possible. To Buckskin Dan he gave great credit, and only in speaking of the trapper was he at a loss for suitable words in which to express his gratitude. When he finished the Major stroked his moustache thoughtfully for a few moments. Then he reached over and brought down a letter from a pigeon-hole above his desk.

"It is strange," he began, "how things do work out. Only yesterday I received this letter, and I have been puzzling my brain over it ever since. It says that several months ago a man died suddenly in England, of heart trouble. Among his papers were found letters which aroused suspicion. A cousin of his, and the heiress to a large estate, was supposed to have been lost in the wreck of the *Tampan* about six years ago. This man, who was next of kin, therefore came into possession of the property. The letters, however, told a far different story. The girl had not been drowned, but had been stolen away by an old woman who was paid liberally by the girl's cousin for her services. The letters of the latest date told that they were somewhere in Northern Canada, and word was accordingly sent to the Mounted Police wherever there is a Division, and in fact to every city or town of any size in Canada, asking for information concerning the missing one. There is now not the shadow of a doubt that the Madeline Normsell mentioned in this letter is the one with the same name you found in Hishu. You knew her in England, so you tell me, and can swear that she is the same person. I cannot commend you enough, Grey, for what you have done, and I am very sorry to lose you from the Force. You may consider yourself discharged with special honours."

Grey found it hard to free himself from his comrades as they gathered at the Canteen to hear the story of his experiences from his own lips.

He escaped at length, however, and made his way to Silas Farwell's house. Many were the thoughts which surged through his mind as he walked along the street. He was free, and Madeline was near, and his.

His footsteps upon the verandah of the house were heard by one who was anxiously awaiting his arrival. Suddenly a vision of beauty stood before him. It was Madeline, dressed no longer in her old tattered garments of the trail, but in a dress more becoming to her trim form. For an instant Grey looked into her flushed happy face, and then enfolded her in his arms.

There was no one to see this sacred meeting, for Mrs. Farwell had taken Donnie away to his own little cot upstairs. Madeline led Grey to a cosy room to the left of the hall, where burned a bright fire in an open grate. In front of this they sat while Grey related his interview with the Major.

"Oh, it is wonderful!" exclaimed Madeline. "To think that Cousin Rob would do such a thing, and that all has come out right at last."

"And we shall go home at once, darling," Grey replied. "We must not delay too long. We can set the wedding day now, and talk and plan for the future."

"But what will become of Buckskin Dan?" asked Madeline. "Perhaps he will go with us."

"Not a bit of it, dearie. His mind is too full of the gold he discovered in that old abandoned mine. He's going back to work it as soon as possible. He wants me to return after affairs are settled in England. He's at the Sergeants' Mess now, and will be here this evening to talk the matter over with us. You won't mind coming back, darling, will you? We shall have a fine house like this in Big Glen, and be so happy here."

"I shall go to any part of the earth with you," and Madeline placed her hand in Norman's as she spoke. "We must never be parted again."

The twilight deepened, and the fire burned low as the two lovers sat and talked of the future. The weary trails of the past were ended, and new ones opened up before them, winding far into the unknown future, shimmering clear and golden in the mystic light of eternal love.

THE END

Ingram Content Group UK Ltd.
Milton Keynes UK
UKHW010647050623
422889UK00005B/959